An Incantation of Cats

A Witch Cats of Cambridge Mystery

Clea Simon

An Incantation of Cats

A Witch Cats of Cambridge Mystery

The following is a work of fiction. Names, characters, places, events and incidents are either the product of the author's imagination or used in an entirely fictitious manner. Any resemblance to actual persons, living or dead, is entirely coincidental.

ISBN: 978-1-951709-31-0
eISBN: 978-1-951709-01-3
Library of Congress Control Number: 2019953160

First trade paperback edition January 2021
by Polis Books, LLC
44 Brookview Lane
Aberdeen, NJ 07747
www.PolisBooks.com

POLIS BOOKS

The Witch Cats of Cambridge series

A Spell of Murder
An Incantation of Cats
A Cat on the Case

For Jon

Chapter 1

Laurel always did like to pretend she knew best.

"Something's not right with this girl," the slender sealpoint sniffed, her chocolate brown nose quivering over the new client's glitter-flecked sneakers. Keds high-tops that still smelled of glue, they provided the only touch of light in the visitor's otherwise all-black outfit. *"She's trouble. I can tell."*

The newcomer, whose ragged raven bob matched her goth-style skinny jeans and oversized shirt, didn't seem to notice the curious feline inspecting her sparkly feet as she sprawled on the sofa. Instead, she remained absorbed in her phone as she waited for Becca, the apartment's human resident, to return.

Laurel's two siblings, who had toys of their own, were not as oblivious.

"Well, of course!" Harriet, Laurel's creamsicle older sister, didn't even look up from her post on the windowsill, where she lay preening her lush coat. *"If something wasn't wrong, she wouldn't be here."* The self-satisfied half-purr in her voice was barely muted as she reached to groom the orange patch that spread across her broad back. *"That's our Becca's job, after all."*

"*Hush, please.*" Clara mewed softly from her seat on the dining table at the big room's far end. The youngest of the three littermates, the plump calico was loath to interrupt her siblings. Although they were only minutes older, both Laurel, whose coloring revealed her paternal Siamese heritage, and the long-haired Harriet liked to assert their precedence.

As the felines murmured quietly among themselves, their conversation taking place in tones beneath those of human hearing, Becca had reappeared, balancing a loaded tray. The sweet-faced young woman was settling the tray on the low table by the comfy, if worn, sofa, and the little calico didn't want to miss a thing.

"Here we go." Becca, whose own brown curls most resembled Harriet's lush fur, unloaded two mugs, a teapot, and a plate of cookies. "Peppermint tea," she said, placing one mug before her distracted visitor. "It settles the nerves. And besides, it smells nice."

"Thanks." The black-clad newcomer didn't look up as Becca poured the fragrant tea. "No, thanks," she added, face down, as her host held out the cookies.

"*Something* is *wrong with her!*" Never one to turn down a treat of any kind, Harriet lumbered to her feet and launched herself onto the sofa, just as Becca replaced the untouched plate on the tray. "*If she doesn't want cookies, I don't know if Becca can help her.*"

"Sorry." The thud of the marmalade cat landing next to her got the funereal newcomer's attention, and she had the grace to apologize as she tucked her phone into her jeans, a sheepish grin making her look suddenly younger. Close to Becca's own age of twenty-six—or about two-and-a-half cat years—thought Clara as she made her own, more subtle approach and sniffed the air. Something did smell off about the newcomer, something besides her somber attire on what was otherwise a bright autumn morning. As much as Clara didn't want to admit it, Laurel might be right.

"No problem." Unaware of her pet's concern, Becca perched on the armchair that faced the couch, notepad open and pencil poised. "Gaia, you said? Gaia Linquist?"

A quick nod, her lips drawing in.

"Why don't we start with what has brought you here today?"

The visitor exhaled noisily, staring down at the plate, eyes heavy with liner. *Perhaps the cookies were to blame,* Clara mused. *Maybe the black-bedecked girl had an eating disorder she hoped Becca could help her with. Or maybe she was in mourning, the inky coloring all over her face signaling some kind of enchantment.* Becca, the cat's person, had started advertising her services as a witch detective only a few months prior, but what that actually meant was open to interpretation. *Does she think Becca can counter a spell?* Clara pondered this with growing alarm as her oldest sister edged closer to the tray. *I hope Becca hasn't promised that she can cast one.*

Harriet licked the nearest cookie, her tongue darting out as quick as could be, but still the visitor didn't react. When she finally looked up at Becca, the unpainted parts of her face were deadly pale. "I think someone wants to use the craft against me," she said.

Even Harriet paused, pink tongue slightly visible as she and her sisters watched to see how their person would respond. Becca was a normal young woman, after all, despite Clara's secret belief that her person's diminutive stature hid a great spirit. But the good-natured brunette who opened their cans didn't respond with the promise of remedial witchcraft, to the calico's relief. Nor did she react with the kind of shock or horror or even disbelief that many of her peers would. Although her eyebrows rose slightly, she continued to write.

"Very well," she said to herself, before addressing her visitor once more. "And would you tell me how someone is attempting to use magic against you?"

With another nod, the young woman reached into another pocket, extracting a plastic bag that she held up for display. "This," she said. "I found it in my mug."

All three cats recoiled as the musty scent spread, and Laurel positively smirked. Becca, being more visually oriented than her pets, reached for the baggie and held it up to the light, examining the knobby root within.

"Do you know what this is?" Becca turned it around, examining it, as Clara forced herself to move closer. "It looks like ginger—or possibly ginseng?"

"I wish," the visitor said with a dismissive snort. "It's wolf's bane. You know, monk's hood? Aconite?"

"You're sure?" Becca took in her visitor, though whether her eyes had widened in skepticism or alarm, her cat couldn't tell.

"Of course. I'm studying to be an herbalist, and I know a poison when I see one." The visitor clicked her tongue as if her profession were too obvious for words, showing off the glint of a tongue stud in the process. "I work at Charm and Cherish."

"Of course." Becca mused. Clara knew her person had visited the little shop outside Central Square. Most recently, she had emerged with the pretty blue stone pendant she wore now. But even though the little calico often tagged along after her person on her errands she rarely accompanied her inside. Packed to the rafters, literally, with "all things Wiccan," the tiny storefront always smelled too strongly of strange dried plants and scented candles for the sensitive feline's comfort. "I knew I recognized you..."

"That's how I got your number," her visitor went on. "I saw your notice on our community board. The one about 'Witch Detective.' I figure, if someone's coming after me using the craft, you're the one who can help."

Becca took a deep breath, and Clara, who loved her, could see the play of conflicting emotions across her face. "I understand," she said

10

at last. She spoke slowly, as she searched for just the right words. "And I have worked on several cases already. But this is serious. And this is more than a simple spell or hex. If you really think someone is trying to poison you, you really should talk to the police."

"And tell them what? That someone put a root in my mug?" The visitor shook her jet-black bob, revealing more metal up the side of her ears. "No, someone is trying to use my own craft against me. I need another witch to help me find out who. I mean, I know wolf's bane is supposed to have medicinal uses. I was reading up on it. But a whole root? If I'd swallowed any part of that, I'd be gone fast."

Chapter 2

"*I don't know about this case,*" Clara mewed softly, whiskers drooping with worry. Even after the new client had left, Becca remained hunched over her notepad, scribbling away as her cats looked on. Every now and then she'd look over at the root and turn it over once or twice. Still in its plastic bag, the knobby piece's odd, musty smell was a source of discomfort to the assembled cats. "*It could be dangerous.*"

"*How dangerous? The stench of that...thing would put off a dog.*" Laurel put her ears back dismissively as she glared at the source of the offensive odor. "*Only a human would be in danger of drinking anything it had been anywhere near.*"

"*I don't see why Becca has to let strangers in here at all.*" Harriet lay on the sofa sulking. The cookies had been brought back into the kitchen once the visitor had left. To make matters worse, Harriet's special pillow—velvet with gold tassels—had been shoved to one side. "*Just when I had the cushions arranged so perfectly, too.*"

"*Well, she does have to earn her living.*" Clara wasn't sure about this new person—or the strange object she had left behind—but at least she understood Becca's motivation. Sometimes, her sisters could be so shortsighted. "*She needs to buy our cans, after all.*"

A slight feline shrug ruffled Harriet's luxuriant creamsicle-colored fur, as Laurel turned away to wash one dark brown paw. Neither would openly admit that their baby sister was right, and Clara knew better than to push her point. That didn't help them in their current dilemma, however.

"She should be able to do that without bringing such filth into the house." Laurel bit at a recalcitrant claw, revealing a sharp white fang. Whether she was referring to the goth-y girl who had recently visited or the smelly baggie she had left behind wasn't clear, and Clara decided the better course was to not inquire.

"Don't expect me to do something about it." Harriet huffed. She didn't look at her youngest sister. She didn't have to. While the large longhair had dispensed with unwanted items in the past simply by eating them, the odor coming off the baggie as well as its size made her draw up her already blunt snout in disgust. Besides, they all remembered how much trouble the fluffy orange and white cat had caused the last time she had used her magic.

"Nobody's expecting you to sacrifice yourself, Harriet." Clara, the peacemaker, decided to put the best slant on Harriet's earlier efforts as she silently leaped up beside Becca to get a better look at the foul root. *"But I do wish that strange-looking girl hadn't brought it. If only we could get rid of this somehow…"*

The idea wasn't entirely far-fetched. The sisters had come to their person's aid before. It was, of course, the feline way—cats always help their people, using techniques their humans rarely understood—and these three cats had an edge. Although they might not look related, through their mother they were descendants of a long line of magical cats. As different as they appeared, all three had specific skills beyond the scope of even the usual feline magic. They also, as they all knew, were expressly forbidden by the laws of their kind from revealing their powers to their human companions.

13

"*We don't have to be blatant about it.*" Thanks to the Siamese in her background, Laurel tended to be chatty. "*I could put it in her mind that that Miss Glitter Shoes was full of it, and that she should simply toss that disgusting thing.*" Her distinctive yowl was muffled by fur as she reached around to lick her café au lait back. Not, Clara suspected, because her sleek torso needed grooming, but to show off how agile she was. Laurel was the slimmest of the three siblings and as proud of her figure as she was of her ability to "suggest" ideas into the minds of susceptible humans. "*It wouldn't be too difficult.*"

"*I don't know if that will do any good.*" Clara's skills ran more toward invisibility, as well as the ability to pass through closed doors. Her distinguishing characteristic, though, was her deep loyalty to the young woman who had taken them all in. "*She thinks her new blue necklace lets her spot a liar when she's wearing it. She thinks she'll hear them or they'll make her ears itch of something.*"

Loyalty didn't mean that Clara fooled herself about her person's abilities. "*Besides,*" she added, "*she has to take on clients.*"

"*She wouldn't have to if you let me give her some better ideas.*" Laurel had railed at the restrictions on feline interference. "*Like letting some nice young man take care of her.*"

"*Laurel, please, no,*" Clara pleaded. After having her heart broken the previous spring, Becca had gone on a few dates, but she was, to the calico, understandably reluctant to rush into anything. "*She's just beginning to date again. We don't want her to settle down with someone who isn't right for her.*"

"*Humph!*" Laurel spit out a tuft of fur, expression enough of her disgust.

Harriet, by then, had fallen asleep, but Clara continued to watch their person. Becca, as she often did, had opened her laptop. Jumping soundlessly to the back of the sofa, Clara could see that she had opened the homepage of Charm and Cherish, the shop the new client

14

had mentioned as her workplace. More New Age boutique than old-fashioned *botanica*, the shop sold everything from magic kits to pricey amulets. Becca's computer also confirmed what Clara remembered, that the shop had a wide selection of various plant products as well, though without the aid of scent, Clara was hard pressed to distinguish one saw-toothed leaf from another.

"Enough of that." Becca closed the laptop before Clara could examine further. It didn't matter. Her cats knew what came next. Ever since Becca had started working as a witch detective three months before, she'd developed a ritual. She'd light some sage to clear the air and then sit, cross-legged, on the floor. Usually, the fragrant smoke sent Harriet and Laurel off to the bedroom, but Clara, who always wanted to help, had learned not to try to climb into her lap during these moments. This was her "clarifying time," she'd explained to her pet, lifting the plump calico off and depositing her on the floor. That really meant she was gathering her thoughts, Clara suspected. Although if she knew that her three pets were the ones who had the magical powers that she so desired, Becca might have felt differently about rejecting Clara's help during her ritual.

As it was, both Laurel and Harriet trotted off as Becca reverently removed the bundle of twigs from its earthenware container—a splurge from Charm and Cherish, Clara knew. The sisters could be heard tussling in the bedroom by the time Becca got it lit and began making sweeping motions through the living room.

"Clarity, come to me..." Becca murmured to herself, before dousing the bundle. She'd learned the hard way how sensitive her smoke alarm could be. The faint incense that remained didn't quite mask the stench of that root, not to a cat, and Clara considered joining her sisters in the bedroom. But when Becca settled into her meditative pose, Clara's whiskers perked up. Her person couldn't tell—not yet—but her brief break was about to be interrupted.

15

Not thirty seconds later, the doorbell rang. "What the...?" A startled Becca exclaimed, rising to her feet. "Hello?" She opened the door to a short, stout woman, old enough to be her mother, dressed in what looked like a vintage double-knit suit.

"You're the witch detective, right?" The woman, whose wiry black hair came up to Becca's nose, pushed in. "That's what your flier says, right?"

"Yes. I'm Becca Colwin." She stepped back, blinking. "May I help you?"

"I hope so." The woman deposited two full shopping bags on the floor and turned to face her host. "I need your services—and fast! Someone has been stealing from me, and I have a good idea who the nasty little thief is."

"Okay..." Becca drew out the word, a furrow of concern creasing her forehead. "Please, why don't you have a seat and we'll start at the beginning."

"The beginning? I don't even know when that was." Despite her exasperation, the woman plopped onto the sofa, right in Harriet's favorite spot.

"Would you like some tea?" Becca responded. "I find that it helps me think things through ."

A loud sigh was her only answer, and so under her calico's watchful eye Becca began her usual routine, retreating to the kitchen to make tea as well as to give her visitor—and herself—a chance to gather her wits. If she took a bit longer brewing the tea—Becca didn't always warm the teapot with boiling water before adding the mint blend she preferred—her pet approved. While neither Clara nor her sisters believed in training pets, they all understood that humans could be encouraged into more civil behavior with a few simple tricks.

Sure enough, by the time Becca had re-entered the living room, tray in hand, her latest visitor had settled down. Her mood, however, had not improved.

"What's that?" She squinted at the pot, which Becca had left to steep.

"My special mixture." Becca smiled as she answered, but then, seeing the scowl on the older woman's face, tried again. "It's a mint blend," she explained. "Peppermint, mostly. All organic, and it has no caffeine."

"Huh." The visitor sniffed as she reached for a sugar cookie.

"So, I don't believe you told me your name." Becca pulled her yellow legal pad toward her. She hadn't had a chance to put it away, so she flipped over to a fresh page as she took up her pencil.

"Margaret." The woman looked at the cookie and then, apparently thinking better of it, put it down. "Margaret Cross."

"Margaret Cross." As Becca repeated the name, her pencil scratched across the paper with an intriguing noise that drew Laurel back into the living room.

"*What's going on?*" She nuzzled her younger sibling. Becca, meanwhile, was asking her visitor to detail her complaint.

"*Another client,*" Clara murmured. "*But something's weird about her, too. Can you hear what's on her mind?*"

It was risky, asking Laurel to use her special powers. Vain about her own lustrous coat, the middle sister tended to focus on Becca's looks—and her romantic prospects. Clara wasn't sure what she'd make of another female, and an older, rather unkempt one at that.

Laurel must have picked up on some of her sister's anxiety, because she turned to glare at the little calico and even showed a bit of fang. "*Of course I can,*" she growled.

"*Sorry.*" Clara dipped her head in a gesture of submission. Laurel, even more than Harriet, could be a stickler about status.

"What's going on with your cats?" The wiry-haired woman was staring down at them, brows like angry caterpillars butting heads over

17

her pronounced nose.

Becca bit her lip. "They're littermates," she said. "Sisters. They fight sometimes."

"Sisters." Her laugh sounded like a bark. "Tell me about it. Where were we?"

"You were telling me what you brought you here today." Becca spoke with an exaggerated formality. It didn't take Laurel's sensitivity to know she felt somewhat uncomfortable with this newcomer and her singularly ungracious attitude. "I'd asked you to start at the beginning."

"You could say my sister is behind it. Behind everything, usually." The client, Margaret, shuffled slightly in her seat. Rather like Harriet did, thought Clara, when she was getting comfortable. *"Or when she's ready to tell a lie,"* Laurel hissed, her voice barely audible even to her sister's sensitive ears.

"A lie?" Clara turned toward her sister, intrigued, if a little disconcerted. Had her sister just read the calico's own thoughts? But a brown paw batted away her question, as just then, the newcomer began to tell her tale.

"She's the one who wanted to open the shop. She's the one with the interest, but then she unloaded it on me."

She glared at Becca as if her host were responsible. Becca, Clara was pleased to see, sat still and waited, much as she or her sisters would when stalking a mouse.

"She's flighty like that," the visitor started talking again. "I should've known it was a stupid idea. When she said 'hire this girl,' I should've known something was up, like maybe they're in on it. But that makes no sense." She paused, lips pursing like she'd bit into a lemon.

"Anyway, at first, I thought it was an error." As she spoke, she picked up her mug. Becca had filled it with the fragrant tea, which would surely rinse the bad taste out of her mouth, her cat thought. But the sour-faced woman didn't appear to even taste it. "You know, in retail, there's always a little loss. The silver dollar given out instead of a quarter. The odd mistake in math."

The mug went back down to the tray as she leaned forward. "Don't get me wrong. I'm no pushover. I can't afford the latest equipment, but I keep a calculator right by the register, and everyone is supposed to double-check their totals, especially if it's a large order."

Becca murmured something that could have been agreement. If she had other thoughts about busy clerks being asked to do the same tasks twice, she kept them to herself.

"I told the girl that she had to be careful. That I was going to start deducting from her paycheck if it kept up." Another scowl, one not even a cookie could have sweetened. "Usually, that brings them back in line."

Laurel tilted her head at that, but Clara was busy watching her person. Becca clearly wanted to respond to her visitor—or, at least, to her visitor's ideas about management—but she kept quiet. Only her cat could see the strain in the skin around her lips. If she had whiskers they would be bristling.

"Then I realized it was following a pattern." The client leaned forward again, but not for a cookie. "Every day, it was a little more. But it was never more than twenty bucks. Until this weekend, that is. Last night, Friday, when we closed, the total was fifty bucks off."

"Fifty..." Becca jotted down the number. "And this has been going on for how long?"

"Oh, I wouldn't put up with it for that long. Three weeks, I've been aware of it." The woman nodded to herself, setting her wiry hair bobbing. "So nearly five hundred bucks. Five hundred bucks!"

Becca's eyes widened in surprise, though whether because of the older woman's sudden vehemence or some other factor, her cat couldn't tell.

In response, the woman scowled again. "That's a lot to a small business owner like me."

"I'm sure it is." Becca rushed to reassure her potential client. "Do you have evidence you could share with me? Account books or surveillance tape?"

A huff of dismissal. "What do you think I am? The Pentagon? No, we're a small business. I just know what I'm spending and what's in the cash register at the end of the day."

Becca took that in. "And you believe you know who the suspect is?"

"I do." The woman sat back with a satisfied smirk. "It's got to be the girl I hired. Gail—Gail Linquist."

Becca jotted down the name and paused. But the question she asked wasn't the one Clara expected. "And did you say you suspect your sister of collusion?"

"What? No." Margaret waved her be-ringed hands like she was fanning away an odor. "Elizabeth's nutty, but, no. I'm sure she's not involved."

Becca paused, pen in the air and a quizzical expression worthy of a cat on her face. "Then, Ms. Cross, may I ask what services you want from me?"

It was a reasonable question, but when Clara looked at her sealpoint sister in satisfaction, she saw Laurel's nose quivering in concentration.

"I need you to catch her, of course." The older woman spoke as if her objective was plain to see, her gruff voice ratcheting up in both tone and volume. "I want her punished, and I need you to figure out how she's doing it and get the evidence. If you can catch her in the act, so much the better."

Clara looked from her person to her sister. Surely, it wasn't just the visitor's volume that had set Laurel's chocolate-brown ears back on her head.

"I understand that." Becca spoke in that calming voice she used when the cats were upset, but Clara didn't think she'd even noticed her pet's distress. Indeed, she was looking down at her notes as she spoke, biting her lip like she was peeved at herself.

"And, believe me, I appreciate your interest, but I'm not sure I understand. You're a small business owner and you believe one of your employees is, as they say, skimming off the top. This sounds like a matter for the police. Why did you come to me?"

"To you?" Finally unburdened, the visitor reached for a cookie. "I thought it would be obvious," she said, taking a bite.

Becca waited, but Clara could feel her rising impatience.

"I figure you'll blend in better than any fat old cop who comes snooping around," the old woman said at last. "I own Charm and Cherish, where you hung your notice about being a witch detective. How do you think I found you?"

Chapter 3

"This is just too much of a coincidence," Becca said as she washed her latest visitor's mug. "Two clients, both with questionable cases, and they both know each other through Charm and Cherish?"

Clara, who sat at her feet, didn't answer, but she was listening. Becca might not think her pets understood everything she said. Still, she'd gotten in the habit of talking to them. To Clara especially, the little cat knew. Which was why the calico remained in the kitchen, even after Laurel had retired for a nap and Harriet had harrumphed off in disgust once the cookies had been placed back in their tin. Something about her mixed-up coloring—the black patch over one eye, orange over the other—made her look approachable, Clara surmised as she gazed up at her person, green eyes wide.

"What do you think, Clara? Do you think something else is going on here? Some kind of personal vendetta? I swear you'd answer me if you could."

The cat blinked, warmed by the acknowledgement.

Becca couldn't know that her smallest cat was teased for her coloring—"Clara the calico? Clara the clown!" her sisters mocked—but if it made her person feel more comfortable confiding in her, she was content. Besides, her spotted coat, especially that whorl of gray on her side, made it easier for Clara to shade herself into near invisibility. This is the simplest cat magic, as anyone who has cohabited with a feline knows. But it was a skill at which Clara excelled, and one that proved particularly useful as Becca finished cleaning up and prepared to go out.

Although Becca had packed up her notes and slid her laptop into the messenger bag she usually carried, Clara knew she wasn't heading to the library, her usual haunt, or even the city's hall of records, where she did so much of her research. She had heard her call Maddy, her best friend, as soon as her second visitor had left. Clarification rituals were all well and good, but sometimes one needed to mull things over with a real person, she had explained to Clara as she donned her hat and coat. Saturday midday, that meant coffee and sweets at her favorite café.

Not that her friend was always as ready a listener as her cat. Or as prompt.

"Those people are crazy." Maddy had been flustered when she'd finally burst into the crowded café a half hour after Becca had claimed a table. As if making up for lost time, she barely let Becca get to the end of her story before chiming in. "You don't even have to finish. Let me guess. You took both cases?"

"Are you okay, Maddy?" Becca answered her friend with a question of her own.

"I'm fine." Becca's longtime friend pushed her normally neat-as-a-pin dark hair back from her round face. "Just bothered. There was some kind of an accident last night, and they've closed a lane on the bridge. I don't know what they were looking for, but I was stuck on the number one bus forever."

"I'm sorry." Becca began to commiserate but her friend waved her off.

"It's nothing—but it did give me time to think about what you told me on the phone. I really hope you told that Cross lady to get lost." Maddy returned to her theme, still clearly aggravated. Clara, who had hunkered down beneath their table, kept a careful eye on her swinging foot. "Cross—appropriate name, huh? And that other one, too. What was her name?"

"Gaia. Gaia Linquist," Becca answered, hoping to calm her friend. But not even the oversized chocolate chip cookie she had resisted breaking into while she waited for Maddy seemed to placate her longtime buddy, nor was the extra caffeine helping to clear the questions that kept rattling around her own head. "Or Gail, as her boss called her."

She ate a piece of that cookie finally and pushed the plate toward her friend.

"Gaia?" Maddy only shook her head. "Crazy."

"At first, I thought it was a coincidence." Breaking off another piece of cookie, Becca circled back to the older woman's visit. Maddy might have reached her own conclusions, but to Becca there were still loose ends. "I mean, okay, they both got my number from the card I put on the bulletin board at Charm and Cherish. That didn't mean anything. After all, it makes sense that the clientele and the staff of a magic shop would be the most likely to hire a witch detective."

Maddy's raised eyebrows said it all, but as a true friend, she kept her skepticism silent. Becca, who had already heard tons from her old buddy about her new vocation, ignored it and moved on.

"And then, when the owner, Margaret, said she suspected her employee, I didn't question it. I mean, I don't know how many people work for her. But then when she started telling me about her sales associate Gail, I had to ask—"

"You had to know Gaia wasn't her real name." Maddy sipped her latte, but her eyes were on her friend.

24

"I assumed it was a name she chose." Becca had a more generous attitude toward self-re-creation. "There's nothing wrong with that, Maddy."

"It's pretentious." With that, her friend succumbed, taking a Harriet-sized chunk of the cookie. "And silly. But enough about her name."

This time, Becca ignored the interruption. "Anyway, when I realized that the woman Margaret suspected of stealing from her was the same woman who had come in to see me earlier, I had to wonder. And there's that thing with the sister, too. Ms. Cross—Margaret—didn't want to talk about it, but she brought it up. Something about how her sister urged her to hire Gaia. Only then she told me not to follow up with her sister, Elizabeth. But how can I not? I mean, it almost sounds like a setup, doesn't it?"

"Either that, or the sisters have some kind of feud going on and they're dragging the poor shop girl into it. They'd probably drag any bystander into it, too." Maddy scanned the nearby tables, but none of the bleary-eyed occupants—students, probably, another sign of fall—looked up. "Anyway, you don't need to get caught up in that."

"No, I don't." Becca took another piece of the giant cookie and nibbled on it. But even Maddy must have been able to see that her friend was barely tasting its buttery goodness. "The thing is, I do need clients." She paused to wipe a crumb from her lip. "And if I can help two members of the Wiccan community, well, those are my people, Maddy."

"Don't." Her friend held up one hand to stop her. "Please, Becca. *I'm* your people. Researchers are your people. Academics are your people, and historians. I know you've gotten into this whole witch thing since you lost your job with the historical society, but please don't go overboard."

"I've solved some cases, Maddy." Her friend cared for her, Becca knew that, but her lack of faith was clearly beginning to smart. "You know I have."

"I know." Maddy nodded, resignation sneaking a sigh into her voice. In truth, Becca had solved the murder of a member of her own small coven. Since then, she'd used her considerable powers of observation and skill as a researcher to help others as well. The fact that her three cats had assisted was something neither of the two friends could know. "I'm sorry. Getting stuck in traffic must have gotten to me. But, really, two clients in one day—and one of them is accusing the other?"

"It is odd." Becca's hand went up to her necklace. "But I think they were both being honest in their fashion." Her brows knotted together in a way that her friend knew, from long experience, meant she was about to reach a conclusion.

"Please, Becca." Maddy made one more last-ditch attempt. "You're going to call these two back, right? Tell them you can't take their so-called cases?"

"I think I have to call Margaret Cross." Becca ignored her. "I have to tell her that I can't accept her case. I should have as soon as I heard her employee's name, but it took me a minute to put it all together. All I have to do is tell her I have a conflict because of an existing client. After all, I took Gail's—Gaia's—case before her boss walked in."

Maddy slouched in her seat. "So you're going to keep Ms. Glitter Goth?"

Becca shot her a look. "I should never have told you about her sneakers. They were really cute, and Laurel couldn't get enough of them. But that's not why—no, I'm not going to drop Gaia Linquist as a client."

"Please, don't say it." Becca had seen Maddy put her mug down in preparation for launching into a speech. "I know I could get a job with you at Reynolds and Associates. But I need to give this a chance—I need to give *myself* a chance, Maddy. I'm good at detecting, even if the witchcraft part is still kind of iffy."

A true friend, Maddy bit her lip and waited for Becca to go on.

"And this is serious. Wolf's bane can kill you."

"So don't you think this is a matter for the police?"

Becca shook her head sadly. "It's a root in a coffee mug. And the complainant is a young girl with dyed-black hair and sparkly sneakers, whose boss may be trying to get rid of her. You didn't believe her, Maddy. Why would they?"

Chapter 4

Clara slipped through the door only seconds ahead of Becca, after a last breathless dash. Her person couldn't have known the little calico had followed her out. Had, in fact, been napping beneath her feet as the conversation had turned to Maddy's job and her ongoing campaign to get Becca to join her, and had trotted alongside her most of the eight blocks home. But she didn't want Becca to worry, in case she called her cats together for a consult upon returning home and Clara had been slow to appear.

"*What did you find out?*" Laurel was at the door and reached her brown nose down to touch her little sister's bi-colored one. "*Was I right about that sneak?*"

"*Is she bringing home any treats?*" Harriet ambled over. Neither of Clara's older sisters had quite the facility that the little calico had with passing through physical barriers, like doors. And neither could quite so easily mask themselves into near invisibility—Clara suspected that skill had to do with her multicolor markings. But Harriet in particular was made of solid stuff. Her own special skill—making physical objects appear—might have been an extension of her corporeality. It wasn't always helpful. In the recent past, she had caused a golden amulet and, at one especially troublesome juncture, a pillow to appear, each time causing havoc in Becca's world.

In addition, because the objects Harriet summoned from the ether were either conjured out of air itself or crafted around some small, pre-existing item, they were never quite as good as the real thing. Which was why the always hungry longhair had given up on summoning treats. Especially since their person was usually so good about indulging them.

"No...I don't know." Clara answered Harriet first, as she panted to catch her breath. As the oldest, the marmalade longhair would expect that. "I ran out as she got up to leave." In truth, the two friends had left most of that cookie, which was unlike them. A sign, Clara knew, of Maddy's distress at her friend's decision—and Becca's determination to get started on the case.

"And, no, she doesn't seem to realize that that first woman was lying." She turned to Laurel, whose blue eyes were so much more clear than that stone.

"Humans!" A delicate sniff bristled Laurel's whiskers. "So silly." But despite her assuming a worldly-wise pose, Clara could see that chocolate-tipped tail lashing, a sure sign that her sister was as concerned as Clara herself. That was one of the other reasons Clara had rushed to get home.

"In fact, she's going to keep that girl Gaia's case." That got even Harriet's attention, and the little calico hastily filled her sisters in, even as her sharp ears swiveled, searching for the sound of familiar footsteps on the stairs.

"I could make this all go away." Harriet batted idly at a toy mouse as she spoke. A sure sign, Clara knew, that her oldest sister was up to something. "If you'd let me."

Clara held her tongue. In the past, she'd done her best to enforce the number one rule of magical cats, that they never let their humans know about their powers. It had led to tension, at the very least.

"What could you do?" The hint of scorn in Laurel's Siamese-type yowl hinted at her skepticism.

"Well, something's missing, right?" Either Harriet didn't hear it, or she didn't care. *"You two are so proud of what you can do. But you know that I can summon just about anything as easily as I'd twitch my tail."*

Laurel sat back on her café au lait haunches and seemed to consider the marmalade's proposal. It fell to Clara to break it to them.

"It wouldn't work," she said, her mew softened with regret. *"That lady didn't lose a 'thing,' per se. Someone took money—altered the accounts somehow—and nothing any of us could conjure up would change her bank balance."*

"Balance?" Laurel, the most athletic of the three, drew out the word, one hind leg stretched out balletically behind her.

"It's not..." Clara paused. Cats may be philosophers, but abstract concepts are difficult for everyone. Still, she did her best to explain about bookkeeping and the crime of embezzling from what she had heard. *"Anyway,"* she concluded, *"that's why the older lady thinks that girl did it, because she works for her and could have changed the numbers."*

"Maybe she tried to poison the girl." Laurel's tail lashed like she was remembering a hunt. *"And when it didn't work, she came to Becca."*

It was an interesting idea, and the three cats were busy considering it, tails twitching in contemplation, when the front door opened.

"Hello, you three." Becca looked down at her pets, beaming. "I'm glad to see you're not fighting anymore."

"We don't fight. We're sisters!" Laurel twined around Becca's legs as she removed her jacket. *"We sometimes have heated discussions."*

"Don't distract her." Clara looked on with concern. From the way Laurel's whiskers were bristling, her sister knew she was working hard to implant an idea in their person's mind. *"She needs to think clearly before she gets any deeper into this."*

"I don't see any treats." Harriet had stood up on her hind legs to sniff the air around Becca, in the hope that a bag of cookies might be hidden on her person. *"Didn't you say she was eating treats?"*

"You three." Becca shook her head. "You'd think I'd been gone all day instead of just an hour. I bet you're hungry. Am I right?"

Laurel turned to Clara with a smirk, letting her baby sister know just who had suggested that thought. Harriet, meanwhile, ran ahead, laser focused on being the first to the kitchen.

"You're not going to distract her from the case forever." Clara took up the rear.

"Bought us time, though, didn't I?" Laurel wrapped her chocolate-tipped tail around her feet as she waited. Harriet was brazenly begging, her wide bottom making it easy for her to sit up in a fashion that her youngest sister privately thought was rather dog-like. *"Time for us to look into the whole poison thing."*

"There you go, girls." Becca laid down Harriet's bowl first, knowing the orange cat would push aside her sisters to take it in any case. Then Laurel's and then Clara's, before washing her hands. Despite the talk of poison, all three dived in. "And now, kitties, I've got to get to work. I've got to call that Margaret Cross and tell her I can't take her case."

For a moment, Clara dared hope. Even the glint of triumph in Laurel's blue eyes didn't bother her. If only... But then Becca turned and wiped her hands dry.

"And then," she said, returning the dish cloth to its hook, "I have to start figuring out how I can help poor Gaia."

She returned to the living room, and Clara lifted her head. Her person seemed to be fussing, her movements growing more frantic.

"You done?" Harriet's fuzzy snout pushed into her dish.

"No!" Clara raised a paw, peeved at the interruption, but she stopped herself from going further. It wouldn't do to smack Harriet. Besides, the big marmalade did need more food than the petite

31

calico, and Clara was aware of her own well-padded form. Any more poundage, and she might have trouble passing through closed doors. "*Well, okay.*" She backed away, ceding the dish, even as Laurel looked at her quizzically.

"*I want to hear what Becca is doing,*" Clara explained. Harriet, oblivious, kept eating. But even by the time the big cat had joined her two siblings in the living room, nothing had been resolved.

"*What's going on?*" Harriet asked as she began to wash her face.

"*A lot of fuss about nothing.*" Laurel yawned as she stretched along the back of the sofa. "*Becca needs to nap more.*"

"*No, it's not that.*" Clara knew better than her sisters what Becca's increasingly frenzied activity meant. "*I mean, I don't think so,*" she added, in deference to her sister.

As the three cats looked on, Becca knelt down beside the couch. Reaching, she retrieved two toy mice and a pencil that Clara hadn't been able to resist batting around the week prior from underneath, but still she did not appear sated. If anything, she looked increasingly distraught.

"You three didn't…" She sat on the rug and addressed the cats. "No, you have too much sense. Even you, Harriet."

The big longhair blinked.

"It must have been when she gathered her bags up to leave." Becca rose to her feet, talking to herself as much as the three felines. "I can't…"

She stopped talking as she bolted into the kitchen, but a thorough examination of the trash, the teapot, and the dirty mugs didn't seem to appease her. When she came back into the living room, she plopped down on the sofa, a dazed expression on her face.

"Well, if this doesn't beat all," she said, one hand absently reaching out for Clara, who had jumped up beside her. "I've got one client who worries she's being poisoned, and another who thinks that the first client is a thief. Only, unless I am very much mistaken, the second client just stole the evidence that the first client brought me."

Chapter 5

"I didn't want to go down to the store." Becca addressed Clara's wordless query. Becca's smallest cat had followed her to the front door, where she was donning her coat. "I mean, I really didn't want Margaret and Gaia to know that I'd taken cases from them both. Not when I realized they worked together. But Margaret's not answering her phone. For all I know, she only came by here to steal that root back.

"I should have known." She paused, mid-button, to rest her hand on the lapis pendant. "Maybe I'm not using this right."

Looking on, Clara thought of her sisters. She couldn't tell for sure if Laurel had helped plant the idea the three cats had shared about the root—and the possibility that that nasty older woman had been behind the attempted poisoning. For a moment, Clara even toyed with asking Harriet to get rid of that stupid necklace, which Becca seemed to trust so much. They all had complementary powers, she mused. Maybe that was for a reason.

But for any of that to be effective, the three would have to work together. And while Clara knew her sisters loved her—at least, she assumed they did—she'd been teased for too long and too often to trust them to follow her guidance. *"Clara the clown,"* she could hear the echo of Laurel's distinctive Siamese yowl. If anything, they'd do the opposite, just to mess with her, not realizing how their actions affected the human they loved. No, the plump calico realized, in this, she and Becca were alone.

Her person seemed to have reached the same conclusion.

"Well, nothing for it." Becca had added a hat to her ensemble. A new addition to her wardrobe, the maroon velvet cloche sported a feather that only Laurel's sense of style had kept intact. "Don't worry, kitties. I won't be out too late!"

"*Cute.*" Clara turned to see that Laurel had come up silently beside her. "*That hat. Don't you think?*"

"*I guess.*" In truth, the little calico hadn't paid much attention to her person's outfit. She'd been focused on her own concerns, as well as the undercurrent of concern in Becca's voice. "*That feather will make it easier to follow her. But I won't touch it!*"

That was to Harriet, who had ambled up beside her, as much as to Laurel. Harriet considered all toys hers by right, and Clara knew she had her golden eyes on the perky plume. With a satisfied blink, Harriet accepted her little sister's capitulation, sprawling in a fur mess on the floor. Laurel, meanwhile, had twisted around to lick the base of her tail, secure in the knowledge that neither would nab the tempting feather without her consent and seemingly unconcerned about anything else her baby sister might do. And so with a shimmy of her hindquarters, as if she were readying to jump, the calico slipped through the molecules that made up the closed door.

This is a trick many cats can do. It's why humans can never find their pets when they first come home, and why those pets always look so pleased as they come out to meet their people. As the descendent of a long line of magical cats, however, Clara had a facility that surpassed most other felines. Inhaling a deep breath and taking a supernatural leap, she made quick work of the apartment stairs and the building's front door to catch up with her person on the pavement outside.

Becca must have felt something—a breeze or the lightest brush of whiskers—because she paused and looked down at the sidewalk, where Clara had landed. Just in time, the calico shaded herself so that her orange spots looked like the splashes of the afternoon sun and the grey whorl on her side its growing shadows. Shaking her head, Becca began walking once more, and if her pace could have been in response to the hour or the growing chill of autumn, the grim set of her mouth revealed both her discomfort and her determination.

Despite the risk of discovery, Clara stayed close to her person as she made her way along the city streets to Charm and Cherish. The Wiccan-themed shop had opened a few months ago to the delight of Becca's coven. Clara had first heard of it during one of their weekly gatherings around Becca's table. The group, which had shrunk to just a few close friends, had been overjoyed to have a nearby source for the candles and incense they so enjoyed. But even though the little shop was convenient, its placement in the heart of busy Central Square made it problematic for a feline, even one who could shade herself into near invisibility when she needed.

As it was, she had several close calls. Becca was walking quickly, and in her effort to keep up, Clara had to weave through the busy weekend crowd. Twice she saw feet only seconds before they came her way, avoiding a nasty, if unintentional, kick only by the kind of agile leaps Laurel would be proud of. After the second time, she even considered dropping her shading. She was a good ten feet behind Becca at this point. Only when she looked up did she realize that being visible would have done her no good. The pedestrian whose boot had nearly caught her in the ribs was so glued to her phone it was amazing she hadn't walked into a lamp post.

Dashing to catch up, she saw that even Becca wasn't immune. At the blast of a car horn, a bicyclist dashed up on the sidewalk, nearly colliding with her person. As Becca stumbled backward, the cyclist, his face hidden beneath a black helmet, reared up on one tire and turned back into the street.

"They're a menace." Becca jumped as another pedestrian took her elbow to steady her. "Are you okay?"

Becca turned to look into warm brown eyes set in a plain, kind face. "Yeah, thanks."

"You be careful." A warm voice, too. Becca glimpsed down as the plain man quickly withdrew his hand. "Sorry. I'm a bit spooked." As he apologized, an awkward smile brought out a dimple in his long, pale face. "There was an accident last night, only a few blocks from here. It was pretty awful."

"I'm sorry. I'd heard something about that." Becca must have recognized something in his face, because she softened her tone. "You were there?"

"Right after." He closed his eyes remembering, and the dimple disappeared. "An older man, a homeless vet, I think, was hurt. The driver had disappeared—just left him. I think he'll be okay, but it was touch and go."

"How awful. I hope you're right." To cement her good wishes, Becca managed a smile, and for a moment Clara thought she was going to take the man's hand. "Thanks."

He reached for hers then and gave it a quick squeeze. "My pleasure. Only, please, I deal with enough accidents," he said. "Be alert."

Becca murmured her assent, but to Clara it seemed her person was even more distracted after that, barely registering the street around her as she started to walk again, her eyes following the stranger as he crossed and turned away. So it was with a sigh of relief that Clara saw Becca came to a halt before a glass storefront in the middle of a commercial block, set between a dry cleaner and a convenience store. Even without being able to read the signage, Clara could have distinguished the magic shop by the colorful zodiac symbols painted on its windows, as well as the funky herbal scent that leaked out despite the closed door.

"Nothing for it," Becca murmured to herself, peering between a bright red lion and a blue crab that appeared to be dancing over an unevenly drawn star. Clara looked up with concern as her person took a deep breath before pulling open the front door. Braving the nasty smells she knew would only intensify, Clara followed her inside as a tinkling bell announced their arrival.

"Hello!" a voice called out from somewhere unseen. "I'm in the back. I'll be right out."

As Becca walked over to the glass-topped counter, loosening her coat, Clara took in her surroundings. Despite its small size, the shop was packed. Below that colorful front window, piles of newsletters—notices of circles and classes—yellowed in the afternoon sun beside a gold-painted Ganesh. Bookshelves along the wall reached to the ceiling, packed with a variety of multicolored bindings. A rack that ran down the center held candles and more books, along with a few strange metal objects—balances and weights, Clara realized, having seen something like that in Becca's kitchen—along with some knives that looked more ceremonial than functional.

Ducking around a table with some small figures—another version of the elephant-headed god, a fat bald man, and, rather to Clara's surprise, a series of felines—she saw Becca leaning over the glass counter. She seemed to be examining the shelves on the wall behind it, where a row of glass jars were displayed. These, one sniff confirmed, were the source of those odd odors, their tight-fitting lids not quite containing the strange and spicy aromas of the leaves and twigs and, yes, roots within.

"Hello, oh!" Becca and Clara both turned to see a familiar black-clad figure—Gaia—step into the room. "Becca, I didn't expect you." She came forward, pulling a door closed behind her. "Did you want to speak with me again about my case?" Even though there was nobody else in the store, her voice had dropped to a conspiratorial whisper. Her black-lined eyes darted back and forth. "You don't have anything yet, do you?"

"No." Becca gathered herself up. "Why? Has anything else happened?"

"No." She shook her head. "But I've been extra careful, lately. My boyfriend—well, he's really just a friend—said he thought he saw someone hanging around the shop."

"He did?" Becca seemed to slide right over Gaia's redefinition of the relationship. Among humans, it could be hard to tell. Clara knew that. Still, she'd heard her person's quick intake of breath. "Maybe I should speak with him?"

"No, I don't think so." Gaia stepped back behind the counter. "Tiger wouldn't want to be involved in any of this. I know him."

"Oh." Becca tilted her head, looking amazingly like Laurel as she pondered. "But if this Tiger saw someone suspicious and can describe him…or her… What's Tiger's full name?"

"Look, I shouldn't have mentioned him. He's just being protective. I mean, there's never anyone in here." With that, she turned to examine the shelves of jars behind her, shutting Becca out. But the young woman Clara knew and loved was not without her resources. "Hardly ever. It's safe as a tomb."

Becca's silence acted like catnip on the black-clad shop girl.

"Okay, a few things have gone missing." The goth girl shrugged and turned once more to eye her visitor. "Not that we have any big-ticket items here. I mean, unless you count the gong."

"Shoplifters?"

A tilt of her head made those ear studs flash. "Someone grabbed something out of the window. I think that's what happened, anyway."

"I see." Becca's tone was soft, but Clara was heartened to hear the suspicion underlying those two words. "Someone took something?"

Another shrug. "I think. It wasn't a big deal."

Becca paused, cataloging the theft—or the other woman's sudden reluctance to discuss it—and moved on, her hand creeping to the pendant in the hollow of her throat. "Well, then, if you don't think anyone has been in here, I have to ask. Looking at all those jars...is there any chance that maybe...I mean, so many of those roots look alike..."

"You think I nearly poisoned myself?" The other woman's eyes went wide. "You mean, by accident, right?"

Becca didn't respond, and Clara knew she was weighing the possibilities. The cat couldn't imagine why a human would choose to make herself sick. Then again, Laurel had eaten a moth once, with disturbing results, and Harriet had no problem coughing up furballs with amazing regularity.

"People make mistakes." Becca's response, when it finally came, was phrased to sound perfectly noncommittal.

"Not possible. I know what wolf's bane looks like." The woman behind the counter turned again, taking in the various botanicals. "We don't even have it here. I mean, why would we?"

"Wolf's bane does have medicinal uses," Becca pointed out. "You said so yourself."

"And it can also be used for harm," Gaia shot back. "You know the rule."

A nod from Becca. "An ye harm none, do what ye will," she recited. "But that doesn't mean botanicas and purveyors to the craft don't stock it."

"We don't." Gaia was firm. "I do all the buying. Well, with Margaret, Margaret Cross. She's the owner."

Becca's face fell and Clara knew why. The kind-hearted girl didn't want to think that the older woman was behind the attempted

40

poisoning—or the attempted cover up. Still, she rallied as she recalled the initial reason for her visit. Finally, she had her opening.

"Of course," she said, and leaned forward, as if about to impart a secret. "Actually, I'm really here to see Margaret. Is she available?"

"You know Margaret?" A quizzical lift of one pierced brow. But as Becca fumbled for an answer, Gaia provided her own. "Oh, yeah, you must have gotten her okay to post your notice. She's not—I haven't seen her or her crazy sister at all today. But is there something I can help you with?"

"No." Becca bit her lip, which she always did when she was thinking. Clara did her best to still her tail, which threatened to lash in anticipation, and watched, waiting to see what her person would do. "It's personal, to be honest. Do you know how I can reach her?"

"I have her cell number." Gaia pulled open a drawer beneath the register.

"So do I," Becca admitted. "She's not answering."

"That's curious." Gaia leaned back, her hands still on the drawer. "Usually, she's on top of everything. In everything, I should say. The woman has no boundaries."

Something about Becca's expression must have given her thoughts away, because Gaia's eyes went wide. "You don't think she's...the wolf's bane," she said, her voice growing breathless.

"You mean that maybe she got her hands on some? And that maybe somehow, by mistake maybe..." Becca's voice went high and tight, as Clara knew it did when she was about to lie, or almost lie. "Would you have any reason to suspect her?"

"Any reason, such as that she has accused you of embezzling." Clara provided the missing words. *"Accused you of stealing from the register you have your hands on?"*

"Suspect?" Gaia tilted her head, looking for all the world like Laurel at her most quizzical. "Why would she...no, that's not what I meant."

Becca and Clara both waited as the other woman shook her head. "I just mean, well, if she's not answering, and she's not here. Maybe it wasn't just me. Maybe someone has tried to poison her, too."

Chapter 6

"Let's not panic." Becca put out her hands in a calming gesture as Gaia tensed, ready to run from behind the counter. "There's no reason to jump to conclusions here."

"But you don't know." The counter girl sounded breathless, gulping her words like air. "I mean, we share mugs. I brew a big pot of tea first thing in the day...maybe it wasn't meant for me. Maybe Margaret..."

"Please calm down." Becca spoke softly but firmly, like one would to a panicked kitten. She couldn't be about to share her suspicions, could she? Clara wondered, when Becca responded with a question of her own. "What was your last interaction with her?"

"Like I said, I spoke to her this morning. She called right before I took my break. She wanted to confirm my schedule."

Becca listened without comment, and Clara didn't need Laurel's powers to know why. The older woman had probably checked in to make sure her staffer was going to be in the store before she visited Becca. That didn't seem to be information Becca was ready to share with her younger client, though. "And you haven't heard from her since?"

"No." Gaia sucked her lips. "But, well, you know I took a kind of long-ish break to go see you. And then, well, I was so upset that I felt a bit light-headed and I thought, maybe, some lunch…"

"Who covered the shop while you were out?" Becca interrupted what was clearly going to be a chain of excuses.

"Nobody," the woman said, like it should have been obvious. "It's not like we have this huge staff or anything. In fact, it's pretty much just me and Margaret's nutty sister Elizabeth. But she just flits in and out. I don't think Margaret pays her. She's always complaining about money, and I know she pays me little enough. That's why I figured, well, if I needed to take some time off…"

"So, Elizabeth didn't cover for you?" Becca tilted her head, looking for all the world like Laurel when the Siamese was trying to figure something out.

"No, I put up a sign, saying that we'd be open again in an hour. I mean, maybe it was closer to two hours. But, you know, who knows when anyone came by? Because if they came by an hour after I left, then it was only…"

"So the shop was closed." Becca might have been thinking out loud, but her words cut the other woman off.

"Uh-huh." She acknowledged. "You think maybe she came by?"

"I don't know." Becca turned, taking in the crowded shelves, with their books and bric-a-brac. "Did it look like anything had changed when you came back?"

A slow shake of that jet-black bob showed the other woman's confusion. "Do you think someone broke in?"

"I'm not sure." Becca spoke slowly. "I was trying to reach Margaret because, well, something was bothering her." As she spoke, she began to walk around the store. She picked up a candle and turned it toward her, noting its blackened wick. "Do you usually light these?"

"Me? No." The idea was met with a grimace. "I don't want to have to shell out eighteen bucks for that."

44

Becca flicked the darkened wick, her finger settling on the shallow cavity surrounding it. "Someone has."

She moved on to the display of Tarot cards. "Was this pack open?" She turned back to Gaia. "Maybe as a display model?"

"What?" Gaia was by her side faster than Clara could pounce, scooping up the open cards. "No, well, maybe. We do let customers look at the cards. I mean, if they seem serious. In fact, maybe that candle…"

Becca was watching her, a puzzled look on her face. Clearly, something was bothering the black-haired girl. Something beyond her concern about being poisoned. "Does anyone else have the keys to the shop?"

A shrug. "Frank—Mr. Cross, that is." Her pretty mouth pouted in annoyance. "But he never comes down here. He's got his own office, and I don't think he thinks much of this place. In fact, I'm pretty sure he wishes she'd fail so he could get another tenant."

"Another—wait, he's the landlord?"

A shrug, as Gaia brushed her bangs out of her eyes, revealing another piercing. "Well, yeah. I can't imagine she'd have this place otherwise. Didn't I tell you? They live upstairs."

Even Gaia must have heard Becca sigh. To Clara, it was a roar of annoyance. "How do I get up there?" She made to go behind the counter, and Clara could tell she was heading for the back door.

"That's just the store room." Gaia headed her off. "And our little break area."

She took Becca's arm and led her toward the front door. "The building entrance is past the cleaners. Hang on." She fished a ring of keys from her pocket, like she was about to lock up.

"Oh, there's no need. I can find it." Becca reached for the door. "Is there an apartment number?"

"It's the fourth floor. They call it the penthouse." An exaggerated widening of her kohl-rimmed eyes showed what she thought of that. "You sure you don't want me to come along?"

"No, thanks." Becca glanced toward the counter. "I feel like I've kept you from your job for long enough today."

This time, Gaia didn't even try to hide it when she rolled her eyes.

***

"There's something odd going on with that store." Becca couldn't have known that Clara was right beside her as she walked past the dry cleaners, its lights glowing in the growing dusk. But maybe she sensed her pet's presence, the little calico thought. Her warmth as the afternoon sun began to fade. And maybe the companionship of the devoted feline was helping her process. "That candle—it made Gaia uncomfortable for some reason. And the way she grabbed at those cards, laid out like that? It was almost like she didn't want me to see something."

Becca had reached a nondescript metal door, marked only with the street number and a grimy inset window. While Clara waited, Becca leaned forward to spy through the dirty glass. Clara could pass through doors but there were limits to her abilities. She could jump, but not high enough to see through the inset window—just as she couldn't read the labels on those jars and bottles. If only she had thought to climb up while Becca was questioning that other woman.

Any regrets had to wait, however, as Becca pulled open the door and entered a small foyer that smelled of dust and rot, undoubtedly from the pile of takeout menus that lay moldering in the corner.

"Penthouse, there it is." Becca examined a directory and pressed a button by the mailboxes. After a pause, she tried again, as the dust settled in silence. Clara, careful not to stir it back up, nosed the interior door, held ajar by a rubber wedge.

She might not have Laurel's power of suggestion, but then again, she might not need it. The foyer was small enough that Becca soon noticed and let herself into the stairwell. As she started up, she pulled out her cell.

"Third time's the charm," she said as she punched in the number. But even before the call could go once more to voicemail, the ringtone was drowned out by a clattering on the stairs as first a pair of clogs and then striped tights appeared.

"You're here!" a tall stork of a woman announced as she reached the bottom stair. Examining Becca over her hawk-like nose, she nodded, her shoulder-length gray hair as wild as unraveled yarn. "Finally!"

"Is it that nasty girl?" The unmistakable caw of Margaret Cross filtered down from above. "Has she come to gloat?"

"Excuse me?" Becca addressed the woman on the stairs as she pocketed her phone. "You must be..."

"Elizabeth Sherman." The gray-haired woman extended a hand. "Margaret's big sister. Come on up."

"I've been trying to reach Margaret." Becca had to step quickly to keep up. Elizabeth nearly sprang up the stairs, despite clogs and the smock-like dress that might have tripped a shorter woman. "And I might have some news she doesn't like but I need to tell her..."

Before she could finish, they'd reached the top, where Margaret, still in her suit, was waiting. "It's the wrong girl," said the more formally dressed woman with a scowl as she turned back into the apartment. "I meant the other one."

Becca's head swiveled between the two women, considering the similarities in the sisters' wild hair, which played so differently with Elizabeth's height and rather hippie-ish attire and Margaret's double-knit suit. For Clara, the main distinction was a faint difference in scent, almost as if the store owner's sour attitude—or maybe her hair dye—had curdled something inside her.

"Mrs. Cross." Becca followed the shorter woman into a large, well-lit living room decorated in wood and earth tones. A shelf that ran the length of the window was lined with potted plants. Without turning to acknowledge her guest, the storeowner plopped down on a nubbly brown couch.

"I'm sorry to bother you at home, but I've been trying to reach you." Becca hesitated, standing on the other side of a cherry-stained coffee table. "I need to talk to you about your case."

She stopped there, looking up at the taller sister, who had clomped past her into the adjoining kitchen, turning on a tap and humming tunelessly as she knocked dishes about. But before Becca could ask Margaret if she wanted to move the conversation to a more private venue, she was startled by a sob. The store owner had doubled over, her face in her hands.

"Mrs. Cross—Margaret, are you okay?" Becca raced to her side, and, shuffling onto the sofa beside her, tentatively reached one arm around the older woman's broad back, patting her shoulders as they heaved up and down with tears.

"She'll be fine." Elizabeth stepped back through the open doorway holding a tray with a teapot and three mugs. "Did you meet him yet? The man?"

Becca looked up. She seemed about to answer, when Margaret broke in.

"There is no other man. Only my Frank." The woman on the sofa sobbed once, with what might have seemed like dramatic emphasis. "He's gone."

Becca patted her back again as she looked to the sister for clarification.

The other woman only shook her grey curls as she placed the tray on the table. "Sugar?"

"No, please don't bother."

Elizabeth disappeared back into the kitchen, leaving Becca with the distraught Margaret—and a confused cat. Becca liked her tea sweet.

"Margaret…" Becca focused on the woman beside her. "Mrs. Cross, I'm sorry. I didn't know. Was it sudden?"

"Was it…?" A bleary face turned up to Becca, trails of mascara mirroring the wild black hair. "Frank's not *dead*. Not yet, anyway."

"Frank's been unfaithful." Elizabeth, returning, put down a silver sugar bowl and three spoons. "I warned you, Margaret."

"Oh." Becca paused, the possibilities sinking in. "And you think that…"

"I know!" Another glare as Margaret pulled a handkerchief out of her sleeve and wiped her face. "That black-haired minx downstairs."

Elizabeth took this in stride as she sat and poured the tea. If she'd looked up, she'd have seen the play of emotion over Becca's face. At first, Clara thought her person would use this very reasonable excuse to leave. But, no. Although Becca was kind, she was also determined. Taking a deep breath, she began to speak.

"Ms. Cross, I've got to ask…" Another breath to get the words out. "If you thought Gaia—Gail—was involved with your husband, well, it would be understandable, if you were angry… If you wanted to… I mean, if you had suspicions…"

"Suspicions?" Becca didn't get a chance to finish. "I've known something was going on for a while. Late nights at that dead-end car lot of his. Like he was really sitting there all alone. I have my sensitivities too!" This was directed toward her sister, who only nodded.

"Car lot?" Becca's face brightened. "Oh, is he—are you the Crosses of Cross Cars, the used car lot down by the river?"

"Don't tell me you ever bought a car from him?" She barked out a laugh. "No, of course not. I'd know if he'd sold any."

The older woman's glare didn't invite an answer.

"Well, anyway." Becca cleared her throat. "I mean, it would be only human if you wanted to implicate the other woman in a less personal crime. Or perhaps scare her…"

49

"Scare her? I'm the one who's bereft." The tears had stopped. Margaret's mood, however, had not improved. "He was out late again last night, and when I came home today, he was gone. He's cleaned everything out."

"Everything?" Becca craned her head around, confused. Although she appeared to be taking in the reasonably full bookshelf, the shelf of plants, and what looked like a high-end sound system, Clara knew she was looking for a particularly stinky baggie.

"What?" The bark of the question pulled her back to Margaret's scowl, which creased her lipstick alarmingly. "This? This is all mine. But his rings, his watches—they're all gone! All the little presents I gave him."

A sudden intake of breath as she jumped up, racing to a door at the far end of the room. "I knew it!"

With a quizzical glance toward Elizabeth, Becca rose. She followed the voice and found Margaret in what was clearly the master bedroom. Leaning over a low vanity, she was staring into an opened jewelry box, whose gold satin lining matched both the curtains and the fluffy duvet behind her.

"He took mother's pearls, Bitsy," she called out, and then pulled a lower drawer open. "And my diamond earrings as well."

With that, she turned, fixing Becca with dark eyes sparking with rage. "If he gave my sparklers to that little hussy, I swear, I'm going to kill them both."

***

"I think we should alert the police." Ten minutes later, and the three were sitting in the living room again. On Becca's urging, Margaret had made an inventory of her valuables. Sure enough, although the electronics were all untouched, everything small and pocketable had been taken. "This might have been the work of a professional."

"It's the work of that little hussy." Margaret had gone from tears to anger and back again, and now slurped her tea. "Believe me, I know."

"I'm sorry, Margaret. But how can you be sure?" Becca turned to the other sister for confirmation, but Elizabeth was pouring the last of the tea into Margaret's mug. When that was done, she rose without a word and retreated to the kitchen. "Have you spoken with your husband?"

"I've been trying him all day. He's not answering his phone."

"You haven't been either." The words slipped out. "I'm sorry, but I was trying to reach you."

"I wasn't in any shape to talk to anyone else." Margaret sniffed. "Besides, I wanted to leave the line free. I don't trust those things."

There was no easy answer to that, so Becca changed the subject. "Maybe he lost his phone? Maybe he's been busy?"

Margaret shook off the idea. "I've had an idea for a while now. I just thought I could catch them before it came to this."

"Ah." Becca turned thoughtful. "Is that why you hired me?"

"What? No." A glare like a hawk. "Someone has been stealing from me, and this just makes me even surer it's that girl. Gail—Gaia—whatever she calls herself. I'm sure that once you start looking into it—"

"That's just it. I can't," Becca interrupted her. "That's why I was trying to reach you earlier today, Mrs. Cross. I have a conflict of interest. That's only one reason I think you really need to talk to—"

"It's that girl." Her gaze was piercing, and Becca squirmed a little, even as she spooned sugar into her tea. "She's hired you, too. Hasn't she?"

"I'm not at liberty to say." Becca tried to sound firm. In truth, she wasn't sure of the etiquette of the situation. Did hiring a witch detective automatically convey confidentiality? It seemed like it ought to.

"She's outsmarted me every step of the way." Margaret looked angry now, rather than sad. Her cracked lipstick set in a tight red line until she started speaking again, and this time her fury seemed directed at Becca. "You do realize what she's doing, don't you? She's playing you. Playing you to get to me. She knew I was going to talk to you. She saw me taking down your number, only she got to you first. What did she say? Did she accuse me of something? Financial malfeasance? Spousal cruelty? I bet Frank spun her some stories about me…"

Becca swallowed, her eyes darting to the kitchen, but Elizabeth did not re-emerge. "I'm sorry," she said one more time. Only this time, her voice sounded a little more resolute. "I understand that this all very difficult, but if you won't let me call the police about the jewelry theft, I don't see what else I can do here. This seems to be a domestic matter that I really don't want to be a part of."

"Oh, you're part of it, young lady. In fact, I'm wondering if you two came up with this together." The scowl deepened into something truly scary.

Becca put her mug down, frustrated. She no longer wanted to drink anything in this house. What she wanted to do was leave. "Wait a minute. You came to me. I have not conspired with anyone. I don't do that," she said. "In fact, as a witch, you should know our basic rule—as long as ye harm none."

"Tell that to Gail." The woman across from her pushed her own mug away and slumped in her seat. Suddenly, she looked no more than an old woman, defeated and in mourning. "Frank wasn't a great husband by any means, but he was the only one I had. Bitsy was right about that girl. She doesn't care about the shop, about the craft. She's just into whatever she can get."

Becca, having witnessed the other girl's lax attitude, bit her lip.

"I knew he was up to something with that lot of his. He never wanted me to come down there. Never mind that I paid for it. She was probably hoping for a free car or something. Wait till she discovers Frank has no money of his own," she said, half to herself. "Then she'll see who's been taken for a ride. I wouldn't be surprised if she gets rid of him before long."

***

When it became apparent that no amount of persuasion would get Margaret to call the cops, Becca stood to leave. "I'm sorry," she said again, heading toward the door, though Clara inferred her regret had more to do with showing up at all than for the other woman's sorrows. "I really have to go."

It was near dark by the time she was out on the street again. Around her, the lights of the city were casting colors over the sidewalk, making it easy for Clara to sidle up to her person with care. Becca might have been oblivious even if her pet had made herself visible, the calico realized, as her person collapsed against the brick wall with a deep sigh.

"Becca?" At the sound of her name, she jumped. Elizabeth was standing beside her. "I didn't mean to startle you, but I wanted to catch you."

"It's no problem." Becca's brow furrowed. "I'm sorry. I didn't hear you come down."

The other woman only smiled. "I wanted to tell you how grateful I am for you coming here today. For your interest in Charm and Cherish."

"But I'm not—" Becca shook her head. "I don't know how much you heard, but I'm not taking your sister's case. I think she should go to the police. Maybe you can work on her?"

"Maybe." A noncommittal shrug. "But she's right, you know. Her husband was stealing from her. Still, there are other reasons…"

"I get that she's embarrassed." Becca filled in the blank. "But she'll have to file for insurance, especially if there are family heirlooms involved."

"Of course, and we are family." Elizabeth reached out, putting her

53

cool hand on top of Becca's. "Be careful, dear."

Becca nodded, a million thoughts playing across her face. "Thanks," she said, and turned away.

"And you, too." Elizabeth whispered, her gaze directed to the shadowed calico at her feet.

Chapter 7

"I must have imagined that," Clara told herself, frozen to the spot. *"Could I have misheard?"*

Fancy rarely got the better of the little calico. Cats in general are extremely practical. But recently Clara had realized that she'd been taking on some of Becca's quirks, most likely because she loved her so—a trait her own two sisters never hesitated to point out. After all, nothing else made sense. So when the older woman turned, chuckling softly, back to the shadowed building entrance, Clara shook herself whiskers to tail, and looked around for Becca.

Her person had paused only a few yards away in front of that colorful Charm and Cherish window, now lit from within as the afternoon sun faded. But although Becca appeared to be considering her options, she didn't pull open the door with its friendly bell. Instead, she stayed on the sidewalk, her round face drawn with concern, as she gazed in at the raven-haired salesgirl behind the counter who appeared utterly absorbed in her cell phone.

Was her person considering warning Gaia/Gail about her employer's rage or interrogating her further about the identity of her not-a-boyfriend? Clara couldn't tell, although the slight frown on her person's face alerted her that some serious thinking was going on. And so when Becca shook her head and kept walking, her pet could only be relieved. It wasn't that late. This time of year, dusk came early. Still, it was time for Becca and her pet to retire. Clara wanted to think through that odd final encounter with that strange Elizabeth. The two sisters might look alike, but Clara had the distinct impression that they were as different as, well, Clara and her siblings. And no matter how nasty that Margaret might be, Clara couldn't help but think that she was the safer one for Becca—and for herself.

Clara was musing about how odd humans could be when she suddenly realized that she had lost her person in the growing dark. Panicked, she dropped her shading for a moment, her back arching like a Halloween cat.

"What the—!" A man in a business suit stopped just short of tripping over her, causing the bike messenger behind him to swerve. The cyclist nearly hit a tree, and while Clara looked up at the businessman in a silent, wide-eyed apology, he had turned to vent his rage elsewhere.

"You're not supposed to ride on the sidewalk!" he screamed at the cyclist. "And you're supposed to have a light."

Hopping on one foot as he righted his bike, the cyclist eyed him coolly, blue eyes wide. Dressed in a black pullover and jeans dyed the same hue, he looked lean and fit, a creature of the growing dark, with a helmet to match and a scent that was vaguely familiar. If these two were to fight, Clara would have bet on the cyclist, despite the businessman's obvious pique. That is, if cats were gambling animals. Which, the plump animal reminded herself, they were not.

Nor was the slender young man the type to take offense. "Sorry, man," was all he said, but his voice wasn't the one Clara was expecting. Her faint memory dissipated as, readjusting his helmet, the cyclist kicked off and was gone. By the time the pedestrian had turned back to Clara, she had shaded herself once again and dashed behind him, desperate to figure out where her person had gone.

Being a cat has some advantages. Small and agile, if not quite as lithe as Laurel, Clara was able to weave through the crowd emerging from the T. Shaded and nearly invisible, she had to be extra careful, especially when a young mother pushing a stroller lost her grip, for a moment, on the hand of her toddler, who stumbled right at the calico.

"Kitty!" The little girl chortled with glee as Clara scrambled up the trunk of a small maple.

Alerted by the cry, her frazzled-looking mother reached over and grabbed her hand. "There's no kitty there, Lily," she said.

Clara didn't have time to puzzle out what had happened. Had she let her shading fade once again, startled by the oncoming stroller? Or did the child have power of some sort? She thought again of Elizabeth and her odd farewell. She'd bring it up to her sisters later, she decided as she craned around. The maple wasn't tall, though its placement broke up the concrete cityscape nicely. And Clara had to maneuver around a squirrel who had already tucked himself in for the night in order to spy through a break in the scarlet leaves.

"*I mean no harm,*" she murmured as the fluffy rodent started in alarm, scrabbling at the tree's smooth bark as he did. For a moment, she thought about uncloaking, then decided against it. From the look on that grey face, the sudden appearance of a cat might be enough to cause him to fall off the limb entirely.

The height didn't help. Even though her feline vision barely acknowledged the growing dusk, Clara couldn't see Becca's curls or her silly velvet hat. Not even that perky feather showed itself above the crowd. That didn't mean she should worry; Clara knew that. After all, maybe Becca had just stopped to pick up some dinner or a treat for later. But something was making the fur along her spine stiffen. Maybe it was the bitterness with which the older woman talked about her employee. Or maybe it was Gaia herself. Something was off with those two women, and every guard hair on her body was on alert. In desperation, she closed her eyes, raising her nose into the air.

Success! She got it—a slight scent of her person, faint but distinct. Over...where was it? Yes, toward the river. Scrambling down the tree in a rush that nearly upset the squirrel, she dashed down into the gutter, the better to make a beeline toward the young woman whose happiness and safety were Clara's main responsibility.

By the time she reached her, the young woman was heading down a street Clara had never seen before. Though only a few blocks away, it felt like a different city. Clara was used to her own part of Cambridge. In their own neighborhood, even the larger red-brick buildings were softened by window boxes and a few stately beech trees. On the main drag they had just visited, at least the lights were colorful, as was that captive maple poking out of the sidewalk.

The street they had just turned down might as well have been on the moon. Treeless—grassless, even—all was hard and dry, and in the growing dark, the industrial buildings that climbed above the concrete sidewalks loomed like watchful giants. Sniffing the air, Clara caught traces of the river, and the reeds along its shore. Even with her superior night vision, however, she could see no sign of such greenery. Not through the high chain-link fence that Becca now approached, or in the cracked asphalt of the lot beyond.

Instead of grass or trees, Clara could see several cars that seemed to be frozen in time, judging from the fine layer of dust on all but one of them. Only minutes from the bustling city center, the strip felt foreign—and dangerous. Every instinct told the small cat not to go farther. But there was Becca, walking through that deserted lot, toward the cinder-block building at its center. The squat building, at least, showed signs of life. Its glass front shown with light, and from where she watched, Clara could see the glow from another opening in the back. And so, gathering up her courage, the little cat dashed over the open tarmac to catch up with her, just as Becca pushed the door open.

"Hello?" The room was dominated by an empty desk and the strong smell of burned coffee. Overhead, a fluorescent bulb buzzed. "Is there anyone here?"

Becca looked around. The window showed only the lot outside, still and dark, but a door to the right stood slightly ajar. More light and the smell of that coffee emanated from within. Raising her voice, she cleared her throat and tried again. "Hello?"

"Calm down!" a man's voice called from behind the door.

"Mr. Cross?" Becca's voice rose with tension as she took a step forward. "I'm sorry. I didn't mean to startle you, but I—"

"Please!" The voice sounded agitated, and Becca stopped in her tracks. On the other side of the door, the man started speaking again, only this time his voice was quieter. Clara, whose hearing far surpassed her human's, made sure to shade herself carefully and crept by Becca. Her person might want to respect Frank Cross's privacy, but it was easy enough for the shadowy calico to slink by, even without additional magic, squeezing through the narrow opening without nudging it further.

The man in the small office might not have noticed her even if she had. Pudgy and sweating, with a skein of brown hair that ran across a glistening pate, he paced, oblivious to anything other than the beige phone squawking in his hand.

"Please, I promise."

As Clara watched, he pushed his damp hair back farther on his head and patted it. If that hair had been Harriet, it would have bit back, the way he kept at it, flattening it out. He still might not have noticed, as focused as he was on the phone, which was pressed so tightly to his ear that only the faintest sound escaped.

"No, you're wrong." He licked dry lips and paused in his pacing. "No." Leaning forward, he caught his desk chair with one hand, and Clara wondered if he was going to be sick. "Please!"

Something was wrong, horribly wrong, and Clara's thoughts went to her person. Zipping through the nearly closed door, she found Becca still standing, caught in her uncertainty.

"Let's leave!" the calico did her best to suggest, thinking of the brisk, fresh air outside. Of the nice warm apartment that awaited. But Clara didn't have Laurel's gift, and besides, Becca was caught up in this interaction, despite being unsure of what to do.

"Mr. Cross?" Her voice was so soft that even had he not been on the phone, Clara doubted he would have heard it.

"No!" So loud Becca started. "I didn't…I wouldn't ever…" A clatter as the balding man slammed down the receiver, and then a loud sigh. Becca gathered herself up to knock on the half-closed door when another sound broke the silence: wracking sobs, like a man overcome with grief or, possibly, shame. Letting her hand fall to her side, Becca stepped back, and then turned and left, as quietly as she had entered.

"Well," she said, once she was again on the darkened street. "Maybe that's settled. It sounds like she reached him!"

She might have thought she was speaking to herself, but the day's curious interactions had Clara thinking. Perhaps she had misinterpreted Elizabeth's odd farewell, or the woman had been disoriented by the dusk. Perhaps the toddler on the street had been confused by the squirrel, or simply liked to yell out "kitty!" Clara had little experience of human kittenhood. But, increasingly, she wondered about her own connection with Becca. The bond between them was so strong, wasn't it likely that her person sensed her presence? At times like this, it was all the little calico could do to resist twining around her person's ankles. Only the knowledge that her sudden appearance here, in this bleak industrial part of town, would give Becca a fright kept her from letting her presence be felt. As it was, Becca appeared more relaxed as she turned toward home.

"Maddy? I've got some good news for you." Clara wasn't crazy about

Becca talking on her phone as she walked. Cambridge was her home, but it was still a big city, and the spotted cat wished her person would stay alert to her surroundings, especially now that the dusk had given way to night. Still, it was useful to eavesdrop on Becca's conversation.

"Uh-huh, I'm still taking Gaia's case," she was saying to her friend. "But I'm free of the other one, her boss's." Clara couldn't hear the other side of the conversation, but from the way Becca was nodding, she could guess that her friend was repeating her advice that Becca drop the whole thing.

"There might not even be a case," she picked up once her friend fell silent. "I mean, Margaret, the boss, was saying that someone was embezzling, but I think she was just angry at Gaia. She thought her husband was having an affair with her. I think she was trying to frame Gaia. And maybe scare her, too." Becca's voice dropped to a conspiratorial whisper. "I think maybe she saw the root that Gaia brought over and stole it."

Slight squawks escaped from the phone.

"It's—no, Maddy, I'm not getting involved in anything criminal. In fact, I'm walking away now. I had a hunch, when she wouldn't let me call the police, even though she was wailing about jewelry being stolen. She was trying to convince me that her husband had taken it and run off. Sure enough, her husband is at work. To be honest, I think he was dodging her calls, but when I walked in, they were clearly having it out. Don't worry, Maddy, I'm not getting between them. I don't know what he did, and I don't want to know. But I can tell you he feels super bad about it now."

Becca paused. "Didn't I tell you? I went to see him. She said something about his lot, and I realized that used car lot over on Putnam had to be his. We pass by it all the time. You know the place I mean— Cross Auto, with that big sign that says, 'Ask Frank! Make a deal!'"

The sounds from the other line were quieter this time.

"No, I wasn't sure what I was going to say. Maybe, 'Call your wife,' or something. I just thought I should drop by. Confirm the facts. I may be a witch, but I've got to do the basic legwork, right? But it didn't even come to that. I was waiting in the front room—I don't know, maybe his receptionist had left already, if he has one—and I could hear him in his office. He must have finally picked up one of Margaret's calls. He was apologizing like anything. To be honest, it sounded like he could barely get a word in."

She was smiling and shaking her head even as she listened to Maddy's reply.

"I don't know, Maddy. I don't think I'd want to be either one of them. I was with Margaret, so I know how angry she can get. Not that she didn't have reason if what she suspected was true. But I figure whatever was going wrong has been put right. I have never heard someone trying to explain himself so fast," Becca said. "I mean, he didn't even sound apologetic so much as he sounded scared!"

Becca was small for a human, but as she relaxed, her stride lengthened and Clara had to trot to keep up. Still, she was grateful for this indication that her person was happier. Even the squawking from the other end of the line sounded quieter.

"Yeah, I know." Becca nodded, as if her friend could see her. "Believe me, I don't want to get between those two either."

Becca broke into a grin as her friend responded, much to Clara's relief. Still, she tilted an ear forward as her person lowered her voice once more.

"I'm going to stay on Gaia's case, though. It's not just that I could use the experience, Maddy. Even if she can't pay me, I signed a contract."

More noise.

"No, I'm sorry, but I have to, Maddy. Because what if I'm wrong about Margaret just trying to scare the girl? What if someone really did try to poison Gaia? And what if they try again?"

Chapter 8

Clara was exhausted by the time she got home, racing Becca the last few blocks. Not that this stopped her sisters from pestering her for news.

"*What happened?*" Laurel nudged her with one chocolate-dipped paw. "*Did you find out anything about that girl Gaia?*"

"*Where has Becca been?*" Harriet sat back, her flag-like tail flicking back and forth with anxiety. "*Doesn't she know how we worry?*"

"*She's on her way.*" Clara made sure to answer her oldest sister first and address her unspoken concern. "*I'm sure she'll feed us as soon as she gets in.*"

"*Humph,*" Harriet snorted, pulling her tail around her toes. She wasn't satisfied, Clara knew. She was, however, a little self-conscious about being so single-minded. "*You think that's all I care about.*"

"*Well?*" Laurel pushed Harriet aside. "*Did she meet anyone cute?*"

The image of the brown-eyed stranger flitted through Clara's mind, and Laurel purred in response. "*He was just someone on the street,*" Clara snapped.

The little calico wanted nothing so much as to bathe. The dust from the used car lot had gotten beneath her fur. Even her whiskers felt gritty. More than that, a good tongue bath would soothe the lingering concerns that had ruffled her fur. Still, Laurel would not be kept waiting.

"*You were right about Gaia,*" she said. "*That girl is trouble.*" Quickly, she told them about the visit to the shop. The fact that Gaia seemed lackadaisical, at best, about her job didn't seem to concern Laurel much. If anything, that seemed quite reasonable to a cat. When Clara got to the storeowner's accusations, however, both her sisters' ears pricked up.

"*She...collects men?*" Laurel interrupted before Clara could get up to the strange interaction with Elizabeth, and the calico flicked her own tail in annoyance. The sealpoint sister had long wanted Becca to be more romantically adventurous, but Clara didn't think this was the way to do it.

"*Other women's men,*" cautioned the calico.

"*Oh, that's not good.*" Laurel's ears lay flat, and she turned toward Harriet.

"*What?*" Harriet turned toward the front door. "*You told me that you wanted to let Becca do this by herself, and now...*"

"*Harriet, what did you do...?*" But it was too late. Even before Clara could finish her thought, her sisters had raced ahead to stand at attention at the door. A moment later, they could hear the familiar footsteps slowly ascending the stairs and then the key in the lock.

"Hi, kitties." Becca's good cheer sounded intact, even if her voice was tired. "How nice of you to meet me like this."

"*You!*" Harriet mewed plaintively. "*Where were you?*"

"I bet you want your dinner, don't you?"

Laurel's eyes closed in satisfaction. Not that she'd have had to work that hard to suggest the idea to their generous human.

"I'll get right to it, as soon as I get my coat and hat off."

"*Thank you!*" Clara twined around Becca's legs, grateful to finally be able to express herself physically. Her person seemed to appreciate the contact, even as she almost tripped, laughing, over the plump cat. It was Harriet who put a stop to the fooling around.

"*Stop that!*" she hissed, cuffing her baby sister on the ear.

Hunger, Clara figured, and accepted the rebuke quietly. But even though her oldest sister made quick work of her can, Clara couldn't help but wonder at her comparative lack of enthusiasm. For a change, it was Laurel who looked over, licking her chops, to see if Clara was going to leave anything behind. Harriet had already raced ahead to the living room.

"*What's with Harriet?*" Clara asked. "*Is she feeling all right?*"

"*Why don't you go see?*" Laurel eyed the crumbs in Clara's dish, and after a moment's hesitation, Clara backed off. Harriet might be a pain, but she was her sister. She trotted into the living room after her.

"Maddy? I'm home." Becca spoke to her phone in much the tone of voice she used with her cats. "Sorry, I should have called you five minutes ago but I had to feed the kitties."

A smile down at Clara warmed the little calico.

"No, I think I'm in for the night. It's been a big day, but thank you." Even as she spoke, Becca shed her shoes and settled on the sofa. "I haven't had a chance to even look at my own work today. You know." She reached to rub her foot, and Clara made a mental note to knead it later. "Those documents about my family."

She was taking up a position near her person's ankle as Maddy rambled on. Something about a party, Clara gathered. A man—or men—that Maddy wanted Becca to meet, and for a moment she found herself remembering the kind-faced stranger in the square.

"I think I'm just not ready yet." Becca could have been talking to Clara, and so the calico bent to her task, kneading the stockinged foot. "I do not want a knight in shining armor, Maddy." The foot withdrew. "I just…well, for tonight, I'm happy with my cats. Have a blast, Maddy.

Tell me all about it tomorrow."

With that, Clara got back to her work, albeit gentler than before. Becca opened her laptop and soon the machine was purring in her lap, as Laurel stretched her tawny length across the sofa's back. Within minutes Harriet had joined them on the sofa and was lounging on her pillow, one paw flicking its golden tassels. Another perfect evening, as far as the calico was concerned.

But even as Clara focused on Becca's foot, she picked up that something was off. It couldn't be her kneading. She was very careful not to use any claw at all. Nor was it the laptop. Although Becca often reacted strangely to the images she'd summoned, tonight she was actually humming as she read, and Laurel, in an ostentatious show of self-restraint, wasn't even trying to bat at its warm and enticing surface. No, it was Harriet. Although to all outward appearances, her oldest sister was as relaxed as usual, her impressive bulk spread out across the pillow, the oldest of the three cats was holding herself back.

She was not only tense, Clara realized, she was concentrating—on the edge of a small baggie peeking out from beneath the coffee table.

"*You returned it?*" Clara chirped softly. Harriet didn't usually admit to mistakes. "*How wise of you.*"

The compliment earned a snort. "*I had to dig it out of the litter.*" Harriet's head reared back in disgust. "*But you were right. Becca seems to think this is important.*"

"*Shall I?*" Clara didn't want to interfere if Harriet had a plan.

"*Go ahead!*"

Clara jumped to the floor and with a well-aimed tap sent the plastic baggie spinning on the pivot of the lumpy root inside. Sure enough, a moment later, Becca was on her knees beside the sofa.

"Well, I'll be…" She grabbed the baggie and examined its odoriferous contents. "I could've sworn I looked under here."

Clara, who was licking her paw, didn't comment. That musty smell carried even through the baggie.

"*How do you feel?*" Laurel peeked over the edge of the sofa, blue eyes wide.

"*A little dirty,*" Clara admitted, even as she dug in between her toes.

"*No dizziness? Shortness of breath?*"

Clara paused, mouth open. "*You don't think that the poison...*"

The feline equivalent of a shrug. "*Harriet's got more mass, shall we say...*"

"*Hey!*" A white mitt slapped Laurel's chocolate ear. "*Watch it!*"

"*Sorry.*" Laurel's face retreated, but Clara could imagine her sister's head ducked in submission. Harriet's largesse only extended so far.

"*I think we're fine,*" the calico called up. "*Only the smell lingers.*"

"*Good.*" Laurel's head appeared over the lip of the sofa again, her eyes slightly crossed. "*'Cause I'm not so sure about Becca.*"

Clara whipped around, alarmed. Sure enough, Becca was sitting on the floor beside her, frowning as she held the baggie up to the light.

"I don't know about this," she was saying. Clara looked up at Laurel, but her sister only shrugged. "And I'm glad I didn't come right out and accuse her. But I do think I owe Margaret Cross an apology."

Chapter 9

"Now you've done it!" Clara was struggling to keep her voice level. Her fur was already standing up along her spine and it was only by holding her tail down with one paw that she managed to keep that from turning into a bottle-brush of fright. *"Becca was off that case, and now she's going to talk to that crazy woman again."*

Her slinky sister eyed her, curious, but Clara turned away. Bad enough Laurel could read human minds. Clara wasn't ready yet to share what had happened at the Cross apartment. That woman—Elizabeth— had unnerved her, as few human beings could, and the moment when she could have disclosed the odd interaction had passed. This left Clara feeling out of sorts, almost as if she were alone in a shelter. Or a trap.

If Becca ran out to confront that woman again, Clara wasn't sure what she would do.

For the moment, though, her fear was allayed. After another examination of the bagged root, Becca set it aside and, after carefully washing her hands, prepared her own dinner, which involved too many plants to be of interest to her pets. More satisfying was the speed with which she finished and settled back on the sofa with her laptop.

"Of course she does that after eating. For her, that's like grooming,"

Laurel noted as she pretzeled herself around to lick her haunches. The part-Siamese didn't quite understand Becca's research—none of the cats did entirely—but Clara saw enough truth in her observation not to correct her. She might not understand Becca's work in depth, but she did know that "doing research," as her person put it, made her happy. Besides, she was too grateful for her person's continued presence to object. For comfort, she joined Becca on the sofa. Harriet was already nestled by her side, her fluffy form stretched not only over her special velvet pillow but extending nearly to the arm rest. But Clara was still too agitated for a nap. Instead, she perched on the sofa's upholstered back, from where she could peer over Becca's shoulder at the screen.

If only Clara could feel as single-minded, or as calm, as her person.

"*What is it?*" Laurel had jumped up beside her, so silently that she startled her baby sister, whose nerves were already on edge.

"*She's looking at pictures.*" Clara knew her sister had difficulty making sense of pixels. Laurel's sense of smell might be better than hers, but her eyesight left something to be desired. "*Pictures of plants.*"

"*How silly.*" Laurel whipped her dark tail around her toes. "*Why look at pictures when she could simply go outside.*"

"*But it's dark out and we don't want her to go...*" Clara broke off.

With a sigh, Becca had closed the herbalism site and clicked open a news alert. "The accident," she murmured. "No wonder the bridge was closed."

She read a moment longer, then clicked and another page appeared, one Clara had seen before. Along with the writing, which might as well be sparrow tracks to the cats, it featured pictures, reproductions of old engravings. This was the genealogy project Becca had been telling Maddy about, Clara realized. The research she longed to resume. Although she had seen her person looking through these pages—what Becca called an "online historical database"—before, something about Becca's silence, or maybe it was her own unsettled mood, showed the word in a new light. Becca was searching for her family. For the small cat, whose only memories of her own mother were few and fading, the search seemed impossibly sad. Yes, Becca spoke to her mother weekly, using one or another of her devices, but she was alone in this city. Alone, except for her cats, Clara reminded herself.

Besides, mused Clara, looking over at her snoozing siblings, blood relations weren't necessarily a requirement for domestic happiness.

Silently vowing to be a better helpmate to her person, Clara pushed her own sibling issues aside and focused in on Becca. As she watched, Becca scrolled down through the database's images until she settled on one that the calico had seen before. In it, a woman sat with a cat on her lap. Something about her face—the bright eyes, perhaps—looked like Becca, only with longer hair and any trace of Becca's curls squashed under a cap. With one outstretched finger, Becca traced the outline of the woman's round face. Did this strange, flat representation bring back memories of Becca's mother? Of herself? Clara couldn't tell. Besides, to the calico it was the feline on the woman's lap who was the real focus of the picture. That cat, who even in the scratchy black-and-white image bore a striking resemblance to Clara, occupied the center of the composition, drawing the eye even as she stared out at the viewer.

Despite the centuries between them, Clara felt the connection—and felt reassured, as if the calico in the picture was somehow reaching out. An older generation keeping watch over Clara and her person. Maybe, Clara thought, there was something to Laurel's gift—a psychic connection that went back generations. Or maybe she was just too tired to worry anymore, and what she took as comfort was simply gratitude that Becca had remained on the couch rather than run out into the night.

It had been a full day, even without that strange confrontation. Brief as it was—only three words—Clara knew that encounter with

Elizabeth was at the root of her desire to keep Becca away from those women. Knew as well that she was hiding the truth from her own siblings. She told herself this was her sisters' fault. Harriet and Laurel complained whenever their person did anything involving other humans or the outside world, or, truly, whenever she left them alone. To give them any more reason to grumble could only lead to further unpleasantness if not outright trouble.

"Why trouble?" Clara turned to see Laurel's blue eyes staring into hers.

"Did you just read my thoughts?" Clara reared up, nearly falling off the sofa. Her sister had startled her—and invaded her privacy. *"Please don't do that!"*

"Oh, please!" The Siamese licked at one dark paw. *"It's almost the same as suggesting thoughts, only, more like inhaling..."*

Clara eyed her sister with curiosity, even as she tried to keep her own mind blank.

"And I did smell something off about that plant, you know. Something that Becca isn't aware of. My nose is very good. I think you did too, only you never focus..."

Before Clara could respond, the woman seated in front of them jerked back and began to type. "Why didn't I think of this before?" The two cats seated behind her exchanged a weighted glance.

"Dear Aunt Tabitha," she murmured as she typed. "I'm not sure if you know, but I'm living in Cambridge now, and being in New England, I've started to research our family history..."

"Our family?" Laurel's soft mew dripped with scorn. In her distinctive Siamese yowl, that first word dragged out into a wail.

"She means hers." Clara translated as quickly and politely as she could. She didn't want Becca to be disturbed, certainly not by the idea that one of her cats was in pain. But Becca had grown used to her cats' strange sounds. With barely a glimpse at the felines behind her,

71

she continued typing. And so, after a moment's pause, Clara carried on, too. *"She thinks that it was her ancestor who got them in trouble with the witch trials,"* she said. Thanks to her particular gifts, Clara had accompanied Becca to both the library and the city's archives, and considered herself well versed in that aspect of her work.

"Well, it was their fault." Another sniff of that neat black velvet nose. Laurel claimed their family history as her own area of expertise. *"Great Grandmama would never have been so careless."*

Clara didn't comment. In part, because she agreed—cats had been caught up in witchcraft trials over the centuries almost always because of mistakes their people had made. In part, because she was also hoping to hear more of what Becca was trying to communicate to this aunt of hers. Although she vaguely understood the idea of writing, she couldn't read. It was only because of her diligence staring at Becca's keyboard that she even managed to make sense of the flat, scentless images that popped up there, seemingly at the coaxing of her person's quick-moving fingers. Thanks to Laurel—even if she was loath to admit it—Clara knew the basics of her own family history. Knew about their ancient lineage and their bond with the special humans with whom they lived. Still, both her sisters had been frustratingly vague about the details of their royal duties. Clara was hoping for more.

So, it seemed, was Becca, from the hopeful lift in her voice. "If you have any information, would you let me know?"

A flourish and a final tap, and Becca sat back with a sigh that would have done Harriet proud. Of course, by then, Clara's oldest sister was snoring gently once again on her special velvet pillow. In truth, Clara was starting to doze, too. But when Becca roused herself to head toward her bed soon after, her smallest cat joined her, knowing her sisters would be along soon.

Chapter 10

It seemed but a moment later that Becca's phone began to buzz.

"Aunt Tabby?" Becca sat up, blinking, as if from a pleasant dream, unsettling the three felines who were stretched out alongside her. "No, wait," she reached for the device, which had begun to skitter across the nightstand like a beetle on its back. "Of course not. Hey, Maddy, what's up? How was the party?"

A few minutes later and Harriet was once again asleep. Laurel had jumped down in search of some more entertaining company, while Clara, eyes still closed, was doing her best to remember a particularly fascinating dream.

"A cute new feline specialist?" Her person's voice reached her through her drowse, but even as she listened, she let herself continue to drift. Something about their mother...or was it their great-grandmother? Becca's voice broke in once more. "Do you mean for me or for the cats?"

A pause, but the dream image was gone.

"Okay, not cute. Sweet. So, did you like him?"

As Becca rambled on, Clara stretched. She had slept through most of the night, which was unusual. The day's adventures had clearly taken their toll, and she'd been grateful to have her person safe at home. If only she could count on a lazy Sunday, she thought, examining one white front paw, all would be well. However, a tingling of her long guard hairs alerted her that something was up, and she sheathed the claws she'd begun trimming. Becca might not realize it yet, but she was about to require her pet's full attention.

"Wait, Maddy, you're not making sense. He does emergency care? Oh, hang on." Becca held the phone away from her ear and studied it with the intensity Laurel would give a bug. "I've got…I've got to take this."

Perhaps to change her view, Becca stood and walked toward the window. "Hi, Mrs. Cross," she said. The smile on her face must have been a little bit forced, but it lightened her voice regardless. "I was meaning to call you. I might have been a bit rude—uh, hasty in some things I said, but I'm afraid I really can't reconsider. I understand that you're upset, but my other client did approach me first. For what it's worth, I did attempt to speak to your husband…"

Becca jumped down, accidentally nudging Harriet, who grunted. "*What's up?*" She blinked up at Clara and then over at their person. "*Why's Becca so awake?*"

"*I think she's upset,*" answered Clara with concern.

"Wait, no. Mrs. Cross—Margaret, please slow down." Becca put a hand out, as if she could physically contain the woman on the other end. "No, I didn't see him. I went down to the lot, though, and I heard him. I thought you two were talking on the phone… What do you mean, did I talk to the police? Mrs. Cross, please—I'm sorry, what? But that's impossible. I was just there. And I know that when I left, your husband was still alive."

***

"*What is she doing?*" Even though Becca had hurriedly served her cats their breakfast, Harriet was fretting. And for once, Clara couldn't

74

blame her. Here it was, Sunday morning, and yet Becca had already grabbed her coat and was in the process of wrapping a scarf around her neck. The three cats circled her uneasily as she searched for her hat. *"Doesn't she know we need her here?"*

"I'm sure she'll be back in time for dinner." Laurel had mastered the feline equivalent of side eye, quite a feat considering that her blue eyes tended to cross when she concentrated. *"What I want to know is why she's bundling up like some arctic explorer."*

"A what?" Harriet scrunched up her already abbreviated nose. *"Oh, you mean the scarf?"*

Becca had found the velvet cloche by then, on the floor behind the sofa. Its distinctive feather was missing.

"It was a fashion decision," Laurel huffed a bit defensively. *"But, no, I meant that awful puffy coat."*

"It must be getting cooler out." Clara didn't want to pick a fight, but she couldn't help feeling protective. After all, her sisters rarely left the house. *"And she doesn't have lovely, thick fur like you do,"* she added in an attempt to mollify her oldest sister.

"There are other ways to get warm." Laurel rolled the last word into a suggestive purr. *"And if she happens to meet someone…"* Clara knew her sister was going to suggest something slinkier, but Clara didn't linger to hear it. Becca had donned her hat and was heading out the door.

"I'm sorry, Maddy, you wouldn't believe what happened." Becca was walking so quickly, Clara had a hard time keeping pace. Only when she paused to call her friend back could the little calico catch up. "That was Margaret Cross on the other line. Her husband has been in some kind of an accident, I think. No, I don't have any details. That's why I'm on my way back there. Maddy, I have to go." Another pause as Becca waited to cross the street. "I was just at his office, you know, that lot by the river, last night, and she wants to talk with me. She's really upset."

This didn't seem to satisfy Becca's friend any more than it did Clara. In the bright morning light, the calico deepened her shading to remain unseen. However, being virtually invisible brought its own dangers, and the little cat's ears and whiskers were on high alert as Becca rushed heedlessly on, weaving between the churchgoers and the students out for Sunday brunch who seemed to congregate on every corner.

"No, you don't have to." Becca seemed to be talking her friend down from something as she race-walked into Central Square. "I'll call you as soon as I know what's going on. I promise."

To Clara's relief, the young woman shoved the phone in her pocket and actually looked around as she readied to cross Mass Ave. with its constant traffic. Down the block, Clara could see the red brick building that housed the magic shop and the Cross's apartment, as well as the blue-and-white Cambridge police cruiser out front.

"Excuse me." Becca began to work her way through the crowd of onlookers who blocked the store's brightly painted window. "I'm trying to reach the apartments."

A uniformed officer stood by the recessed entrance, blocking the building's metal door. "Are you a resident?"

"No, but I know a woman—"

"Residents only." He resumed his sentry position, staring over her head once more.

Becca stepped back as another couple pushed forward, either to try their luck or to pass through the crowd. Clara, who had hung back to avoid getting stepped on, saw Becca focus on Charm and Cherish. From this side, she could see the shop's colorful glass window and the lights that signaled it was occupied, if not open for business. Those lights seemed to draw Becca, and Clara couldn't help worrying as her person turned and began to make for the little shop's door.

"Gaia!" Becca called, and waved, perching on her toes to be seen above the crowd. Inside, behind the zodiac symbols, Clara could now see the black-haired shop girl talking to a man in a trench coat. "Over here!"

In the shop, the man had stepped away, and Gaia resumed her customary slump back against the wall, with its shelves of leaves and roots. Seeing an opening, Becca stepped forward, until a hand reached out to stop her.

"I wouldn't." Tall and lean, with black bangs that hung over a pale and serious face, he smelled vaguely familiar to Clara. Something about him must have gotten Becca's attention, too, the calico realized, as her person peered up at him.

"Excuse me?" She pulled her arm away as she spoke.

"I'm sorry." The flash of a grin as he ducked his head in an apology that even Harriet would understand. "I just…I think maybe it's better to stay out of this."

"But I know Gaia," Becca started to explain. "I mean, not well. I've been helping her. It's complicated." Becca turned back to the shop, which now appeared to be empty. Gaia and her interrogator had either stepped into the back or left through another exit.

"I get it." That smile again. Almost wolfish, Clara thought, especially against that dark hair. "Things with Gaia can be complicated." If he didn't exactly roll his eyes, he came close, before covering by brushing his hair back from his face.

"You know her? Wait, you're the bike messenger. The one who almost ran me over yesterday."

"I did? Gee, I'm sorry." His light blue eyes widened, dominating his pale face. "Really. Are you okay?"

"Yeah." Now it was Becca's turn to chuckle. "I guess neither of us were paying attention." She paused to take in the man before her. That hair, which could have come from the same dye package Gaia used, tended to distract from his prominent cheekbones and a generous mouth set in a serious line. "You're not Tiger, are you?"

77

He paused, regarding her with those icy blue eyes.

"I should explain," Becca rushed ahead. "Gaia told me she had a friend who was concerned for her." Clara noticed her use of the word "friend." She also saw the smile that had returned to the young man's pale face as he turned, once more, to take in the woman in front of him.

"Yeah, I guess I had reason to worry, huh?" As the import of his own words had hit him, the last of the grin disappeared. "Man, poor Gaia." He shook his head as they both regarded the colorful shop window. "So, I think I'm missing something." He turned away, and his face fell into shadow. "You said you were helping her?"

Becca nodded slowly, a contemplative look coming over her. "She hired me because she was worried about—about something. But she didn't expect this."

"No, she didn't." He must have seen the sadness there, because he reached out to gently brush her arm once more, and Clara saw long fingers with nails bitten down to the quick.

"I'm Becca, by the way." She looked down at his hand, which dropped to his side. "She didn't say anything about hiring me?"

"She…" He shook his head. "No, I'm sorry."

"She implied that maybe you two weren't spending as much time together."

An embarrassed laugh as he wiped that hand over his face. "Yeah, well, you know."

"I do." Becca's voice grew soft, and Clara knew she was thinking of her own on-again-off-again ex, as well as the young man she had dated a few times last spring. Laurel always had a lot to say about human romances, but Clara thought their person was only being sensible to be so careful with her heart. "I'm glad you came over when you heard about Frank."

Becca paused, as if listening to her own words. "Did she call you?"

"No." That half-smile again as he shook off the idea. "I wish, but I was just in the area and saw all this." One wave took in the police, as well as the crowd.

"You must have been worried."

A shrug. "She told me he had a bad ticker. It's too bad, though. Poor guy. I don't think we're going to get to see her. Not this morning, anyway."

Becca scanned the crowd. The storefront remained as bright and still as a museum diorama, and although the crowd was beginning to disperse, the uniformed cop standing in front of the residential entrance seemed in no hurry to follow.

"No, I guess you're right." Becca sighed with frustration. "Though this seems like an awful lot of fuss if he simply had a heart attack."

"You call 9-1-1, they send out all the emergency services. Especially if the caller isn't clear." He shrugged, then turned toward her, brightening with inspiration. "Hey, why I don't take your number? If I hear something, I'll give you a ring."

"Thanks." Becca smiled back automatically, though she forced her face back into something more somber as she punched her digits into his phone. "I don't know how this will effect Gaia, but if you do get to speak with her, please let her know I'm on the case."

Chapter 11

"Tiger, huh?" Laurel was at her slinkiest, weaving herself around Becca's legs as soon as the young woman returned home. *"I always liked tigers…"*

"Please." Clara sat back, restraining her tail by wrapping it around her paws. It was bad enough that her sister read her thoughts. To have Laurel interrupt her as she filled her sisters in on the strange encounter was unnerving, to say the least. *"We don't know this man, and he may still be involved with that other girl, the client."*

"Don't be a kitten," her sinuous sister purred. *"He was interested in our Becca. I'm picking up traces of his interest still! He touched her, didn't he?"* Before Clara could even answer, Laurel continued. *"That's how they show their interest, silly! He wants to claim her as his own."*

"Nonsense!" As Becca stepped carefully over her furry welcoming committee, they were joined by Harriet, who was having none of this. *"Becca is our person,"* she huffed, lifting her foreshortened nose up to sniff Becca's hand. *"If this Tiger wants a person, he can very well get his own."*

Clara couldn't have agreed more and stepped back to give Harriet pride of place as the small party proceeded into the kitchen.

She remembered all too well how sad Becca had been when her last romance had ended. And although their person had gone out a few times with a local painter—Clara had enjoyed the tangy pine smell of the turpentine he used—Becca had cooled on him recently.

"*What about the man who caught her arm? The one with the good teeth?*"

Clara jumped and wheeled on her sister. "*Don't do that!*" Her fur bristled when she was startled.

"*Yes, she met someone with a nice smile, but they didn't even talk, really,*" Clara said, as much to settle her fur as to explain. "*He was just being kind. He helped her when that cyclist nearly knocked her over.*"

Laurel only flicked her tail, but the message was clear. Two men, both fighting over Becca, even slightly. That got the sealpoint's interest.

"What's gotten into you three?" Six eyes—green, blue, and gold—looked up in surprise. "I'd swear you'd think I'd been gone for weeks."

"*Now you've done it.*" Harriet batted at Laurel. "*Bad enough you destroyed her feather. She won't want to give us treats now!*"

"*Shhh...*" Laurel hissed. "*She doesn't know what happened to the feather.*"

Clara wisely sat that one out. In truth, the cats had already had their breakfast, before Becca left. But to Harriet's delight, she headed once more to the kitchen, as Laurel assumed a particularly self-satisfied smirk.

"No, I couldn't speak to Gaia either." Becca cradled the device against her shoulder as she scooped out the savory feast. "The cops were talking to her. I wonder if Margaret said something about her and, oh, never mind. Speaking of, Maddy, I meant to tell you. I met Gaia's ex. He's a bike messenger named Tiger."

She paused then as she laid down the dishes for the three felines. But, looking up from her own second supper, Clara noted the strained expression on Becca's face.

"You going to eat that?" Harriet's face pushed close, distracting Clara just when she wanted to listen.

"Hush!" Clara pushed closer to her food, but kept her ears tipped.

"Yes, Maddy, a bike messenger..." Becca was leaning back against the counter, eyes back with exasperation. "No, you've got the wrong idea. I mean, sure, he's cute. But what's more important is that he might be helpful to the case. He might know who would want to hurt Gaia."

The buzz coming from the phone sounded like a bee was trapped in there.

"They're still friends," Becca explained. "They talk. That's good, right? I mean, it's civilized. Anyway, she had told me that he was worried about her, so it was natural to start to chat with him. He's my first lead."

A pause so weighted that even Harriet looked up.

"I told you, I'm not interested, Maddy. And even I was, I wouldn't be poaching. I happen to have it on good authority that Gaia was already seeing someone else. Someone she shouldn't have been." The three cats exchanged glances. Becca rarely used that particular tone. "Anyway, I have to go now. My coven is meeting here this afternoon. At least they believe in me!"

***

In truth, Becca had several hours before the coven's circle—if the informal and somewhat reduced gathering could even be called that. The unsettling events of the previous spring had shaken the group, and in the wake of a summer wedding and an August break, attendance at the weekly meetings had become a bit irregular. Two of the coven, Trent and Larissa, were now such infrequent attendees that Becca hadn't bothered to ask them about rescheduling their usual Tuesday night to a Sunday afternoon until the day before. Whether it was a fit of pique or a real conflict that caused Larissa to text back a curt excuse, Becca couldn't tell. Maybe the wealthy older woman really was spiriting away her younger boyfriend for the weekend. The two remaining witches—women about Becca's own age—were the ones she wanted to speak with anyway.

Besides preparing for her guests, Becca did have work to do. Despite what she'd told Maddy, the fledgling investigator was feeling a bit more desperate than defiant. Money was tight, and her unemployment was running out. If she wanted to make being a witch detective a going concern, now was the time.

Clara might not understand the details—finance being of little interest to a cat—but she picked up on her person's intensity as she huddled over the laptop for the next few hours.

The first was spent on what Becca called "old-school research."

"I can't rely on my sensitivity for everything," she had whispered to Clara. What that meant, as far as the cat could tell, was typing in people's names and seeing what came up. Gaia/Gail Linquist seemed to have an awful lot of photos. With, Becca noticed, an awful lot of young men.

"Tiger can't have been that serious," she said, with what to her cat sounded like a happy upward lilt. Clara wasn't sure how she felt about this development. A few clicks later, though, she did agree that the goth girl's jet-black hair was a more striking look than her original mouse brown.

Margaret and Frank Cross seemed to have less of an online profile. "Makes sense," Becca said. "Given their ages."

Once again, Clara couldn't make heads or tails of the comment, or of the few photos that popped up. One, back when the used car salesman had more hair and his wife's mouth had been smiling rather than puckered, made her sad, though. She leaned on Becca, and the two sat quietly for a moment with that one the screen.

When Becca rose to fetch the smelly baggie, Clara became concerned. Her person had stuck it in the refrigerator, and her cat had hoped it would disappear there, never to be seen again, like that lettuce from last month. She was relieved to note that its smell had faded, somewhat, after its time in the chill—and even more so when she realized that Becca was only going to look at the thing, through the plastic, rather than touch or taste it. When she put it aside to return to her laptop, Clara considered her options. Harriet's actions might have been troublesome, but her instincts were dead on, her calico sister realized. If only there was a way to get rid of the thing that didn't draw attention to the feline sisters' powers or otherwise break the rules against involving humans in their magic.

"*I'm sure Harriet could bury it again.*" Silent as a shadow, Laurel had jumped up to join Clara and Becca on the sofa. "*She doesn't have to make it look like anything. She could just dig.*"

"*Becca would worry.*" Clara didn't even want to admit the truth to herself. "*She'd only turn the house upside down.*"

"*Well, we can't have that.*" Laurel drew back in distaste, any kind of frenzied human activity, including housecleaning, being anathema to a cat.

Before they could decide on any other action, Becca had picked up the bag once more. Holding it close to her laptop, she seemed to be comparing it to one of the odorless images. Clara and Laurel could only trade worried glances as Becca typed madly and then stared long and hard at the screen.

After what seemed like an eternity to the cats, Becca finally put the specimen aside, and with a tantalizing dance of her fingers, the screen before her changed. That picture again—the woman and the cat—moved as Becca read. Although she didn't have Laurel's gift, Clara thought she could make out a few stray thoughts as she focused on her person. "*Ancestor...*" The little cat tried out the word. Yes, that was right. "*With her familiar...*"

Could Becca be close to understanding? To comprehending, at last,

84

that her cats had a history of power and had protected their people as best they could? Clara closed her eyes to concentrate and found herself visualizing her own mother. Those last days at the shelter...

"*Witch.*" No, she wasn't hearing Becca's thoughts. Her person was whispering to herself, reading, Clara realized, the text on the screen. A story that seemed to dismay her, from the way she blinked and then closed her screen.

She rose, then, but her mood carried over from whatever she had seen. Although their person remained quiet, the set of her mouth indicated trouble, Clara thought, as did the way her brows had pulled together. When she went for the vacuum cleaner, pulling it from the back of a closet where Clara and her sisters had hoped it had gone to die, she and Laurel made themselves scarce. Even Harriet woke in the ensuing tumult, blinking and affronted as they all crowded beneath the bed in safety.

By the time they emerged, Becca had gone into full-on hostess mode, arranging her small apartment for the arrival of her friends. The three cats took refuge on the sofa, until an extra vigorous fluffing of pillows sent Laurel scampering once more, and an aggressive wiping down of the table had even Harriet hesitant to hover, no matter what tempting crumbs might have gone flying.

Only Clara remained, to show her support as her person fussed. She might as well have been invisible, however, as Becca nearly tripped over her in her frenzy.

"I'm sorry, kitty." She reached down and scooped up her youngest cat. And although the embrace was a tad awkward—Clara's foot stuck out and she could feel the bulk of her body already sliding through Becca's arms—she began to purr. Clearly, Becca was still bothered. Whether that was because of her friend Maddy or because of what she'd found on her laptop, Clara couldn't tell. Still, any opportunity the plump calico had to soothe her person was worth a little discomfort.

85

"Hang on!" At the sound of the doorbell, Becca shifted, and Clara managed a decent landing on the floor.

"Graceful," Laurel snarled quietly from under the sofa.

"I just wanted to make her feel better." Clara sat and began to groom the fur on her back, where Becca's embrace had ruffled it.

"I thought you wanted her to give up all this witch silliness." With Becca safely at the door, Laurel ventured from her hiding spot. *"Give up the idea of being a detective, too. Too dangerous, you said. Too risky for a human to try. And that root..."*

Clara paused, tongue hanging out between her discreet white fangs. It was true that she had hoped that Becca would go back to being a researcher. The idea that she, or any human, could have magical powers was silly. Any cat would agree.

The worst part, of course, was that Clara and her sisters were responsible for Becca's obsession. It had been Harriet's summoning of a pillow—the golden velvet pillow that had been plumped up so vigorously—that had started the trouble, when Becca had misread its appearance as the manifestation of her own attempt at a spell. But recently, she'd come around to the idea that her person might be more like, well, like her cats. And if there were humans who had powers, then their Becca should be one of them.

"You look like a dog, with your tongue out like that." Harriet emerged from the sanctuary of the bedroom to saunter past. Clara quickly closed her mouth as her oldest sister began snuffling up the crumbs that had gone flying. *"Not to mention the way you tag along after her,"* the marmalade added as she licked up a particularly tasty morsel.

"It's not like you need to." Laurel appeared alongside her and, with a wiggle of her hindquarters, launched herself to the tabletop. *"Together, we could—"*

"Kitties! No!" A loud clapping made Harriet put her ears back and Laurel leap to the floor. Only Clara looked up to see the tall, slender woman who was laughing behind her hands. The first of the guests had arrived.

"Honestly, Becca, they're fine." Ande, a member of Becca's self-styled coven, wiped tears of laughter from cheeks that were a shade darker than Laurel's fur. "I mean, if you didn't have cats, maybe you wouldn't have your powers."

All three cats stopped at that and stared up at the newcomer as she walked past them into the kitchen. Even Becca froze, mouth open as if about to phrase a life-altering question.

"That's so funny you would say that," Becca managed, her voice breathless. "I was just reading—"

"Yoo-hoo!" Before Becca could elaborate, another voice rang out. "Everything okay?"

"Marcia." Becca turned to greet the petite newcomer who bounded in, dark eyes wide. "How're you—I mean, merry meet!"

"Merry meet yourself, Becca. But you shouldn't leave your door open like that!" Taking off her ever-present Red Sox cap, she ran a hand through her brunette pageboy. "I got scared there for a minute."

"Why?" Ande stepped back into the apartment's main room. She was holding the teapot that was always filled for the coven's gatherings. "What's up?"

"Don't you come through Central Square?" Marcia looked from Ande to Becca in disbelief. "Something's happening at Charm and Cherish."

"Oh, yeah, I was down there this morning." Becca took the teapot from Ande, who stood stock still, and proceeded back into the kitchen. "Are the police still there?"

"Yeah." Marcia dragged the word out as she looked from Ande to Becca. "You okay?"

"Of course." Ande managed a smile. Laurel, meanwhile, had re-emerged and began sniffing at Marcia's high-top sneakers. "Becca, what were you saying?"

Marcia wasn't waiting. "Did you hear anything?" She tagged after Becca, stepping over the cat. "Is it related to that hit and run? I got an alert that the police are on the lookout for a red sports car with out-of-state plates. I guess the poor guy is still critical. It's a good thing there was a vet nearby."

"Good thing he knew emergency medicine." Becca raised her voice to be heard over the running water.

"Yeah, well, that's part of the training, isn't it?" Marcia looked at Ande. The taller woman simply shrugged. "They're calling him the hero vet."

"Isn't that redundant?" Becca waved Marcia off as she reached for the kettle. "But, no, that was down by the river. The reason for all the fuss around the shop is because of Frank Cross, the owner's husband. He's…well, it seems he's died." Clara could hear the water reaching a boil. With her superior feline senses, she could also hear Ande's startled gasp. "I'm sorry, I didn't mean to startle you. I hear it might have been a coronary."

"And you were there?" Ande's voice was tense with dread. "At the shop?"

Becca shook her head as she counted out scoops of the fragrant mint tea. "Three. Four. Uh-huh," she said. "No, not when it happened. I mean, I was at the shop earlier, but I think he was at his office when— oh, bother."

"You'd gotten to five," said Marcia. "And it's just us three today."

"Well, there'll be seconds." Becca shot her friend a grin as she poured the water into the teapot. "But, anyway, Margaret had wanted to hire me for a case—she had a problem with the shop. I told her I had a conflict and I couldn't take it. But there was one thing I thought I could straighten out for her, just to put her mind at rest. It involved Frank, kind of, so I went down to his office—you know that car lot on

Putnam? Anyway, he was alive then."

"Well, this must be something different." Marcia turned her Sox cap in her hands as she thought. "There were a ton of cops by the shop, not an ambulance or anything."

"Margaret did tell me some valuables had gone missing," Becca confided, her hand going up to the blue stone pendant. "She thought maybe Frank had taken them. That was…well, that was part of what I was looking into."

"Speaking of, nice necklace." Marcia reached over. "Lapis?"

"Thanks. It's supposed to help discern truth from lies."

"Interesting." Marcia eyed the necklace as Ande stepped closer. "How's it work?"

"When did you speak with Margaret?" Ande's question saved Becca from having to confess her ignorance.

"Late this afternoon." Becca reached for the mugs. "I went there right after talking with Margaret. She lives above the shop and—"

"Becca," Ande interrupted her, her face serious. "Tell me you told the police about this."

"I didn't get a chance to," her host said as she fit the mugs and the teapot onto a tray. "I was trying to get to Margaret, but the police wouldn't let me in."

"Of course they wouldn't." Ande took the tray from Becca and handed it off to Marcia.

"What are you talking about?" Becca turned from Ande to Marcia, who looked as puzzled as Becca did.

"I don't know if it was just a coronary, Becca." Ande's brow furrowed. "And I am so glad you're not working for her."

Becca shook her head in confusion.

"You don't get that many cop cars for a medical emergency." Ande pulled Becca back into the living room and sat her on the sofa.

Marcia followed up before Becca could protest. "Ande's right," she said, setting the tray on the table. "You said there was some kind of a problem and that Margaret thought her husband was stealing from her? Maybe his heart didn't simply give out. Or not by itself, anyway."

Chapter 12

The three cats scurried as the three humans all began talking at once.

"That makes no sense." Becca stared, wide-eyed, at Marcia. "She loved him. She was afraid he was leaving her."

Marcia couldn't help but roll her eyes.

"Oh, goddess help me, you don't think that my turning down her case drove her to do something—"

"Hold on. Is anyone saying that Frank Cross's death wasn't natural?" Ande turned from one to the other. "Anyone besides us, I mean?"

"No. This is pure speculation." Becca was trying to be the voice of reason. "Besides, I was with her—"

"When he was still alive!" Marcia voice belied her size, and her exasperation along with it. "But it all fits. I saw a cop questioning Gaia—you know, the girl who works at the shop? And they took Mrs. Cross out the back."

"That doesn't mean anything." Ande was only repeating what Becca had said, but the emphasis she put on the words made both her friends turn. "The way things were between them, she wouldn't even necessarily know."

That brought Becca up short. "Ande, what's up?" she asked.

"Wait, you know them?" Marcia followed her friend as she moved over to the sofa. As she sat, the three cats emerged from under the table. The shouting, at least, seemed to be over.

"I've done some work for the Crosses." Ande, who had settled beside Becca, was staring at her hands. Almost, Clara thought, like she wanted to groom. "And, yeah, I've gotten to know them a bit."

"Work?" Marcia, who had settled in the easy chair, turned from Ande to Becca. "You mean, you've done their taxes or something?"

"I've done hers." Ande glanced up, her hands unlicked. "And the store's. Not his business, though there's some overlap. I'm sorry, I really shouldn't say anymore."

"That's interesting." Becca drew out the word. "So you didn't do the books for his car lot?"

"No." Ande shook her head, her dark face grave. "Becca, you're not looking into anything at that lot, are you?"

"I'm not," she answered, her voice still thoughtful. "Margaret Cross tried to hire me because she thought someone was embezzling. I couldn't take her case because I had a conflict of interest, because something else came up—but when I went to tell her it all got mixed up with her husband."

"Oh no." Ande was shaking her head, as if this were worse. "You're involved in that whole mess between Frank and Gaia, aren't you?"

***

The flurry of questions and exclamations that followed sent Laurel leaping to the top of the bookcase again, while Harriet remained under the table. Only Clara, who had ventured out to the edge of the sofa, dared the torrent of voices.

"*What are they on about?*" Harriet was getting annoyed. "*Are we going to have to stay here all night?*"

"*It's about a man, isn't it?*" From her perch, Laurel's blue eyes glowed. *"I'm sure it's about a man."*

"I think it's about money." Clara, like most cats, had only the vaguest ideas about finance and budgeting. She had learned a little, however. They all had when Becca had lost her last job as a researcher. Once she had set herself up as a witch detective, their person seemed less worried. At any rate, she spoke about it less frequently—at least until recently—and Clara didn't think that was only because of the time she spent on the computer doing what her buddy Maddy called "freelance."

"Money, huh!" Harriet snorted, and curled up on herself. Clara suspected that her older sister was even less clear on the topic than she herself was, but she didn't try to explain. She also knew how grumpy Harriet could get when she was due for a nap. Instead, she turned her ears forward and tried to pick up the thread of the conversation.

"So, you don't think Margaret Cross did something. Do you?" Marcia's gaze swiveled between Ande and Becca.

"I know she was angry with him." Becca's voice was cautious, and Clara's tail began to lash in sympathy. "But not that angry. She was worried about him. She thought he'd gone missing."

"And that was in the afternoon, when she was home with her sister. But you found him easily enough. And you knew she was upset." Marcia's eyes fell on Becca's necklace.

"Yeah, I did." Becca reached for the stone. "But, honestly, I believe she just felt bad because he was cheating on her."

"Like he was going to leave her. Only someone made it permanent." Marcia turned back to Ande. "You knew something was up."

"Yeah," the tall accountant acknowledged, a rueful note creeping into her voice. "I know they were having…issues. But Frank would never leave Margaret. He couldn't." She bit down on her lower lip to stop herself from saying any more.

"It was her money." Marcia put two and two together. "So even if he kept on fooling around—"

93

"Wait, you know about that?" Becca broke in. Her two friends looked at each other. "Did everybody know?"

"I made the mistake of going down to his lot once. Luz thought we could get a good deal on a car, but he had no inventory," said Marcia. "What he had was a roving eye."

"And roving hands," Ande added. "I learned early on never to be in his office alone with him."

"He's lucky he hasn't been sued," Marcia piled on. "Then again, nobody would get much. Or it would be Margaret's money. What?"

Ande had made a face. "He was talking with some other investors," she said. "If you can call them that. Anyway, I stopped working with him."

"Good for you." This from Marcia.

"I didn't realize he was so creepy. Still, this doesn't look good for Margaret, does it?" Becca drew her knees up and hugged them to herself, prompting Clara to inch closer. *If only these other people would leave.*

"I think she was really upset when she couldn't reach him." Becca didn't even look down as her calico nosed her toe. "But if he cheated on her and might have cost her money, too… I don't know. Especially if…"

Now it was her turn to clam up. Her friends noticed and began prodding her.

"If what? Come on, Becca, it's all in the coven."

"I've probably told you more than I should have already, but this is all going to come out, most likely." Becca's forehead was creased, though if that was concern over breaking a confidence or worry about her client, Clara couldn't tell. "The reason Gaia hired me is that she thought someone was trying to kill her. Or, maybe should I say, kill her, too."

"And once the police hear that, they'll wonder if they're connected." Marcia filled in the blanks.

"Why did she think that?" Ande, the voice of reason.

"Well, her ex-boyfriend told her that he'd seen someone hanging around, like a stalker. She said she didn't think anything of it, but now she says she thinks someone put wolf's bane in her tea." Becca looked from one of her friends to the other. "An entire root. I know it sounds preposterous, but the tincture is really dangerous—a tablespoon or two can kill—and I don't know how much would be in a raw root."

"But who would put a root in someone's tea?" Ande pinpointed one of the issues that Clara knew had been troubling Becca. "I mean, it's kind of blatant. Like, wouldn't you notice it when you lifted your mug? That sounds more like what you do to scare someone than to seriously hurt them."

"Not only that, but I'm not convinced it's actually wolf's bane." Becca looked around at her sister witches. When nobody spoke, she continued. "Gaia said it was, said she's an herbalist. But I've been doing some research online. It doesn't look right, and also, there's something about the smell."

"Wolf's bane doesn't smell," Marcia said softly.

"Yeah, I mean, I didn't want to taste it, obviously. Hang on." Becca ducked into the kitchen and returned with the baggie. "Smell that."

Ande opened the bag and recoiled.

"I should have left it buried," Harriet muttered.

"That smells familiar." Marcia wisely didn't put her face too close.

"I know. Asafetida, right?" Becca looked around for confirmation. "So maybe Margaret wanted to scare her. I mean, she was really upset about Frank, and if she thought Gaia was the other woman…"

"What about this ex-boyfriend?" Ande tilted her head at a quizzical angle. "He might be the one trying to scare her. Convince her that her new romance is too risky and that she should come back."

After a moment's thought, Becca shook her head. "Could be, he is the one who's been looking out for her. Maybe he's playing both sides,

95

scaring her and then offering to take care of her. But he's been warning her about a stalker, not poison. Plus, I get the feeling that he's over her. Of course, that doesn't mean the crimes aren't connected. Gaia really thought it was wolf's bane. Maybe Frank did, too. Sometimes, accidents can be deadly."

Neither of her friends had a response to that.

"The first thing I have to do is get this tested." Becca put the bag on the table. "But after that, well, I think I've got to hand it over to the police."

Ande and Marcia exchanged a look. "Becs, I think you should just hand the baggie over now." Ande spoke in the conciliatory tones of someone breaking bad news. "I know she's a client, but this is serious."

"Yeah, you're right." Becca sighed. Whether it was doubt or concern over a man they only tangentially knew, a pall hung over the rest of the gathering, even as the three friends settled down to their wiccan routine. When Ande suggested a purifying ritual, Becca appeared visibly relieved. Laurel fled to the bedroom and Harriet recoiled, drawing one mitten-like paw up to her sensitive nose as Marcia waved the smoldering sage and Becca sprinkled salt. Clara made herself watch, however. These humans had no real powers, she knew that. But something about their rituals was vaguely familiar, even if it was simply that their ancestors had witnessed similar foolery through the centuries, at times with a tragic result. Clara hadn't heard of any such nonsense in Cambridge. Not this century, anyway. But she wasn't taking any chances. Besides, the way the three women waved their hands was positively entrancing. Almost like one of them was about to throw a toy for her to fetch.

"Look at your cat, Becca." Clara looked up to see Ande smiling down at her, brown eyes warm with—could it be?—humor. "I swear, she's trying to learn the ritual."

"There is something uncanny about her." Becca sounded unusually thoughtful as she knelt to stroke Clara's multicolored back. "Even more than her sisters, I feel like she's an old soul."

In response, Clara licked Becca's hand. Salt might not have any magic powers, but it did taste good.

Chapter 13

The ritual did not have the desired effect. Becca slept badly, tossing and turning to the point that her cats fled their regular posts by her feet long before dawn to sleep instead on the sofa.

"*I knew she shouldn't go out!*" Harriet kneaded her velvet pillow before settling down. Her complaining came more from concern for Becca than from any real discomfort. At least, that was Clara's hope, as she nestled on a footstool. "*That's what started all of this.*"

"*She could at least bring a new man home.*" Laurel stretched to her full length along the sofa's back, a luxury she could rarely indulge in when the three shared their person's bed. "*Then things might get interesting.*"

Clara, knowing how her sister could get when she was overtired, didn't comment. Bad enough the sealpoint had sussed out Becca's exchange with Tiger, Laurel's imagination was already a tad overheated. Hoping to keep her sister from reading her mind for more, the plump calico jumped up to the windowsill and watched as the rising sun warmed the red brick across the street to a rosy glow. Not long after, Becca herself rose, a tad rumpled, and promptly provided breakfast. But even as she brewed her own coffee, her gentle face seemed to firm into resolve.

"What's up with Becca?" Once she'd cleaned her bowl, even Harriet noticed.

"She's deciding something." Laurel lashed her tail. More out of habit, Clara suspected, than because it served any purpose of concentration. Laurel was good at suggesting ideas to people. Whether she could always accurately fish them out, however, was a subject of debate. At times, Clara suspected her middle sister of inflating her own skills so Clara and Harriet would take her more seriously.

Even if it was simply a good guess, Laurel purred with pride when Becca muttered something about "getting it done," and went to get dressed. Hoping for a bit more insight, Clara hopped down from her perch to follow the young woman as she prepared for whatever was to follow. Her usual attire of jeans and a sweater offered little clue, and even Laurel seemed disappointed when she joined Clara to observe their person from the bedroom doorway.

"So it's not that new man yet." The Siamese's rumbling purr began to slow.

"Her new what?" Clara turned toward her sister in alarm. *"Laurel, you can't know—please don't push Becca into something. We don't know this Tiger."*

"Tiger." The purr was back at full volume, Laurel's whiskers bristling as her eyes closed in delight.

"What?" Harriet ambled up beside them. But Laurel was enjoying her private musing and Clara was inwardly kicking herself for feeding her middle sister's fantasy as Becca reached for her coat and hat and, stepping over her pets, set out on her mystery mission.

"See if you can steer her toward this Tiger." Laurel didn't even look up as Clara summoned up the power to shimmy through the front door. *"I do like the sound of him!"*

Harriet's round yellow eyes were the last thing Clara saw as she passed through the door.

***

After their previous outing, Clara was careful to keep Becca in sight as she made her way down the brick Cambridge sidewalk. The scents and sounds of a city could be overwhelming, but the way the young woman walked—a happy bounce, most days—made her easy for the little feline to follow. Today, however, that bounce was almost gone, replaced by a more purposeful gait. Becca was heading to the Cambridge police headquarters, a multistory brick complex in the heart of Central Square.

Despite her best intentions, though, her steps slowed as she entered the busy commercial area—and not just because of the pedestrians. While Clara looked around for stray bicycles or anything else that might trip her person up, Becca's pace had eased to an amble.

"She is my client." Clara could hear Becca's justification, as well as the sense of doubt—or was it guilt?—in her voice. "I should tell her first, so she can relax. Besides, the cops are going to want to talk to her."

At that, Clara turned from the sidewalk to take in the storefronts. They were walking down the block that held the magic shop as well as the apartment where the murdered man had lived.

"Gaia?" To Clara's relief, Becca opted for the former, turning in at Charm and Cherish and calling out for the sales girl even as the tinkling bells announced her arrival. "Are you here?"

"As always." The raven-haired waif appeared from the back room, her smile softening the untruth. When she saw who her visitor was, she brightened further. "Becca! You missed all the excitement."

"Excitement?" Although her voice had dropped, Becca's distress could still be heard.

"Oh, I didn't mean…" Gaia waved her hands, as if to clear the air. "Not poor Frank. Oh, that was a terrible shock. I gather you…well, you know about that?"

100

Becca nodded. "That's why I came to see you, actually."

"Me?" The other girl's voice squeaked, rather like a mouse that had briefly gotten into the apartment. Unlike that tiny invader, Gaia didn't immediately scurry beneath a counter, never to be seen again.

"Yes." Becca began to sound more confident. "I have some good news. But in light of all that's happened, I was wondering if you still wanted to continue your case." A pause, and Clara could see the shadow of doubt crossing her face. "I took a moment to examine the root you dropped off, Gaia."

The sales girl's gaze dropped to the counter before her, as if she could hide behind those blue-black bangs.

"I'm not an herbalist, but I'm pretty sure this isn't wolf's bane." Becca spoke gently, but with purpose, as she held the baggie up. "But I was thinking I should bring it over to the Cambridge police, just to be sure. Because even if it isn't poisonous, somebody was trying to scare you, and that could be dangerous. Especially in light of what happened with Frank."

Gaia didn't look up, so Becca took a deep breath and continued talking. "I like to think no actual harm was intended. But sometimes a scare could cause someone to, well, you know…especially if that someone already has a health condition. Like a heart condition." The more jumbled she got, the lower Gaia's head hung. Clara waited, hoping her person would just come out and explain her theory—that Margaret, or maybe even Tiger, had planted the root to scare Gaia and had, in fact, planted something similar for Frank to find, but with more serious consequences.

"I'm sorry. I'm making a hash out of this. I just wanted to let you know that I don't think you were ever in any actual danger. I guess I should just go tell the cops."

"No." Gaia raised her head finally, eyeing first the front window and then the back door, looking at everything, it seemed, except Becca.

"No, you don't have to do that."

"But if Marg—I mean, if someone accidentally provoked…"

Something in Gaia's face stopped her short.

"You knew this wasn't wolf's bane?"

The slightest motion of that dark head indicated her assent, as Gaia turned back to the front of the shop, hoping perhaps that help would walk in the door. "Yeah." Her voice as soft as a kitten's. "It's asafetida."

"And you knew that because…" Breath escaped in one long, drawn-out "oh" as comprehension washed over Becca. She rested the bag on the counter and took in the young woman before her. "Would you like to tell me what happened?"

"Well, when I said I'm learning about herbalism, I really meant it. I mean, I'm going to." The shop girl exhaled noisily. "Okay, I bought a plant, right? I was at that Spirit of Change festival and it was really pretty. It had these blue flowers and spikey leaves, and I figured this place could use some livening up. So I brought it in. I mean, I knew it had power. The lady who sold it to me said it was a healing plant. I thought it looked nice in the window."

Becca waited without comment.

"Then Elizabeth, you know, Margaret's sister? She came in all furious, talking about how my new plant was poisonous and how could I leave it where a child could get at it, and blah-blah-blah. She showed it to me in one of those books." A pointed look at the packed shelves. "Hey, there's lots there. I can't read everything. Anyway, I was going to take it home, only then it disappeared."

"You said some things had gone missing."

"Yeah, okay, one thing—my plant. Maybe someone took off with it. It was really pretty. But I can't help but think Elizabeth, that old witch—I mean, in a bad way—took it. I'd told her I was going to take it home."

"She may have seen it as a danger."

"I guess." Gaia didn't sound convinced. "Anyway, I got so mad and then, well, Margaret started sniffing around, and I thought I might need some leverage. I figured she'd found out about Frank, though we were already basically over and—"

"Hang on." Becca reached into her bag for a pad. "When did this all this happen?"

Gaia rolled her eyes. "I don't know. Maybe, like, five days ago? Yeah, I got it last weekend and that old—Elizabeth saw it, like, right away."

"So you thought about it for a few days?"

Gaia winced. "It wasn't like that. Only, it wasn't until, like, Friday that Frank started wigging out on me. Talking about taking off for Mexico or someplace. I wasn't going to go with him, but I figured something had happened."

"So you saw him on Friday?"

"Barely." The aggrieved girlfriend. "I mean, he said he had to go back to work. That's usually what he tells *her.*"

Becca bit back her response.

"I mean, I'd made the place nice and everything."

"The candle that I asked you about?"

A shrug. "Maybe. They all cost too much anyway. But he wasn't into it. Just kept going on about having to take care of something. Told me to be ready to go."

"And were you?"

"You kidding? I know about their arrangement. I figured he was just trying to scam some more money out of the old bag. I mean, he was just wigging. And his old lady was already all over me, so…" Another shrug, like the response was self-evident.

"So you came to see me, to put the blame on her."

"Look, I was under a lot of pressure. But I'll be okay now, I think."

"You think you'll be okay?" Becca tilted her head. "What do you mean?"

"I wasn't making it all up." Gaia leaned in. "I mean, Tiger says he's still worried about me, but really...after the latest?"

Becca waited. Clearly, the woman in front of her was drawing out her story for dramatic intent.

"Maybe you didn't hear, but the neighbors are saying that the wife is always the obvious suspect." When Becca still didn't respond, Gaia went on. "Of course, they don't even know about her sister, most of them. Everyone just knew Margaret and Frank weren't getting along, and that she had a temper. Though they could've been in on it."

"You think she—they *made* him have a heart attack? They brought it about?" Becca's voice trailed off. Clara looked up, waiting. Surely, her person was going to bring up the previous night's discussion. The subtleties of poisonings seemed inconsequential to a cat. The only real way to dispatch something was with a good, fast shake. But cats would never be so brutal to one of their own, anyway. And secretly, Clara had always been grateful for that one mouse's speedy retreat.

"Some heart attack." A dramatic eye roll dismissed that. "Tiger thinks there's something else going on, maybe something with Frank's business, such as it is. Some kind of conspiracy, even."

Becca looked faintly green, but Gaia didn't seem to notice.

"Makes me kind of glad her old witch of a sister got rid of my plant. Right? Because otherwise they might be looking at me."

"I–I guess." Becca's brow furrowed, as it did when she was thinking.

"So, we can toss this, right?" Gaia poked at the baggie as if it were a hairball. "I mean, I'll pay you for your time."

"You don't have to." Becca sounded relieved. "Though maybe Tiger should talk to the police. I mean, if he's seen someone suspicious hanging around..."

"Yeah, that's not going to happen." With a shrug, the goth girl dismissed her sometime boyfriend's concern. She seemed lighter now and was already turning toward the shelves behind her, ready to re-start her day. "He's a bit of a drama king, anyway."

Her own concerns dismissed, the young woman didn't seem to think anything of it as Becca nodded and left the shop without another word. Clara, however, thought the behavior odd. As she watched, Becca strode, quickly but not breaking into a run, back toward the end of the block. Before Clara could catch up, however, she stopped cold, inches from a dark opening in the brick wall at the edge of the storefront. Carefully shading herself, Clara passed by and immediately saw what had caught Becca's eye.

A shadow—no, a person had slipped into the yawning alley and was moving slowly along its wall. That had been what Becca spied outside the window while Gaia had been going on about the store's owner, Clara realized. Someone walking too slowly and too close to the store to be an ordinary pedestrian.

Clara kicked herself for not paying attention. She could have easily slipped out and followed the figure in the shadows. Even if she couldn't have passed along her findings to Becca, she might have prevailed on Laurel to convey some message. Only now, it was too late. There was no way that Clara was going to leave her person.

Instead, she stood by, guarding faithfully while her person waited, frozen in place, as the figure crept to the end of the alley. For a moment, he was caught in the sun   blond tipped hair, denim jacket, and eyes wide with fright as he turned the corner and disappeared.

Chapter 14

"*No!*" Clara wailed as Becca took off down the alley. "*Becca, don't!*" Of course, being a cat, her mewl of horror came out as a caterwaul—a faint one at that, her ordinary cat voice muted by the magic that helped her blend into the shadows around her. More like the wheeze of a passing bus or the squeak of a bicycle's brakes than a cry of panic, her yowl blended in with the street noise of the busy Monday morning and died away, unnoticed.

Not that this mattered. Even if the young woman in the alley could have heard her terrified pet, she wouldn't have understood her. Not unless Clara could suddenly assume Laurel's gift of implanting ideas in a human's mind, her pet thought with growing frustration.

But Clara had no time for envy or even the most natural sibling resentment. And so, although her own fur was standing on end with fear, Clara darted after Becca, determined to do what she could to aid the person she loved.

"Bother!" Unseen by Clara, Becca stopped short, and only by a quick leap sideways did the little cat manage to avoid colliding with her at the passage's end. Panting, more from the stress than the exertion, the calico looked up as her person craned her head, peeking beyond the brick wall. The alley, Clara could now see, opened onto a paved lot, barely big enough for the two cars and the dumpster parked there. Unaware of the faithful feline nervously shadowing her every move, Becca slipped out to make a careful examination of the space. She started with the cars. As Clara watched, the young woman crouched beside the first, rising up so that only the maroon cloche and the few curls that escaped were visible as she peered through the windows. She needn't have been so careful. These vehicles were empty; their passenger compartments gave off no vibrations, their engines cool and still. Clara could have saved Becca the effort—and the worry—of examining them so carefully had she been able to communicate with her person.

That lack continued to try the pet's patience, but her own superior senses helped her keep her temper. By the time Becca had progressed to the dumpster, checking around the back before peeking inside, Clara had even begun to relax. Just as they hadn't picked up any signs of life in those cars, her whiskers hadn't picked up the vibrations of anything man-sized between the metal receptacle and the brick wall. Becca might not like the family of rodents who had made their home in the storm drain tucked in the corner, but Clara knew they were no real threat to her person, even if their presence might make her squeal.

If Clara was hoping that Becca would ignore the metal door that led out to the alley, however, she was disappointed. As she watched, the young woman strode up to it and tried the handle. Locked tight, the latch barely responded to her energetic pull; the dull gray door not at all. With a sigh of exasperation, she proceeded to examine the frame and then the wall. A frosted window to the right of the door was set too high for her to reach, and no bell or buzzer could be seen. Increasingly exasperated, Becca rapped on the door with her knuckle, but the thick metal only gave up a dull thud in return. Only after a few more tries did she finally give up. But instead of moving along, as her pet would have hoped, Becca began to backtrack. Perusing the little lot and the adjacent street one more time, she peered down the alley and then started the longer walk around the block back up to the store's front.

"Her boyfriend was right." Becca was speaking to herself, but Clara, trotting to keep up, heard her loud and clear. So clearly, in fact, that she found it a bit unnerving. Becca's words could have been her own. "I need to reach her," she was saying. "To warn her..."

But all the cat could do was tag along back to the brightly painted little shop, which was now locked tight.

"Gaia?" Becca called as she knocked on the glass door, and then leaned in, trying to peek through a green and yellow yin-and-yang symbol. "Are you there?"

Becca squinted. The morning sun reflected off the glass, making it difficult for her to see if her former client was inside or, indeed, if the little shop's lights were even on. Clara could have told her that nothing was stirring, but the neatly lettered sign taped to the door—*Back in Fifteen!*—should have been enough. Still, Becca kept at it for at least that long before turning with a sigh and slumping back against the metal frame.

Clara waited with her, tail curled around her paws, willing herself to be grateful for the respite. But although she would have appeared the model of patience if her person could have seen her, the little cat fretted. The shop girl had made no attempt to hide her own erratic work habits. The fact that she had a sign to post should have reminded Becca of this. Besides, if something had happened—Clara's ears flicked in search of any indication of a struggle that she might have somehow missed—there was little her person could do about it now. As Becca waited, one foot tapping in impatience, Clara found herself channeling her sister Harriet. Maybe it would be better if Becca never left the house.

Laurel would argue with that, of course, and as the minutes ticked past, Clara found herself wondering just what her slinky sister had been able to discern. Could her part-Siamese sibling have picked up traces of that young man, Tiger? Or had she somehow implanted a willingness to flirt in their person? Clara had long felt pretty sure of the extent of her own powers—the shading and the ability to pass through doors pretty much went paw in paw, as if her corporeality was tied in part to her visible self. What her sisters could do, though, she wasn't completely sure. Harriet was so lazy, she rarely pressed her powers. Summoning up a pillow or a new toy was apparently all she was interested in. And while Clara had been reasonably confident that Laurel's abilities extended only to implanting suggestions in the minds of humans, her middle sister's recent brags had the ring of truth.

If only her siblings trusted her more, Clara thought, her ears beginning to sag. If only they shared more. Acted more like family. Then maybe she wouldn't worry so much about the person they had all adopted. If only Laurel weren't so obsessed with Becca's love life. The tawny sister was awfully quick to incite interest in just about any possible suitor, Clara thought. Although there had been that one man...

Her musings were interrupted as Becca's phone rang, startling her out of her thoughts.

"Hello?" She answered with something like suspicion. "Becca Colwin."

She stood up straight as she spoke. A sign, Clara knew, that she might be addressing a potential client.

"Oh!" An outburst of surprise as her posture relaxed. "Tiger. Of course I remember you."

Clara strained her ears forward, hoping to catch the other side of the conversation. From the faint color that rose to Becca's cheeks, she suspected it wasn't about business—or not completely. But as Becca put her shoulders back, clearing her throat, Clara realized that perhaps her person had made a decision. Whether it was going to be a good

109

one, the little calico couldn't tell.

"Why, yes, I'd like to get together." With that, Becca began to walk, leaving the colorful storefront behind.

Clara's ears flicked back in alarm. *"This is Laurel's doing!"* A low growl rose beneath the white fur of her chest. *"Not every man is good boyfriend material."*

Worse, Clara realized as she trotted along behind her person, Becca wasn't going to the police station. Despite what she'd told her coven, what she'd promised Ande and Marcia, Becca was heading home. For the first time in Clara's memory, the familiar path didn't fill her with joy. Between the plans she was hearing and the direction Becca had chosen, it was clear her person was getting more deeply involved, just when they had all hoped she was pulling back from the investigation.

"Lunch sounds great," Becca was saying. And there was nothing the little cat could do.

When Becca's phone rang again, Clara dared to hope. But the young woman didn't even slow down as she took the call.

"Hey, Maddy. What's up?" Clara picked up her own pace, hoping to hear Becca's friend talk some sense into her. "Yeah, I know. I was just at Charm and Cherish. No, wait…"

Becca rolled her eyes as her friend interrupted. It was a move Laurel had tried on occasion, with comic results. But while Harriet had chuckled, Clara kept her jaw firmly clenched. Laurel was trying to relate to their person, at least, and her youngest sister believed such an impulse should be encouraged.

"No, that's just it." Becca was speaking again. "I'd already told Margaret that I couldn't take her on as a client, and I went to tell Gaia that she wasn't in any real danger. Her case was, well, I can't get into details, but let's just say we both decided that I shouldn't pursue it. Only, Maddy, now I'm not so sure."

The faint squawking from the phone stopped her in her tracks.

"No, it's not like that." Becca started walking again, albeit slowly, her voice as thoughtful as her face. "I mean, yes, I don't have clients to spare. I'd hoped to make this a going concern by the time the unemployment ran out. And, you know, I've done some good—"

Another burst of sound, a little softer, cut Becca off.

"Thanks, Maddy. I may need to pick up some freelance after all." Becca sounded so down her cat was beginning to regret her own wishes. "But, you see, I can't come down to the office today. No, I'm not going to the police—or not yet. I'm having lunch with Tiger, that bike messenger I told you about."

From the sounds coming through the phone, Maddy was as surprised and upset as the calico.

"It's not a date." Becca emphasized the last word, even as her cheeks grew pink. "I mean, I do believe he and Gaia are over, but still, that would just be too awkward."

Becca raised her hand, as if her friend could see her. "Maddy, listen. Gaia told me that she and Tiger still talk, and he told her that he thinks she's still in danger. And when I went down to tell her about the root, I saw someone hanging around the shop. Lurking, actually. So I want to talk to Tiger, hear why he thinks Gaia's in danger and if it has anything to do with whatever happened to Frank Cross. I gather he's not keen to talk to the police, but maybe he'll talk to me and then I can take it to the cops. Because this guy? He wasn't doing anything criminal, but he was clearly watching the entrance. It was creepy."

"No, Maddy, I didn't call 9-1-1. The guy disappeared as soon as he saw me watching him. And I couldn't just tell Gaia. That's the problem. I tried to, but when I went back to the store, it was all locked up. No, I think she just she took off. She has a habit of doing that. But just in case, or in case there is some connection to Frank, I want to hear what Tiger has to say. And I want someone who cares about her to know what I saw."

111

Chapter 15

"*We've got to do something.*" As soon as Clara slipped into the apartment, she rounded up her sisters. Waking Harriet from a nap was never easy, but the sense of urgency that had set her fur on end had made the calico fierce. "*Becca's getting more involved with this Gaia girl, and there's something weird going on!*"

"*I thought you didn't want us using our powers?*" Harriet wasn't happy about having her nap interrupted. "*Don't let the human know, you always say. Your sister and I have been trying to give you some leeway on this, you know.*"

"*I know.*" Clara dipped her head in a hasty feline apology. "*But I'm worried. And if Becca gets in trouble, who knows what will happen to us?*"

"*Maybe we'll find someplace better.*" Laurel had been sleeping, as well but Clara knew better than to mention it. The slender Siamese liked to present herself as always watchful. "*Someone who leads a more interesting life.*"

Clara bit down on her initial response and took a deep breath through her bi-color nose instead. Laurel was always cranky when she woke up, she reminded herself. "*Part of this trouble might involve a new man.*" Clara offered up the half-truth like a small mouse, the kind likely to interest her flirtatious sister.

"*I knew it.*" Laurel stretched seductively, then began to groom, her customary calm returning. "*And this is a problem, why?*"

"*It's not the man,*" Clara began to explain when Becca came into the room. "*It's something he told—*"

"Look at you three." Becca beamed down at them. "So nice to see you're not fighting for once."

"*Don't smirk.*" Clara couldn't help it. Laurel had a way of arching one eye that drove her mad. "*Please,*" she muted her criticism. "*I'm trying to think of what we can do—what we ought to do. I mean, within the rules.*"

"*Good luck with that,*" her middle sister purred and sauntered off, tail high, to the bedroom. Clara knew Laurel was going to get involved in Becca's wardrobe choices. What she didn't know was how to stop her.

"*This isn't a date.*" She trotted after her sister, her mew softening with a slight pleading tone. "*She wants to talk to him.*"

"*Exactly.*" Laurel leaped to the bed without sparing her sister a glance. "*And he'll take her so much more seriously if she would only lose that chunky sweater. I mean, who doesn't like Angora?*"

"*Angora?*" Harriet lumbered in. "*You mean that pink sweater?*" She reached up to groom her wide face, revealing a few silky, pink strands stuck in her claws.

"*You dragged it down from the shelf.*" Clara closed her eyes, but not before she saw Harriet pull the fibers free and swallow them.

"*Silly!*" Laurel hissed. "*I had plans for that sweater.*"

"*So did I.*" Unruffled by either her sisters or the pink yarn, Harriet continued bathing, straining to lick what on any other cat would have been the small of her back and nearly toppling over in the process. "*It was very soft.*"

"*You missed a spot.*" Resigned, Clara reached over to hook a tuft of the super-fine wool in her claw.

"Clara! What have you gotten into?" The little calico gave a startled mew as hands reached around her middle, pulling her up in the air. "Is that from my new sweater?"

Unable to explain, Clara could only blink in silent apology. On the bed, Laurel's blue eyes closed in a satisfied smile.

"*I could let her know, you know. Point out that Harriet was the one to pull that sweater down from its shelf.*" Laurel's low feline muttering was too quiet for human ears. "*I could also suggest to her that we're more than she knows. That we are, in fact, royalty.*"

"*Please don't.*" Clara turned toward her sister in silent appeal. It was too late. Becca was carrying her to the bedroom doorway, and then she closed the door behind her.

With mounting frustration, she waited outside as Becca got ready for her lunchtime meet, knowing full well that Laurel, if not Harriet, would be turning the situation to their own ends. Pacing outside the shut door, and unable to pass through without alarming Becca, Clara fumed, and then began to blame herself. Of course Laurel had jumped on the romantic potential of lunch with a new man. Clara hadn't explained the situation properly. In part, she had to admit, that was because of her own confusion over what was going on.

For starters, Becca had said that her meeting with the bike messenger wasn't a date. But even without the astute feline hearing that picked up a quickening heartbeat and a slight shallowness in her breath, Clara knew her person well enough to sense that she was intrigued by the dark-haired man. More intrigued, the calico feared, than she had been by anyone since her longtime boyfriend had broken up with her the previous spring.

That had been touch and go for a while, too. Matt, Becca's ex, had regretted their breakup, even though he had been the one to initiate it.

The computer programmer had, in fact, tried to woo Becca back, and there had been moments when Clara had feared he would succeed. But the puppy-ish programmer had cheated on Becca, and, cute as he was, she knew he couldn't be trusted. For a long while after that, Clara had worried that Becca would never again trust any man.

That didn't mean she wanted her person to just jump into something with this Tiger. And despite what Laurel thought, that wasn't simply because of his name. Clara knew she was more protective of Becca than her middle sister would like. But Laurel hadn't been the one who had stayed by Becca's side after Matt had broken up with her. Laurel and Harriet both knew the faithless Matt had done their person wrong, and they had taken the insult personally, as all good cats would. Still, it had been Clara the heartbroken girl had cried with, cuddling her close as if her soft fur were the only comfort she would ever find. Clara didn't know if she could find a way to explain how sad that time had been. Laurel might be her sister, but sometimes she felt like she and her littermates were not only not a real family. They were like different species entirely.

Chapter 16

Tiger was waiting when Becca arrived at the coffeehouse forty minutes later. Clara smelled the bike messenger—that mix of sweat, gear grease, and sandalwood—even before she spotted him uncoiling a heavy chain from his bag.

"Tiger! Thanks for coming out." Becca walked up to him as he squatted to weave the chain between the spokes of his front tire and the body of his pared-down bike. "Are you working?"

"What? Oh, the bike?" Tiger blinked up at her. "No, I ride everywhere."

As he stood, she noticed a phone-like device attached to his belt. "Is that a pager?"

"You've got a good eye." He tilted his head, looking rather like Laurel as he took her in. "Yeah, my boss is old school. But, hey," he said, unclipping the device and tucking it into his pocket, "like I said, I'm not working."

Becca inhaled, and Clara looked up in anticipation, not knowing if Becca had another question or was simply going to respond. But Tiger had already reached for the coffeehouse door, which he pulled open. "After you."

"Thanks," she said, even as Clara waited for more, and led the way to a butcher block table in the corner.

"Not a date." Clara repeated Becca's words, hoping to impress them back on her person.

The corner table offered a modicum of privacy, the better to discuss the case. Clara didn't need any of Laurel's powers to follow her person's reasoning. But Clara had also seen her color rise as she walked by Tiger. The bike messenger was handsome in an outlaw way, with that dramatic dark hair and long, lean muscles sculpted by hours on the bike.

"Just a conversation," the little cat murmured from the shadows as they placed their orders—a turkey sandwich for Becca, a veggie wrap for Tiger. Even as she settled in to observe while they ate, Clara found herself once again wishing that she had more of Laurel's particular power.

"I wanted to talk because I gather you're worried about Gaia." Maybe it was simply that her part-Siamese sister was on her mind. Maybe it was the blue eyes, but as the bike messenger ferried their sandwiches over from the counter, it occurred to Clara that he really did look like Laurel. Maybe it was the way he tilted his head as he waited, silently, for her to continue. "Do you think she's in danger? I'm sorry, I don't mean to pry, but she and I were talking."

A nod. "She told you what's going on?" He raised his brows.

"She said that you two still talk…" This time, there was no mistaking the question behind Becca's pause.

"Well, yeah." The man sitting opposite her shrugged. "We're friends."

"I know how hard it is to stay friends with an ex."

The deep sigh that followed turned into a chuckle. "Tell me about it," he said, the relief giving his deep voice a lift. Then, seeing Becca's wide-eyed response, he caught himself. "You don't have to. I mean, I'm just glad you understand."

"I do." Becca lowered her eyes as Clara scrambled to her feet. There was nothing the little cat could do. Not here, where she was, for all intents and purposes, invisible, and suddenly appearing would only distress her person. Still, she couldn't resist reaching up with one paw. Maybe she should touch her person. Distract her from the intense young man facing her. If she only reached out...

For a moment, Clara wondered if perhaps her ardent desire was enough. Or perhaps, she told herself, Becca had more resolve than her pet gave her credit for. Because, after taking a deep breath, Becca dove in. "Anyway, I am kind of still working with her, and I'm hoping you can share why you're still worried about her."

"Well, just because we broke up doesn't mean..." He shrugged as he took a bite of his veggie wrap.

"No, I'm sorry. I meant if you had specific reasons to be concerned." Becca leaned in, her own sandwich forgotten. "I'd like to know what they are."

Silence while he chewed and took another bite.

"She said you saw someone hanging around?"

"I don't know." He shook his head even as he tore into the wrap. "I don't know if I should be talking about this."

"If it helps, I think you may be on to something." Becca spoke softly, although Clara's sensitive ears had no trouble picking up the intensity of her tone. "And it worries me, because I don't think Gaia is taking your concerns seriously." No response. "I've heard that maybe Frank Cross didn't die from natural causes."

That got his attention. "Like an accident, or that he was killed?"

Becca shrugged. "There were an awful lot of cops around for what was supposed to be simply a medical emergency." Her voice dropped to near a whisper. "Someone told me that Margaret Cross was taken in for questioning."

Tiger leaned in with a speed that set Clara's fur on edge. "You think she's a suspect?"

To her pet's relief, Becca sat back in her own chair, considering. "I don't know," she said, her focus on something Clara couldn't see. "I wish I understood what was going on better. I don't see Mrs. Cross as a...a dangerous person."

"She might have had motive." Tiger's words got her attention back. "I'm sorry. I didn't want to say anything, but, well, it's true."

"I think I may know what you're talking about." Becca bit her lip. "But please, tell me what you mean."

Now it was Tiger's turn to stare off into space, as if he were gathering courage from the list of coffees available. When he turned back, he seemed to have made a resolution. "Frank was having a fling with Gaia." He stated this as fact, although Clara knew how much this could hurt a human. "That wasn't why we broke up," he was quick to add, almost like he could hear her thoughts. "I mean, we were never that serious. But this thing with Frank? Well, I think he was kind of obsessed with her."

"And you know this...how?" Clara could have leaped into her person's lap and begun to knead, she was so happy. Becca's question showed that she was being smart *and* careful.

Tiger dropped his gaze, but he didn't seem to see the remainder of his lunch. "I'm not a stalker, okay? But my boss has had a lot of deliveries for Mr. Cross recently. I've been down at that car lot of his a fair amount, as well as around here most days. So I see when someone keeps showing up."

Becca gestured for him to continue, waiting.

"And I heard some of the fights he had with his wife." Tiger was talking to the table, one long finger tracing the wood grain. "'Margaret, cut it out! Margaret, please stop!' I heard him yell that a lot. And he wouldn't think to protect himself from her."

"So you think Margaret might have hurt him?" The words came slowly, as if Becca were trying them out.

Tiger shrugged. "Maybe."

"But I thought they were making up. I heard him on the phone with her the day he died. He started off by telling her she was wrong, that she should calm down and everything. But I think he was basically apologizing."

He shook his head slowly, his blue eyes sad. "I don't know," he said. "I mean, I don't want to think it was anyone. But you said that word is his heart attack was suspicious, right? Well, they do say that poison is a woman's weapon."

Becca recoiled, and then broke out into laughter. "Sorry," she said as he stared, his handsome face blank. "I thought maybe you were in on it."

"Excuse me?" His voice was barely a whisper.

"Gaia." Becca sighed and shook her head. "She shouldn't have, but it didn't go anywhere. Maybe I'm not such a bad detective after all."

"I'm still missing something here."

"Gaia's case. The reason she wanted to hire me. The poison in her mug." Faced with Tiger's baffled stare, she explained about the root and how her coven identified it as asafetida, as well as her friends' suggestion that her ex-boyfriend might have played a role. "Even when she confessed, I wondered if maybe she was covering—covering for you. You know, if you'd wanted to scare her. And so when you said poison…I'm sorry." Becca was trying to dig herself out. "In conclusion, it was stupid, but it was harmless."

"Ah." Now it was his turn to chuckle, and he picked up his sandwich again. "Yeah, that sounds like Gaia, all right."

"Anyway, I know she was hoping to frame Margaret—and I'm not saying Margaret doesn't have reason to be angry. But I'm more concerned about someone else."

"Someone else?" Tiger leaned forward. For a moment, Clara thought he was going to reach for her, and she strained to see over the edge of the tabletop.

Becca's head bobbed enthusiastically. "When I left the shop, I was sure I saw someone—a man with light hair. Maybe dyed blond. He was acting strange. Lurking, kind of, like he didn't want to be seen. I followed him down the alley, but then I lost him."

"Did you tell Gaia?" Tiger attacked his sandwich with renewed fervor.

"I didn't get a chance to," Becca confessed. "She was gone when I went back. And then you called, and I remembered that she said you'd been worrying about her. And I thought she said you'd seen someone hanging around too?" She paused, waiting for an answer.

Tiger only laughed, a small, sad laugh. "Gaia," he said the name softly, more to himself than Becca. "Yeah, I did. But she's not the type to listen to anyone. Certainly not her ex. And what was I going to say? That I was afraid her new romance was going to get her into trouble?"

"You wanted her to be careful." Becca repeated the words. "And you didn't want her seeing her boss's husband, right? So you didn't see anyone?"

"I wanted her to be careful. I didn't expect any of this." Tiger tilted his head. It wasn't a nod, exactly, and it wasn't a shrug. It was an acknowledgment of an awkward situation. Still, as Becca watched her lunch partner's face, she must have wondered. Clara certainly found herself considering the options. Gaia had already shown herself to be a liar. Might she be covering again? Lying for her former lover? What, after all, did Becca know about this man and his motives? About his strangely spicy scent? Tiger had clearly wanted Gaia to quit seeing Frank. Might he have gone to other lengths? Done something desperate to stop her? Or to shield her from an injured wife's wrath?

121

Chapter 17

"I'd really like to talk to Margaret."

True to her word, Becca had called Maddy to check in after the lunch. But while she did her best to reassure her friend that the meeting had not been a date, she wasn't able to put her fears entirely to rest. "I know you don't want me involved in this, Maddy. And I tried to get out of this case—these cases—but I am involved, whether I like it or not. And, well, I know what Tiger said, but something about it just doesn't sit right. I mean, I don't see Margaret Cross as a murderer."

From the way Becca held the phone, Clara could tell that her friend was yelling. While that had to be unpleasant—no cat liked loud noises—she was grateful that Maddy felt protective. And relieved that Becca wasn't taking the bike messenger's story at face value.

"Don't worry! I am going to the cops. I'm on my way now." Becca was beginning to sound exasperated. "I just wish I could talk to Margaret first. I mean, I knew she was angry. I could almost understand it if she'd lashed out. But would she really have killed him? Have planned it in advance?

"When Tiger said poison, I figured he was simply referring to Gaia's, uh, incident." Becca might be addressing her friend, but Clara had the feeling her person was really talking to herself. "But now I'm wondering… There are some poisons that would induce or mimic cardiac arrest. I was reading…"

More yelling stopped that train of thought. But Becca kept walking, even as she appeared to change her approach. "You're right, Maddy. I'm not going to get involved in what happened to Frank Cross. I'm leaving that to the police. But maybe I'll just stop into the store first. Because Gaia really ought to be talking to the authorities too, and maybe I can get her to come with me. She and Frank were involved, and she might know something. Maybe she heard him talk about an enemy or someone who had a grudge or something."

The voice on the other end of the line sounded nominally less frantic. Or maybe, Clara realized, Maddy was simply tired.

"No, I didn't ask her about money. I'm leaving that to the police, just like you said." Her voice dropped to a near whisper. "Besides, between you and me, I don't think he had much of a business. Margaret kind of implied that, too. But still, Gaia might know more than she thinks she knows, if you know what I mean."

That one almost made Clara stop cold. Becca was beginning to sound as logical as a cat. Only as she caught up with her person did she realize that the young woman hadn't yet aired all of her concerns.

"There's more, Maddy. That root? It wasn't wolf's bane. It wasn't anything poisonous at all. Gaia planted it in her own mug to get back at Margaret." She stopped walking. "I guess that's all going to come out. I don't want to get Gaia in trouble with the police. It sounds like it was just a stupid prank. But especially if the cops are now saying that Frank's death was something other than a heart attack, then they should know. I wish I could give Margaret a heads-up about that. Or her sister. A sister might see things that a wife wouldn't, and that Elizabeth seems pretty sharp to me."

She paused, and Clara waited. But Becca didn't bring up the

other possibility that she had considered out loud—that Gaia hadn't put the root in her own mug but knew who had. That Tiger had done it to scare his ex into giving up her new lover, or at least to take his warnings seriously. Clara didn't know if Becca had taken the bike messenger's shrugged denial as truth, or if she still suspected him of some complicity. She did know that her person was smarter than her sisters gave her credit for, though, and the implication that she might be protecting the handsome young man for some reason made the loving feline uneasy.

But even as she mulled over this possibility, Becca kept talking.

"Besides, Maddy, I can't help but wonder, what if Gaia didn't plant that thing herself? I mean, Gaia admits to having an affair with Frank, so maybe it was a warning, someone trying to scare her. And that could mean she's in real danger."

***

Becca picked up her pace after that, heading back into the heart of Central Square, where the Cambridge police had their precinct offices. Clara had accompanied Becca to the red brick building before, and they'd both come out unscathed. Still, the little cat found herself on edge, every whisker alert, as they drew closer. Sure enough, Becca's pace slowed ever so slightly as they entered the bustling business district. It was only coincidental, Clara told herself, that they were also approaching the block that held both the Cross's apartment and the magic shop where Gaia worked.

"*She's only thinking that she wants to talk to Gaia again,*" the little cat thought. "*She wishes she could have gotten her to come talk to the police with her. She told her friend that.*"

But even though Clara trusted her person more than Maddy apparently did, Clara couldn't help but feel a shiver of fear as they neared the brick building. After all, Becca had also talked about stopping back at the widow's apartment and trying to enlist her sister. Clara didn't relish another encounter with the weird Elizabeth, especially now, when Becca should be handing this case over to the police. There was something eerie about that woman, thought the cat. Distracted, she nearly collided with her person as Becca stopped short at the corner.

"Gaia?" The name burst out in surprise. Sure enough, the salesgirl was standing on the sidewalk, one hand pushing her jet-black hair back from her face. From the looks of her eyeliner, she'd been crying. "I was going to stop by the store—"

"Good thing you didn't." She turned away, as if to wipe her face. Then, with a defiant toss of her head, she grabbed Becca by the arm. "Let's get out of here."

"Why? What happened?" Becca resisted, looking back toward the glass storefront with its colorful symbols. The skulking figure from before was nowhere in sight, but Gaia acted like she was in a hurry, pulling at her as she began to walk quickly away.

"I've been fired. That's what. At least, I think I have." She mugged, trying to smile. Only it didn't quite take. After they'd crossed the street, retracing Becca's steps, the goth girl slowed her stride and let her head hang down.

"I'm sorry." Becca immediately went into comfort mode. "What happened?"

Clara looked from her person to the downcast girl at her side. All the options—the absences from her post, the possible theft, the philandering—ran through her mind. Becca had to be aware of these, and yet she appeared as focused and concerned as she'd be if one of Clara's sisters had started to limp. Becca was tender hearted, Clara knew. She loved her for it, but at the same time, it made her worry about her person, too.

Gaia took so long to respond that they'd reached the end of the block. By then, Becca had her arm around the other girl. Taking a deep breath, she asked, her voice gentle, "Was it because of Frank?"

125

Gaia started, and her quick intake of breath must have been audible even to human ears. Exhaling even more noisily, she nodded, and reached up to wipe a tear that had escaped to roll down her cheek. "What a jerk," she said.

Becca's eyebrows went up at that, but she held her tongue. After another pause—not so long this time—Gaia began to speak.

"That was stupid," she said, staring off down the block as if she could transport herself even farther away. "I didn't even really like him that much, you know?"

Becca wisely chose not to respond. Sure enough, Gaia kept on talking. "He was funny. He used to come into the shop all the time and flirt with me, even though he was this little pudgy bald guy. Like he had all this confidence, you know? He'd bring me a muffin when I opened in the morning. He used to say I was too skinny. I needed someone to look after me. He'd tell me I should get more sleep. Take more breaks. At some point, he started massaging my shoulders. And, you know, he was really good at it. And then he asked me to read the Tarot for him. A private reading in the back, even though he knew I couldn't really read the cards."

She broke off and blinked back more tears, though if they were for the man who had died or the job she had lost, Clara couldn't tell.

"Anyway, it wasn't more than a couple of times. It wasn't like I was going to be his girlfriend or anything." Clara saw Becca open her mouth to comment and then close it again, unable to find the words. "If it weren't for that old witch of a sister-in-law showing up, I don't think anyone would have found out."

"You mean Elizabeth?" Becca latched onto the name.

"Yeah, it was right after she stole my plant. She marched in and said something about 'dangerous friends.' I knew then the jig was up."

For a moment, Clara thought Becca was going to speak out. Gaia was being as unreasonable as Laurel or Harriet. When she didn't, Clara

126

had to wonder once again at the similarities between them. When Becca finally did respond, it was in a deliberate tone that Clara knew meant she had put some thought into her words.

"Gaia, we need to go to the police." When the other girl started to speak, Becca put up her hand to hold her off. "Not about the asafetida. I understand that you were upset, and I think we can just pretend that didn't happen. But about what you heard or may have heard about Frank. And now with this about your plant... I spoke to Tiger."

The other girl stared at her like she'd grown a second head, the black smears around her eyes adding dramatic emphasis. "Tiger? How did you...?"

"I am a witch detective." The corners of Becca's lips twitched. She didn't, Clara noted, mention her lunch with Gaia's ex. "And I'm sorry if I overstepped. But you did hire me to look into what was going on, and then you said that he was still worried about you, and I saw—I might have seen—someone hanging around the shop after I left this morning."

"That might just have been Tiger."

Becca shook her head. "I know you said he worries too much. But maybe he's got reason. I gather that he knew about your affair with Frank."

"Tiger? No, he didn't..."

Becca cut her off before she could continue. "Maybe he didn't want you to know that he knew, but he did. I don't know if that's connected. But he told me he thinks there was bad blood between Margaret and her husband. Really bad."

A shrug led Clara to believe the black-clad girl didn't care that much about the other woman's distress. "Frank wasn't serious about me. He was never going to leave her."

It wasn't a question, and Becca didn't answer.

Gaia acted like she had heard something, though. Kicking at a pebble, her lower lip jutting out like a toddler's, she glanced over at her companion. "I guess I messed up, huh?"

Becca held her tongue and the two walked in silence for a bit, until Gaia stopped and turned toward Becca. "You think that's why she tried to frame me?"

"Frame you? Did you ever, um, meet at his office?"

"No." Gaia looked miserable. "I went down to the lot once, but I didn't like the sleazy guys he worked with. Is that where he...?" For a moment, the death of her former paramour seemed to register, before she brushed it away as if it were a mere annoyance. "No, I didn't mean...that. Poor guy. Just that she tried to set me up for stealing." She bit down on the words. "Why she told you, told everyone, that I was taking money out of the register."

"And you weren't?" Becca's voice was as soft as kitten fur. "Not even as a loan?"

"Me? No." Gaia scoffed at the idea. "I don't care about money. If I did, you think I would have stayed in that dead-end job? Besides, Tiger's always telling me I can work with him. He makes pretty decent money."

"Do you like to ride?" Clara couldn't tell if Becca was curious or slightly miffed. The little calico found herself relieved by the idea that the pale messenger still harbored feelings for this pale and painted girl.

"What? No, in sales. I'm good behind a counter," she said, waving off any evidence to the contrary. Even as she did, the reality of her situation seemed to hit home. "Not that I'm going to get any kind of a reference now," she moped.

"It does seem like maybe it was time to move on." Becca spoke as gently as she could. "But you said you weren't even sure you were fired."

Another shrug. "I don't know for certain. I mean, it's Margaret's shop, but I think her sister is really behind it. She's the reason Margaret hired me."

"She is?"

Margaret's words came back to Clara as she watched her person take this in.

Gaia stretched out her black-clad arms. "I guess I look the part. Or I thought that's what was happening anyway. Margaret said something about her sister telling her to get 'that girl,' like she had me in mind, special. Only I think Elizabeth had it out for me for a while. Just last week, I heard her telling Margaret that she'd made a mistake. That she'd hired the wrong girl. Actually, she kind of liked you."

Gaia regarded Becca with a gimlet eye.

"Me?"

Gaia nodded. "She must have seen you when we talked. Or maybe it was when you came in to hang up that flyer. Anyway, she was all excited that you'd come back to the shop. Wanted Margaret to reach out to you right away."

Becca bit her lip, and Clara knew she had to be thinking about Elizabeth and her sister. Margaret had reached out to Becca, all right, but as a client. And Becca had sent her away.

"Anyway, I don't know for sure what's going on, only that she came in and told me to get lost. That I was gone. But I don't know. Truth is, I think she's going senile. That old bat couldn't even get your name right. She kept saying she was waiting for Clara."

"Well, that's curious." Now it was Becca's turn to look distracted. But Gaia didn't give her a chance to think it through.

"Wait a minute." She reached out for Becca's hand again. "Something doesn't make sense."

Becca shook her head, waiting.

"If Tiger was only warning me because he wanted me to be more careful around those Cross witches, then why is he still worried? I mean, it's not like I'm still going to see Frank. Unless..." Even under her smudged makeup, the goth girl's pallor was obvious.

"You don't think that Margaret, that that crazy lady... Or maybe she's working with her sister. Maybe they did do something to Frank, and now they're going to come for me."

"But you just said that Elizabeth basically threw you out of the shop."

"Yeah, she did. But maybe she did it because she knows something—something about Margaret." Gaia held Becca's wrist in a death grip as she leaned in close. "She wants me gone before I can find out what really happened. Or before her crazy sister can kill me, too."

Chapter 18

"We're going to the police." It was a statement, not a question. Still, Gaia tried to wriggle out.

"I'm sure it's nothing," she quailed. "I was being silly. Tiger always says I overreact."

"Tiger should be coming with us, too." Becca pulled her phone out.

"No, please." Gaia reached for her hand, but it was a plea not a grab for the device. "Let's leave him out of this. I'll go with you."

Becca thought for a moment, then accepted with a quick nod. It must have taken all her self-control not to hold the other girl's arm, Clara thought as she turned and started back into the square. At the end of the block, she slowed. The brick building that housed the shop and the Cross's apartment lay straight ahead.

"Why don't we duck behind the store?" Becca asked, turning toward Gaia. "Just in case."

Gaia managed a wan smile in return, and the two turned down the side street that would take them past the back of Charm and Cherish. This was a boon for Clara, as the smaller one-way was both less trafficked and, at this hour, shadowed by the block of buildings. The lack of light appeared to have affected the two young women, however.

As they passed the neighboring structures, they walked in silence, each lost in her own thoughts.

Once they neared the small lot in the rear of Charm and Cherish, Becca paused to look up the alley that ran alongside. But the narrow passageway was empty now except for shadows. Still, Becca was so preoccupied that she almost missed Gaia's sudden intake of breath.

"What?" Becca turned to her.

The other girl appeared frozen in place, as if her glittery sneakers were glued to the sidewalk.

"I can't," she said. "I really can't, Becca."

She was staring ahead at the tiny lot. Only one car was parked there now, a battered tan Toyota that was rumbling as it belched out clouds of blue smoke. Over the top, Becca could see a wiry head of grey hair.

"Elizabeth." Becca sighed. The older of the two sisters had clearly just exited the shop, that gunmetal gray door propped open behind her. The light from the small window just past the door shone down through the shadow, highlighting the silver in her hair. "Well, she's probably just taking out the trash."

Clara peered up at her person. Even from here it was apparent the older woman was speaking to someone in the car. Gaia must have seen it too, because she emitted a faint groan.

"Maybe it's just someone asking for directions." But sure enough, the Toyota began backing out with a scraping sound that didn't speak well for the exhaust. As it turned, Becca strained to see. There was something familiar about the driver, Clara thought. But with the windows up, she could catch neither scent nor sound.

"Funny." As Becca looked on, the car headed away, leaving the small lot empty except for the dumpster. Elizabeth turned back toward the building, then paused to examine a plastic milk crate that had been left beside the door. A moment later, she stood, shaking her head, and left it there as she went back inside, letting the door shut behind her.

"Anyway," said Becca, "she's gone." With that, Clara's person turned to her companion, only to find that the goth girl had disappeared as well.

***

"Gaia?" Becca called quietly, whirling around to check up the alley. But the black-haired girl was nowhere in sight.

"I may as well talk to Elizabeth." Becca sounded resigned. "At the very least, she can fill in some blanks for me."

With that, Becca walked up to the alley and, after a moment's hesitation, followed it up to the street, Clara hard on her heels. When she paused on the street out front, Clara waited. For a few seconds, Clara thought she might even have thought better of her errand and decided to continue on her original mission. But to the little cat's dismay, Becca was only once more looking around for the missing girl. And possibly, she realized, strategizing. Then, pulling herself upright, to make her petite frame as tall as could be, she walked up to the colorful store and entered, to the now familiar jangle. Clara had no choice but to follow behind, passing through behind her before the bells had quieted.

"Hello." The shop appeared empty. Although Clara could make out sounds, nobody stood in Gaia's place behind the counter or between the packed shelves. "Anyone here?"

"Coming," a familiar voice called from the back room, and Becca headed toward it. But if she was hoping to check out the storeroom, she moved too slowly. Elizabeth stepped out, pulling the door shut behind her. She was wearing a smock and work gloves, and in one hand held a pair of secateurs. "Becca, dear," she said with a smile as she pocketed the pruning shears. Although she was fully shaded, Clara ducked behind a display of crystals as her person stepped forward. "Welcome."

"Elizabeth." Becca was smiling, Clara could hear it in her voice. She could also hear the strain underneath. This was a ploy, she realized. Her person was trying to disarm the older woman. "I was hoping to

133

speak with you or, perhaps, with Margaret."

She stepped forward, toward the back room. Elizabeth didn't move. "I'm afraid Margaret is indisposed," she said. "I'm sure you understand, what with Frank and all."

"Of course." Becca agreed. "I'm wondering if the police have shared any information with you?"

"The police?" Elizabeth's voice rose as she began to pull off her gloves. "Why would they tell me anything?"

"Well, I gather you're here, taking care of your sister..." Becca caught herself before she finished the sentence. She wanted the older woman to reveal herself, Clara realized with admiration.

"I don't take care of Margaret," Elizabeth said so quickly that Becca caught her breath. "I do try to advise her, of course. But it's not like she ever listens to me."

"I gather you didn't like Gaia, the girl who was working for her."

"That fake?" She brushed her hands together, dismissing the shopgirl like a last bit of dirt. "No. I had no use for her. I told Margaret."

"And I assume you shared your suspicions with the police?"

"Of course." Elizabeth sounded very matter of fact. "But that doesn't mean... Oh, dear! Becca!"

Clara started forward in time to see Becca begin to fall, her knees buckling. She grabbed the counter just as Elizabeth raced around to catch her.

"*Poison!*" The calico stared, wide-eyed, unsure of what to do or how to help.

"I'm fine." Becca leaned heavily on the older woman. "I just got a little light-headed. If I could just sit down for a moment?"

"Of course." Arms still around Becca, she began backing up, kicking open the door behind her. And as Becca apparently regained her strength enough to walk through it, Clara relaxed. The move had been a ruse, a trick to get into the back room.

"Would you like some water?" Elizabeth asked, showing Becca to a worn couch. Despite its sprung upholstery, it looked comfortable, Clara thought, with deep cushions and soft velvet that still retained some of its pile. As her acute nose informed her of its other recent usage, her ears went back. This, then, was where Frank and Gaia had their assignations.

The odors were too faint for Becca to notice, however. And as Elizabeth hurried over to a corner, where a sink and hot plate made for a makeshift kitchenette, she took in her surroundings. In front of the sofa, a scarred wooden coffee table held two dirty mugs as well as an opened deck of Tarot cards. Metal shelving lined the walls, stuffed with books and boxes, several wrapped in cellophane. The door to the shop remained ajar, as did one by the sink, revealing a small lavatory below a smoked-glass window. As Elizabeth ran the tap, Becca craned around to see the exit to the street. Her view was nearly blocked by large cardboard boxes, some open, others taped shut. Someone was in the midst of packing, though whether that work would require pruning shears or gloves, Clara didn't know.

"Here you go." Elizabeth slid onto the sofa beside Becca, handing her a plastic beaker of water.

"Thanks." Becca managed a smile but did not, Clara was glad to see, drink. Instead, she turned to face the open boxes. "Are you, uh, changing out the inventory?"

"That? Oh, yes." Elizabeth appeared flustered, as if she were seeing the boxes for the first time. "I'm afraid Margaret let things go, and so I figured that while I'm here I would try to get things in order. There's so much that's outdated and nothing has been taken proper care of. Of course, it would be a huge help if we had a proper staff."

Becca nodded. "I ran into Gaia."

Elizabeth sighed and shook her head. "That girl," she said. "She didn't belong here. She had no feeling for the craft."

135

Becca's eyes narrowed. For a moment, Clara thought, she resembled Laurel. "That's why you let her go?"

A startled laugh. "You thought—because of Frank? No, she did Margaret a favor, though my sister doesn't see it that way. Frank was a liability from the get-go. She'll be much better off now that he's gone."

Before Becca could respond, the jingling of bells announced the opening of the store's front door.

"Elizabeth, are you there?" a voice, nasal and a little whiny, called.

"Margaret?" She rose and turned. "Coming!"

Becca followed her back through to the front of the shop.

"Glad you're feeling better." She greeted her sister with a hug.

"What? Oh, hi, Becca." The shorter sister had her coat on, and her pink cheeks attested to a longer walk than the half block from her apartment. Still, she bobbed her head toward her sister. "Yes, thank you, Elizabeth. The nap did me good."

Becca looked from one sister to the other, but bit back whatever response she was about to make. "I'm glad you came by," she said instead. "I've been meaning to offer my condolences. I'm so sorry for your loss."

The new widow sniffed, a bit dramatically. "Thanks. It was a shock."

When nothing else followed, Becca leaned in. "If you're up for it. I was also hoping to ask you a few questions."

"Questions?" Even a human couldn't have missed the way the two sisters locked eyes. But if Becca saw anything, she chose, once more, not to comment. Instead, she simply smiled and waited. "Of course," said Margaret. "Elizabeth, would you make tea?"

With another glance at Becca, the taller of the two sisters retreated into the back. Margaret, meanwhile, removed her coat and carried it around the back of the counter. Although she sniffed again, Clara suspected that had as much to do with the chill outside that had pinked her cheeks as with grief. Surely, Becca had to notice that the widow had

136

seemed more upset at the idea of her husband leaving her than at his death?

"With everything that's going on, I can't believe that Elizabeth fired my only employee."

"I thought she was following your wishes?" Becca spoke quietly, so as not to be overheard by the woman in the back.

"Elizabeth?" Margaret shook her head. "Hardly. She thinks she knows best. As always."

As she settled onto a stool behind the counter, Becca leaned forward. "She was telling me about Gaia." Another quick peek, but the older sister still had not emerged. When the widow sniffed once more—perhaps she had a sinus condition—Becca hesitated. But when Margaret only dabbed at her eyes with a balled-up handkerchief, she began again. "I'm sorry. I'm not interested in gossip, but Gaia's been having some problems, and you have to see how this looks. I was thinking that if, perhaps, someone was angry at Gaia, she might have thought to scare her a little."

The wiry-haired widow sighed, and for a moment Becca looked like she was about to apologize. Clara understood—Becca was a sweet girl and inclined to be sensitive—only just then she hoped she'd hold firm. *"Please, Becca, you need answers,"* she muttered in a low feline rumble. If only she had a little of Laurel's powers of persuasion, the calico thought yet again, as she concentrated as hard as she could.

"Have you spoken to the police about the theft?" It sounded like a digression, and Clara stared up at Becca, wondering what her person was aiming at.

Margaret seemed to deflate further, and Clara realized there was, indeed, some kind of connection. "Frank," she said, as her bowed shoulders rose and fell once more. "He was a dreamer. He thought bigger than he was. What else can I say?"

"So you didn't report the jewelry? The watches?"

A single sad shake of the head. "It doesn't matter now, does it? I mean, to anyone but me."

"But if you think someone was stealing…" Becca's tone stayed even, her voice soft, but she wasn't giving up.

"Someone was. Only, well, that's all over." Another brush of her hand, as if larceny were a pesky fly.

Becca sucked in her lip. Clara recognized that move. It meant she was thinking about something or, no, regretting it. "Margaret, when I said I couldn't take your case, it wasn't because I didn't think it was legit."

"It doesn't matter, dear." The large eyes raised to meet Becca's were dry but sad. "I did some silly things, too."

"I was wondering." Becca's voice, already quiet, grew powder-puff soft, as gentle as a kitten's paw, and Clara waited. "Was that what happened with Frank, Margaret?" Becca glanced quickly toward the door, expecting Margaret's older sister to emerge at any moment. "Tell me, Margaret. Did you want to scare *him* a little? Bring him back in line?"

"Frank?" Margaret's head went back as she screwed up her face in confusion. "You think I…that I made him sick? You think that's why he left? You can't, possibly…"

Becca reached out to take her arm. "I don't mean it was anything intentional. Of course not." Becca remained quiet, the voice of sympathy, though Clara could hear how tightly controlled her breathing was. "But if there was an accident with one of the herbs from the shop, maybe? I mean, I would understand."

"No, I don't think you do." Margaret pulled away, any trace of that brittle giddiness gone, replaced by an acid scorn. "I don't know where you get your information, but I didn't dose my husband with anything. Not from my shop, not from anywhere. I've never hurt anybody, not even that cheating little trollop you seem to have become friends with."

Becca started to protest, but Margaret cut her off.

"I'm extremely glad I didn't spend any money on your so-called psychic services." Her dark brows descended as she glared at Becca. "It's pretty clear you're no good at detecting anything. Frank's heart gave out, you silly girl. He was a cheater and a loser, and it's his own fault if his guilty conscience finally caught up to him."

***

"Why don't we step outside?" A hand gripped Becca's upper arm and she turned to see Elizabeth, who proceeded to march her toward the door. "Shall we?"

Clara bristled, ready to spring. But as soon as she had Becca out on the sidewalk once more, the older woman released her. Blowing out her lips, she reached up and pushed that wiry hair off her face. "Stupid girl." It sounded more like frustration than a reprimand.

"I'm sorry." Becca still seemed stunned by Margaret's outburst. Or perhaps, thought Clara, by the widow's lack of grief.

"Not you—that Gail. Gaia, as she calls herself." Elizabeth peered back into the shop. Checking for her sister, Becca thought, and giving Becca a moment to collect herself. "She was a menace."

"You mean, because of the wolf's bane?" After Becca threw out the name of the poisonous plant, Clara could hear that she held her breath, waiting.

"So foolish." Elizabeth frowned. Her bushy black brows arched like a cat's back, but she didn't pretend not to understand. "You do know that aconite can bring about arrhythmia, a heart attack, don't you? If the police found that plant in the shop...well, Gaia should be happy I made her get rid of it."

"You made her get rid of it." Becca repeated the words to make sure she heard them correctly.

"Didn't she tell you?" Elizabeth barely noticed. "Yes, I tried to make her understand the danger. Not that a girl like that takes anything seriously. I was glad when it disappeared."

"Disappeared?" Surely, thought Clara, the older woman would notice the emphasis her visitor placed on the word.

"Re-homed. Tossed. Whatever. As long as it was no longer sitting right there in the Charm and Cherish window. Stupid." She shook her head again, but slowly, as if consumed more by disappointment than anger.

"So you didn't take it?" A tilt of the head.

"Me?" Elizabeth laughed, face up in an appeal to the heavens, and then focused those dark eyes on Becca. "You should know better, Becca. You more than anyone. But never mind." She turned and reached for the door, ready to rejoin her sister. "Just stay clear of this, okay? It's not safe."

Clara looked up at Becca then, but her person simply stood there, too stunned to respond. The little calico, meanwhile, couldn't help but notice how the older woman's eyes flickered under those heavy brows as she nodded once more to Becca, and then slid over to the cat who stood at her side.

"Especially with your family history," she said.

Chapter 19

"You've been gone all day!" Harriet greeted Clara at the door with an eager sniff. *"This is as bad as when Becca had that job of hers. We haven't eaten since breakfast."*

"Did she spend all afternoon with that Tiger?" Laurel circled, her tail lashing with the excitement of the hunt. *"Is she bringing him home soon? Are they going to his place?"*

"No!" It was all Clara could do to contain her temper. *"Everything's gotten so much more complicated! You don't understand, either of you. Ow!"*

That was in response to Laurel, who had batted her ear. Harriet merely stared, affronted, her own flag of a tail flipping back and forth in annoyance.

"There's a lot you don't understand, runt." Laurel was not going to forgive easily. *"Especially about men and women like our pretty Becca."*

"No, it's not that. It's this whole situation." Clara looked at Laurel and then Harriet. The time for secrets, she realized, was over. *"There's something I haven't told you. A lot, actually."*

With her ears tuned for Becca's footsteps on the stairs, Clara filled her sisters in on what had happened. The lunch, running into Gaia, and, more disturbing to the little calico, her interaction with both Margaret and Elizabeth. As she described the older woman, tall with that wiry silver hair and a beak-like nose that seemed to draw her dark eyes close together, Harriet rose to her feet. Thinking that her oldest sister was simply getting restless, Clara hurried to finish.

"*That look was bad enough,*" she said, ears flicking backward at the memory. "*But then that Gaia said something that really freaked me out. She said that this Elizabeth was looking for Becca, only she called her Clara. Like maybe she was really looking for me.*"

"*Huh.*" Eyes closed, Laurel sniffed dismissively. "*Like the runt of the litter, Clara the clown, would be the feline she sought.*"

"*I'm the one she saw,*" Clara offered, hoping to appease her sister. She had her own thoughts as to why the wiry-haired woman had asked for her, but there was no sense in antagonizing her sisters. "*Becca's smart. She must have figured it out. Elizabeth is taking over the shop. She's getting rid of stuff, and it looked like she was maybe gardening. That could mean she was doing something else with that poison plant. Plus, she said that her sister was better off without Frank.*"

"*And she fired Gaia?*" Harriet took a while to understand, sometimes.

Clara resisted the urge to nip her older sister. "*The girl is lucky! At least she got out alive. But that's not the strangest thing. This Elizabeth, it's like she staged all this to bring in our Becca. She spoke as if she knew Frank was going to die. As if she was already planning—*"

"Well, what's going on here?"

Clara turned. Harriet sunk down onto her belly, and Laurel jumped as Becca shut the door behind her. They'd all been listening so intently to Clara they'd missed the sound of their person, who now stood, smiling down at her three pets.

"It almost looks like you three are having a conference. Or, should I say, a convocation?"

"More later," Clara mewed softly as she turned toward her person.

"No sign of poison." Laurel had already rubbed her face against Becca's legs and now stood to bury her brown snout in Becca's palm. *"She's clean."*

"Well, that's a mercy!" Harriet made a desultory pass. *"There are some odd scents on her though."*

"Really?" Clara pushed in, earning a slight snarl from Laurel.

"Hey, I'm working here!" One brown paw raised to bat her little sister.

"Just when I thought you were all getting along so well." Becca's tone was enough to make Clara slink off, tail down. "Ah well, never mind, kitties. Let me get you some dinner. I've got some strategizing to do."

"Sorry." Clara slipped in behind Laurel as the three cats followed their person into the kitchen. *"Can you…?"*

"On it," said Laurel. *"Something about this 'strategizing' I don't like."*

"Gaia?" Even before the third can was down on its mat, Becca had her phone out. "Call me please."

When the phone rang only a few minutes later, Becca grabbed it. By then, she was on the sofa, feet up, with her computer on her lap. Laurel was bathing on the armrest, while Clara, at her feet, sat up at attention. Harriet could still be heard in the kitchen, hoovering up the last few crumbs.

"Hey, Maddy." As Becca closed the laptop, she put one hand over her eyes. "No, I didn't get to the police today. I was on my way when I ran into Gaia outside the shop. I was hoping to get her to come to the cops with me, but she bolted, and I ended up talking to Margaret Cross and her sister, and it all got complicated. I'll go tomorrow, I promise. With or without her, but it would be better if she'd come with me."

As Clara listened, Becca ran through the events of the afternoon. When she got up to her decision to come home rather than continue on to the police station, Clara couldn't help but feel like her person was intentionally leaving something out.

"You just don't want to admit that she messed up." Laurel, stretched along the couch back, managed to mute her usual Siamese voice.

"You weren't there." Clara shifted. *"She was afraid. That woman— Elizabeth—seemed to be warning her off."* It made her uncomfortable when Laurel eavesdropped on her thoughts. Besides, she wanted to listen to the conversation.

"Like that's any different?" The distinctive yowl grew a bit louder.

"Hush, now." Harriet landed with a thud and, seeing that Becca had taken up most of the sofa, began to knead her instead.

"Come to think of it," Becca was saying. "I'm going to try Gaia again now."

Laurel glared at Clara, but Clara only had eyes for Becca as she punched in the by-now familiar number. Something was very wrong. She could feel it.

"Hey!" With a startled mew, Harriet leaped sideways to avoid the laptop, which slid to the sofa beside her. *"What's going on?"*

Neither of her sisters answered, although Clara joined Laurel on the sofa back as Becca rose and began to pace.

"Hey, Gaia. Thanks for picking up." Becca was doing her best to be casual. Clara could hear the slight sing-song cadence of her voice. Until she stopped and stood up straight. "Gaia, what's wrong? You don't sound good. You—what? Did you say 'numb'? Where are you?" She started looking around, and Clara rolled a pencil out from under the sofa for her person to grab. "I'll call you right back."

"Emergency? I just spoke with a friend at 932 River…" As Becca spoke, she headed toward the door, grabbing her coat as she did. "You need to send an ambulance there now."

Chapter 20

Clara didn't even consult with her sisters. As quickly as she could fade her orange spots to gray, she followed Becca out the door and down to the street, where Becca hailed a passing cab. Overcoming her natural feline distrust of motorized vehicles, Clara even managed to scramble onto the black vinyl seat beside her.

"Mount Auburn Hospital," Becca told the cabbie. "I'm sorry, I don't have the address."

"Emergency?" The cabbie's voice emerged from his darkly shadowed jowls.

"What? No, I'm fine."

"Emergency room, I meant." Dark eyes caught hers in the rearview. "Don't worry. I actually drive for a living."

"Of course." Clara didn't understand the slight blush that crept into Becca's cheeks. She did know that the car was moving more smoothly than Becca's usual ride shares. In the seat beside her, Clara was taking no chances, however, and dug her claws into the slick upholstery. The small risk that Becca would notice the indents was worth not being thrown around should the car stop short.

"Uh, miss?" Clara needn't have worried. Becca was so distracted that she was halfway out of the cab before the driver called her back.

"I'm sorry." Becca fished out her wallet and handed the driver a bill. "And thanks."

If Clara thought the ride was bad, the scene that met her when she followed Becca through the sliding glass doors was worse. Beeps and blats, along with a terrifying array of smells stopped her in her tracks. Only the rattle of wheels alerted her to jump to one side in time to avoid being run down as some kind of a trolley rolled by, propelled by four white-clad feet clearly in a hurry.

"Gaia—Gail Linquist?" Becca's voice, over by a window, made Clara focus once more and she hurried to join her by the safety of the wall. "Has she been brought in?"

"One moment, please." Considering all the noise and activity, the woman who responded sounded surprisingly calm. "Are you family?"

"No, I'm a…a friend." Becca leaned in. "I'm the one who called an ambulance for her."

"Becca Colwin." A male voice, deep and oddly familiar. "Why am I not surprised?"

"Detective Abrams." Becca, breathless, barely got the words out as Clara identified the large and rumpled man who had come up behind her. Clad in a tweed jacket that sagged at the elbows and wrinkled khakis, the man smelled of stale coffee, the dust of paperwork, and the sweat of many, many hands. In other words, he was a cop. That he was familiar with Becca, and she with him, put the small cat somewhat at ease. She, too, remembered the unexpected gentleness of the big man. "I'm so glad you're here." Becca's voice lifted with relief. "I've been meaning to come talk to you."

Eyebrows like untrimmed hedges rose as the detective sipped from a paper cup.

"I shouldn't be surprised." A rumble like the wheels of that trolley. "Only when your name came up, I thought I would insert myself into

146

this…situation." He motioned with the cup. "Shall we go have a chat?"

"I can't." Becca looked over the window, but from all Clara could see, the woman on the other side did not respond. "I'm waiting to hear about Gaia. Gail, I mean. She's a friend. A client. Well, sort of."

"Let's go chat, Becca Colwin." One large hand reached out behind her to propel her along. "I think you'll want to talk to me about this 'Gaia Gail friend client sort of' of yours."

Chapter 21

As relieved as Clara was to leave behind the noise and traffic of the waiting room, the idea of her person heading off with the rumpled cop wasn't exactly comforting. Yes, she knew—or hoped she knew—that the big man was both kind and fair. However, he did work in a building that resembled a giant cage. Also, as he walked Becca along, one big mitt behind her as if to stop her from escaping, he propelled her first through a set of double doors that threatened to close on the skittish cat and then a long passage that smelled of chemicals, all the while herding Becca like a determined sheepdog. Even as she paused, looking back toward the loud room, he kept his sad, dark eyes on her, taking in everything, Clara thought.

In the past, this large man had proved himself more gentle than his rough exterior suggested. Still, Becca was clearly ill at ease, looking up at him as they walked, and so, despite her own discomfort with their surroundings, her loyal cat stayed close, waiting for a chance to break them both away.

"Why don't we have a seat?" Holding out a hand the size of Harriet's water dish, he directed Becca toward a row of molded plastic chairs in relatively quiet alcove. Apparently carved out of the hallway, it appeared to be a waiting room, though for what, the little cat could not tell. It had no windows, and she couldn't read the signs that hung overhead. It also had no carpet, and no plants for cover, and so Clara focused hard on her shading as she ducked around her person to take up position beneath an orange seat.

Looking as skittish as Laurel, Becca perched on the edge of one of the hard plastic chairs like she was readying herself to leap.

"Let's start at the beginning, shall we?" Abrams fished a pad out of his jacket as he settled, more heavily, beside her. "What brings you to the ER this evening, Ms. Colwin?"

"I told you. I'm here for Gaia—you probably know her as Gail." Becca glanced back down the hall. "When I called for an ambulance, the EMTs said they would be taking her here."

"And you know this Gail, how?"

"She hired me. She thought—well, it doesn't matter now. It can't. Not really."

The big man leaned forward.

"It was a stupid prank. That's all. But when I went to talk with her again, I saw something."

The big man's capacity for stillness was impressive, thought Clara. He's a hunter, she realized, waiting for small prey to emerge. Waiting for...Becca?

Clara jumped to her feet, the fur along her spine rising as her back arched. Eyes wide and whiskers flared on the alert, she eyed the hallway. If she darted out, she could turn and jump. She had no hope of holding the large man, but she could create a distraction. Buy a few seconds, maybe, that would allow Becca to escape. Her ears picked up that Becca's tone had risen and she could feel the air as she gestured. She was helpless, and only Clara could help.

Only Becca didn't seem to realize the danger she was in. In fact, the calico realized as she readied to spring, her person was leaning toward the big man and almost touching him as she explained the day's events.

"So that's why I was trying to reach Gaia," Becca was saying. Her voice, Clara realized, was raised in excitement or frustration, perhaps. Not fear. "I wanted her to come with me to talk with you. Something odd is going on, and I don't know how it all ties together. But both Gaia and Margaret Cross were accusing each other of the most awful things, and Gaia was involved with Margaret's husband—"

"Hold on, please." That big hand went up like a stop sign. Even Clara had sat to listen by this point. "What exactly is your role in this?"

"I'm a witch, ah, investigator." Clara's ears flicked as Becca stumbled over her customary title. "Because these women are in the community, they asked if I could help them out."

A slow nod made Clara think that the big man understood more than he was letting on.

"So both Gail and Margaret hired you?"

"Well, they both tried to. I told Margaret I couldn't work for her because Gaia had hired me first. That was before Margaret lost her husband."

Another nod. "And how exactly did you come to be here, at the hospital, this evening?"

"Well, I had been trying to reach Gaia. She and I were going to come talk to you about…about, well, something I saw. And a plant. It's a long story. Honest, but when I finally reached her, she said she was feeling funny. Her mouth had gone numb, and she was slurring her words. So I called 9-1-1." She'd glided over the part with Gaia slipping away, Clara noted. The way the big man waited made her think that he'd noticed something was missing from her story, too.

"You were coming in to speak with me?" His voice flat as a stepped-on mouse.

"Yes." Becca paused, and Clara thought she was going to explain, then, about seeing Elizabeth—about the missing plant and Gaia bolting. Instead, she simply forged ahead. "She and I had talked about it. Her ex-boyfriend—I'd just met with him. He was worried about Gaia. He thought someone was out to get her, and I guess he was right."

"This boyfriend have a name?"

She nodded enthusiastically. "Tiger. I mean, that's probably a nickname, but that's what everyone calls him. Have you spoken with him? Because he thought that someone was stalking Gaia. He warned her to be careful."

"And you've met this Tiger?" His voice was still soft. His eyes, dark and kind. Maybe it was the way he leaned forward or some undefinable note underlying his questions, but Clara's fur began to rise once more.

"Yes, we had lunch and he told me that he thought that Margaret maybe, but no..." Becca shook her head, picking up on the shift in tone that was causing Clara's unease. "I just saw her, and Tiger's wrong, at least about Margaret and her sister. I mean, she was angry at her husband. And at Gaia, too. But she didn't put the root in her mug. Besides, it was just asafetida, which smells awful but isn't dangerous."

"I'm not talking about this Margaret or any smelly root," Detective Abrams interrupted gently, as if he were correcting a kitten. "I'm talking about you, Becca Colwin. Because before you arrived, I interviewed the victim's friend, this so-called Tiger. And he says he hasn't spoken to you. In fact, he says he's never met you at all."

Chapter 22

"That's crazy." Becca sat up, her eyes turning once more to the double doors at the end of the corridor. "He's upset. Or maybe he's pretending? He and Gaia have broken up, but our lunch was, well, I had the feeling that maybe he thought it was a kind of a date, and maybe he…"

Becca's theory petered out under the big man's skeptical gaze.

"Okay, then. Let's move on to some other questions. Shall we?" The detective flipped a page in his pad. But as he did, the double doors slammed open, and a dark woman in pink scrubs came striding through.

"Is there a Becca Colwin here?" She craned her head around, and Becca stood to greet her. "Becca Colwin?"

"That's me. Did something happen?"

"The patient has been asking for you." The nurse beckoned, then paused, turning to the portly man at her side. "And you are?"

"Abrams." He tilted his head, taking her in with eyes that were suddenly smaller and quite sharp. "Detective Eric Abrams."

"Well, Detective Eric Abrams, I need Becca here to come with me. Gail has woken up."

Becca turned to the large man. "I'm sorry, Detective. I really should go. But I will come down tomorrow and speak with you."

"Like you were going to today?" A note of skepticism.

"Becca?" The nurse was waiting.

"Go." The hand holding the pen rose in dismissal, while the other tucked the pad away, and Becca went.

"We're hoping you can answer some questions for us." As the doors buzzed, the nurse shepherded Becca through. "After you speak with Gail."

Steeling herself against the noise and odors, Clara ducked in behind them into what looked like another hallway, with curtains sectioning off more scents and sounds than the little cat had ever encountered. Blood and other bodily fluids in excess. But also something sharp and chemical, all hard to process as a series of high-pitched beeps kept up their frantic call.

Even Becca didn't seem immune. Her head swiveling, she took everything in, wide-eyed, even as the nurse strode ahead. She didn't go far, though. At the fourth curtain, she stopped and short and motioned Becca, who had scurried to catch up, ahead. As Clara, unseen, pushed in beside her, she slid behind the curtain where the goth girl lay on a narrow hospital bed, her dark, damp hair pushed back from a face that was nearly as pale as the pillow she reclined on.

"Hey, Becca." A ghost of a smile spread her bloodless lips. Her voice was so soft even Clara had to strain to hear. "I owe you. I guess Tiger was right, huh?"

"Oh, Gaia." Becca stepped forward, but stopped herself even as she reached for the other girl's hand. Needles and tubes extended out of her right forearm and into an IV bag suspended above. "What happened?"

"I'm not sure. I had some tea, and I started to feel funny. My lips got numb. I knew something was wrong, but, I don't know, maybe I was too confused. Then you called…" Her eyes closed for a moment

153

before flitting open again. "I guess just firing me wasn't enough."

"What?" Becca drew back.

"The tea. It came from the shop. I figure Margaret added something. Or her sister." Her voice dropped even lower, more breath than sound. "Maybe I gave her the idea, huh?"

"But that's crazy," Becca responded in urgent tones. "I spoke with Elizabeth. She says she didn't take the plant. She thought you got rid of it."

The pale girl pursed her lips as she considered. "Who else could it be? Margaret hates me, and that sister of hers…" Gaia lay back, her eyes slowly closing once again. "My wolf's bane…"

"That's why I wanted us to go talk to the police." Becca leaned in, dropping into a conspiratorial whisper. "I know you faked that first poisoning and anyone else who knows might try to discredit you. But this proves it. Someone really is trying to hurt you."

"Excuse me, miss." A young man in scrubs had slid inside the curtain, his eyes on a monitor that pinged regularly. "She needs her rest. You have to go now."

"Will she be okay?" The ping was accelerating, like an agitated cricket.

"Now." Another set of scrubs pushed in front of her, and she looked around for the nurse who had brought her in. But that nurse had now joined the others, reaching for a metal tray.

"Miss?"

Becca started toward her and stopped. Hands on her shoulders were turning her. Propelling her past the curtain, through the steel doors, and back out to the waiting area.

Chapter 23

"Becca! Did you get in? Did you see her? They won't tell me anything."

Becca turned at the sound of her name. But even before she registered that the harried male voice didn't belong to Detective Abrams, Clara had identified the newcomer. Panting and wild-eyed, the bike messenger had apparently rushed into the ER waiting area only moments before.

"Tiger!" Becca started back, mimicking Clara's own reaction. Although the calico was still shaded, her presence a mere flicker of color and shadow in the busy, brightly lit room, her instincts had taken over. As she had started, stiff-legged, her back had arched and her fur begun to bristle from tail tip to head, to make herself appear larger in the face of an oncoming threat. "Wait." Becca held her hand out, stopping the man in his tracks.

"What?" He looked like he might rush the door through which Becca had just emerged. "Is she—"

"They're taking care of her." Becca grabbed his arm, and he turned. But if Becca—or Clara at her feet—were concerned that the slim man could be violent, his next words put those fears to rest.

"Please," he pleaded, taking her hand in his. "Tell me. You've seen her?"

"Yes. She's in there." Tiger pulled away, turning toward the window. This time it was Becca who reached for him. "They're working on her now, Tiger. They just kicked me out."

Maybe it was her voice, gentle with concern. Maybe her words had sunk in. Clara couldn't tell, but she followed as the lean young man let himself be led to a quiet—well, quieter—corner of the room.

"How is she?" Tiger searched Becca's face for answers. "Did the doctors say? Is she...will she be all right?"

"She was awake but weak." Becca bit her lip. "But then she started to fade. I don't know."

With a cry, he pulled away and would have charged the closed doors. Only Becca's hand stopped him, turning him around once more.

"So you were with her?"

"Me? No." He looked toward the attendant's window, the cords of his neck distended with the strain.

"But the detective said you spoke with him." Becca frowned as she glanced around the room. "Detective Abrams. He was just here."

"Oh, him? Yeah, well, I came by after. She was already feeling sick by then, and I, well, I just have my bike, so I went for help. I thought that's what you meant."

"Oh, she didn't tell me..." Becca bit her lip, a sure sign, Clara knew, that she was holding herself back. "I'm sorry," she said after a moment's pause. "It's just that the detective was questioning me. And he said that you didn't know me."

"Excuse me?" She had his attention now, but the pale man appeared as confused as Becca.

"The detective," she said, speaking slowly, like one would to a child. "He said he was just talking to you, and that you didn't know me or know anything about me."

"That's…no." Tiger shook it off. "That's not what happened."

Becca tried again. "I was telling the detective what I'd learned, and your name came up. He said you had no idea who I was. And you were just talking with him."

"I'm sorry." He pushed the hair off his face, revealing his bunched brows. "This is all just so much. He was…it was all very fast."

"I gather he heard my voice messages or saw my number on her phone…"

"Yeah, I was just so flustered. The paramedics had just taken her." He strained to see behind him, but the door was still closed. "I had to follow, and I just got here."

"You might be able to go in." Becca felt for him. That much was clear. "You should go ask."

He sighed and gave something between a nod and a shrug. "I'm just hoping…." He licked dry, chapped lips and then, perhaps distracted by the noise of the room, turned back toward Becca. "I'm sorry. You said you learned something? Something about Gaia?"

"Yeah." Becca agreed. "Elizabeth has it out for her, all right. You know she fired Gaia, and she made her get rid of her plant. And she had those shears… But I don't think either Elizabeth or Margaret could be behind this."

"What are you talking about? What shears? Who else could it be?" As Tiger spoke, his voice rose, and Clara became aware of several bystanders turning to stare. "You've got to tell the cop that!"

Becca stepped back, one hand reaching up to her lapis pendant. "I think Elizabeth was telling me the truth. She was angry. Her sister's devastated, but they're not killers."

"Yeah, of course. I'm sorry." Tiger reached out, touching Becca's arm with his fingertips. "I'm upset. That's all."

"Of course you are." Becca didn't draw back, not immediately, but she didn't sound convinced either. Instead, she raised her hand to her pendant, shedding his fingers along the way.

"I just..." The pale young man craned around, as if suddenly aware that he was the center of attention. "I wish we had more information, you know? I guess I was hoping that, with you being a detective, that you could, maybe, find out more."

"I *have* been speaking to people." Becca sat back, stung. "I ask questions." Her voice dropped to a conspiratorial whisper. "I did find out the truth about the asafetida."

"Of course." Tiger reached to take her hand. "I'm sorry. I mean, I guess I always thought of detectives as people who looked for physical clues."

"I do that, too." A bit stiff.

"No, please, I understand." A shake of the head. "I would never expect you to put yourself at risk by sneaking into someplace or anything like that. That's not the kind of detective you are."

"How dare you! You're talking like I'm some timid bookworm rather than a woman of power." Becca pulled herself up to her full five-six. Towering to her pets, but surely not to this tall, muscular young man. And yet, he appeared to back down.

"I'm sorry." He even stared down at the ground like a submissive kitten. "I shouldn't push. I guess I'm worried. I feel guilty, okay? Gaia and I are through, but I still care for her, of course. Only, I think maybe she thought we could be more again. Now that...well, you know."

"You mean, now that Frank is out of the picture."

A half-hearted smile said it all.

"That's kind of a quick turnaround." Becca bit her lip against the sharpness of her rebuke, but the words were already out.

"I didn't mean that she had no feelings for him. I know she did." His voice had gotten quiet again. Clara was reminded of Laurel's attempts to modulate her Siamese yowl when she was trying to get

158

treats from Becca. "I think turning back to me was more about comfort and familiarity. She was really shaken up by everything that happened."

"I get it. It has been a lot." Becca's eyes strayed, recalling the week before. "Her boss turning against her, then Frank, and getting fired."

"Exactly, and, well, there's something else." As his voice grew quieter, Tiger stepped forward and slid his hands down so that his fingertips gently cupped hers. "I know you two are friends, and I respect that."

Becca started to speak. Clara thought she was going to argue with that definition of her relationship with the goth girl. But—maybe it was because of the way Tiger's long fingers were gently stroking hers, maybe it was a furball—only a choking sound came out.

"And, like I said, I still care about her. As a friend. And so I wanted to be honest with her and tell her first. That's why I went to see her today. Becca, I know this has all been very sudden, but I feel there's something here. Something between us. Don't you?"

Chapter 24

Becca's eyes went as round as Harriet's. But before she could respond in a more articulate manner, a short shriek caused her to spin around, and the ensuing clatter had everyone in the waiting area rushing over. Ducking through the crowd, Clara could see white shoes and legs clad in lime green scrubs splayed on the floor.

"Are you all right?" A large hand appeared.

"Careful." Another set of scrubs pushed by. "What happened here? Do you feel lightheaded or dizzy?"

"What? No." The woman on the floor, a slight thing who seemed more surprised than hurt, waved off the outstretched hand. Instead, she flipped onto her knees, the better to gather the various surgical tools that had emptied out all over the floor. Clara leaned forward to sniff at a small clamp. Disinfectant, rather than blood, she noted with relief.

"I thought I saw...never mind." Green scrubs turned to reach for the clamp. Clara ducked back, holding her breath as the orderly, her voice lowered to be nearly inaudible, explained to her colleague, "Dale, I thought I saw something scurry by me. You know, like a rat."

"A rat?" The distinctive yowl made Clara spin around. Sure enough, two blue eyes were staring from beneath one of the chairs.

"*Hush!*" The calico raced over to join her sister, crowding in beneath the orange plastic seat.

"*These people.*" Even though Laurel's body was nearly shaded, Clara could make out the toss of her apple-shaped head, the blue eyes closing briefly in disgust. "*They're all listening to those machines. They wouldn't hear me if I sat up and caterwauled.*"

"*I'm sure you're right.*" Clara knew it made more sense to humor her sister than to argue. "*But, Laurel, why are you here?*"

"*Because of Tiger, of course.*" The blue eyes were momentarily veiled as Laurel dipped her head. "*I knew he would come after Becca and I wanted to see what would happen.*"

"*You wanted to influence her.*" The words slipped out, as the truth will. "*Laurel, we don't know this man.*"

"*We know he likes her.*" Even muted, Laurel's voice rose in that distinctive Siamese yowl. "*You heard what he just said.*"

Clara didn't respond. Instead, she turned to look out at Becca. On her knees only feet away, she was reaching for a small silver object she must have fished out from underneath the couch. As Clara watched, she stood, handing the metal tool to the orderly, and Clara couldn't suppress a slight purr. Her person was always helping others.

"*That's why I want what's best for her, too.*" Laurel's voice, softer now, broke into Clara's reverie. "*I know you love her. We all do. But, little sister, believe it or not, hanging out with us is not the way she should spend her life.*"

"*I know.*" Clara sighed, her purr dying away. "*If only we knew this Tiger better.*"

"*Well, now's our chance.*"

Clara felt a damp nudge as Laurel nosed her ear. She turned to look at the young man, who had hung back even as Becca had raced forward, his pale face unreadable. Was that rejection, Clara wondered?

Or was he simply unsure how to approach the woman he had just bared his soul to? A quick sniff might answer some questions, Clara realized. But as she started toward him, another familiar voice boomed out and sent her scurrying under the nearest chair.

"Becca? Becca Colwin?" The detective had emerged from the double doors. "Oh, good, you're still here."

"What is it?" Becca stood and started, looking past him at those doors. "Is it Gaia?"

"A moment, please." The detective motioned her forward with a scoop of his big hand.

Becca turned back, to take in Tiger. But he had gone deathly pale and only nodded. And with that, she turned and followed the detective back into the treatment area, with Clara close behind.

***

"What's happened?" Even as the doors were swinging shut behind them, Becca was demanding answers. "Please tell me. Is Gaia...is she going to be okay?"

Instead of escorting her back to that fourth cubicle on the left, the detective herded Becca over toward the right, where two chairs faced an empty bed.

"Why don't you have a seat?"

"No." The edge to Becca's voice made Clara's ears tilt back, even if she understood her person's impatience. "Not until you tell me what's going on with Gaia."

The big head bowed in assent. "She's talking," he said. "So I don't know for sure, but I figure that means she's going to be all right."

"Thank the Goddess." Becca flopped into one of the chairs and leaned her head on her hands.

"That doesn't mean you're out of the woods, young lady." If anything, the large man's tone had grown more serious.

"What do you mean?" She swallowed.

"You've told me about this Gaia and about Margaret Cross, and yet you failed to disclose that you saw Frank Cross shortly before his death."

"But I didn't." Becca's voice rose to a pitch reminiscent of Laurel's.

"We've had a report that you were seen at his place of business." It was a statement of fact, not a question.

"His…" Becca paused to correct herself. "Yes, that's right. I went down to his car lot. Margaret was really upset and I was hoping to figure out what was going on. But I left without seeing him or speaking to him. I overheard him on the phone. He was in the next room. That's all."

The cop waited, silently.

"It sounded like he was talking to his wife, so I left." It sounded lame. It was also the truth. "It sounded personal, so I thought I should keep out of it."

If the man in front of her mumbled something about that being a good idea, Becca didn't hear it. Besides, he had more to say.

"That's not all, though, young lady. You're working as a private investigator without a license." One hand went up to stop her before she could protest. "Don't argue with me on that. The laws exist for a reason, you know. And one of those reasons is that you're not equipped to deal with an attempted murder."

"But it wasn't." Becca closed her eyes. "Gaia just faked it because she wanted to get Margaret in trouble. That's all."

"Faked it?" Those large eyes scanned Becca's face. "You were by her bed when she nearly crashed just now, Becca. Do you really think that was faked?"

"No." Becca shook her head, staring at the empty bed as if the answer would be found there. "I'm sorry. The first time. She was trying to frame Margaret."

"We know." Abrams sounded tired. "We understand that there

was bad blood between the women even before Mrs. Cross's husband was killed."

"But you can't think that Margaret... She loved her husband..."

"I'm not saying anything. It's not my place to charge anyone with a crime. We will be talking with Ms. Linquist, and we have people at her apartment looking into what may have sickened her at this moment." The detective leaned forward, bringing his large dog-like face close to Becca's. "Which is our job. This is serious, Ms. Colwin. People are being hurt, and you are not qualified to investigate who is doing it or why."

"But I'm part of their community." Clara could see that Becca was struggling to explain without seeming like a flake or, worse, a dilettante. At times like this, she wished she could rub against her person's shins, or even jump into her lap and butt her head into Becca's hand, knowing that whenever her person massaged the velvet base of her ears, they both felt so much better. "And I promised them." Her voice had a dying fall that broke Clara's heart. "I promised to help and be fair to everyone."

"I understand." The detective didn't attempt any physical contact, but a certain warmth in his voice made Clara think that maybe he did comprehend some of what her person was saying. "And I'm glad of it. After all," he said, hands on those tree-trunk thighs as he pushed himself out of the plastic chair, "that might be the only reason you're still alive."

Chapter 25

"That's ridiculous!" Becca spoke with a sharpness that set Clara's ears back. It wasn't just her tone. While it was true that Becca was addressing a nurse who had, in fact, been ignoring her repeated requests to be let in to see Gaia. And it was also true that this nurse was now staring at her computer monitor like Becca was no longer standing right in front of her, the uniformed woman who was very clearly avoiding Becca's fierce gaze really hadn't earned this rather loud outburst of temper. Not from Clara's normally very polite person.

Her ordinarily sweet young woman was at the breaking point, the calico realized, bringing her ears back up to a perky point, and she believed she understood why. When the stout police officer had first called Becca's name, she had seemed to welcome the interruption. Tiger's declaration, as flattering as it might be, had disconcerted Becca, Clara could tell, if in a different kind of way. As he had spoken, her cheeks had pinked up, and she had looked down and then away, unable to find the right response.

However, the respite the detective offered had proved short-lived and maybe, her pet realized, not altogether welcome. He had cowed her, especially when he implied that she might be at risk legally because of her attempts to set herself up as a private investigator. The suggestion that she might be in danger had thrown her, too, although after he had walked away, she had muttered something about how he was simply trying to scare her away from the case.

On top of all that, the bike messenger had disappeared by the time the detective had released her. Embarrassed, perhaps, or regretting his hasty words, which Becca had finally had a chance to absorb. Clara didn't know how her person would respond, though she was pretty sure Laurel would want to weigh in, but she could see Becca's increasing frustration as she scanned the room. And now she couldn't get in to see Gaia either. Maybe it was understandable that her person had lost her cool.

Following her outburst, it did appear as if she were trying to be reasonable. "Please, can you at least tell me if she's being admitted?"

From her tone, her pet realized, Becca was close to tears, and her tender feline heart went out to her person as she tried once more to explain why she should be given this really quite basic information. Already, she had told the nurse that she had been visiting with Gaia only minutes before. That it had been her quick action that had resulted in her friend being brought in to the ER. It did no good. Becca wasn't authorized to receive confidential information. And so, no, she couldn't even tell her if Gaia was being admitted or what her status was.

"I gather there's a security issue," the nurse said without looking up from the screen. "And I'm not going to say anymore. Do I have to call security?"

"No." Becca admitted defeat as the other occupants of the waiting area quickly returned to their phones. It really wasn't surprising that her person had lost her temper. And since all she had done was raise her voice, Clara didn't think that any person, no matter how sensitive, could blame her.

"I'm not blaming her."

166

Clara jumped. She had forgotten Laurel.

Shaded into near invisibility, her sister was crouched beside her, under one of the waiting area's molded chairs. *"Really, Clara, sometimes you act like you're the only one who cares."*

Clara rounded on her sister, ready to hiss. It had been a trying day, and having her sibling read her mind was the final invasion of privacy.

"I'm trying to help, silly." Laurel's blue eyes, the only part of her visible, flared as she backed away. *"You could tell she was thinking of Tiger."*

"She shouldn't be." Clara felt her ears go back. *"The last thing she needs now is to be romanced by some stranger."*

"No, silly," Laurel started to explain, but just then Becca turned and walked out into the night, and the two cats leaped to follow. Although Becca was striding swiftly, Clara caught up to her as she exited the hospital grounds. But while she wished with all her heart that her dear person would simply go home, her desires lacked the power of persuasion. Worse, Becca stood on the sidewalk, staring at the passing cars, long enough for Laurel to make her way up behind them. The Siamese might be nearly silent, but Clara was determined not to be taken by surprise again.

"What's the matter?" Clara couldn't resist. Even though she had no problem shimmying through the door that had swung closed in Becca's wake, she had seen her sister struggle. *"Did you find another man for Becca?"*

"Hush, baby sister." Laurel's tail might be invisible, but Clara could see the swirls of dust as it lashed back and forth. *"She's about to—"*

"Who told the police I was down at the car lot?" Becca might have been talking to herself, but her voice was clearly audible to the cats' sensitive ears. And as she looked around the darkened parking area, Clara could feel her sister's eyes on her. "And why did Tiger run off?"

"Enough!" Clara was ready to take on her sister, precedence or not.

167

But before she could even raise a paw, a car pulled up.

"Becca Colwin?" As their person climbed inside, the two feline sisters exchanged a glance and jumped to follow her. Out of habit, as much as anything, Clara even waited for Laurel to go first. If she had to, she knew, she could sidle into the trunk, even as the vehicle pulled away.

She didn't have to. Becca, it seemed, had changed her destination. "I know I said that car lot down by the river, but it's late." She leaned forward to explain to the driver. "I think I'll just go home, if you don't mind."

"It's your ride." With a shrug, the driver took off, and Clara began to relax.

"*This is incredible.*" Laurel, meanwhile, was entranced. Now that she knew where to look, Clara could just make out her sister's outline. Standing with her forelegs on the car door, the sealpoint was staring out at the street, her eyes wide as she watched the world go pass. "*No wonder you like this.*"

"*I don't go out in the world because I like it.*" Clara, whose nerves were a bit frayed, wasn't so easily mollified. "*I do it because I worry about Becca.*"

"*Yes, but...*" Laurel adjusted, as the car took a turn. "*I've got to tell Harriet about this.*"

Clara closed her eyes, regretting all the times she had wished her sisters shared her concerns. Bad enough that she had to deal with Laurel and Harriet's interference at home. If the two of them really did start to follow her out in the world, protecting Becca was going to become exponentially more difficult.

"Maddy?"

Clara woke with a start.

Becca was speaking quietly into her phone. "Are you free tomorrow? I need your help with a kind of experiment. Call me?"

Clara looked around to see Laurel staring back, eyes wide with curiosity.

Nothing the rest of the evening made Becca's plans any more clear. As soon as she was home, she reached for her laptop.

"Nothing new on Frank Cross." She clicked on the keypad. "They're still looking for that driver though."

Within minutes, she'd gone quiet, and when Clara slipped behind her, she could see that Becca was focused on an image she had often spent time with before. Laurel had gone to sleep on her usual shelf by then, exhausted, Clara figured, by the outing. Even though she could feel her own lids growing heavy, Clara remained perched behind her person, determined to figure out what she was up to.

"*I don't understand why that thing is so fascinating to her.*" Harriet landed with a thud on the sofa and began kneading her pillow by Becca's side. "*She can just as easily look at us as at those pictures.*"

Clara started. Yes, it was true. The familiar engraving that Becca often consulted was more detailed than she had first noticed. The odd flatness of the computer screen had obscured its details, as did the technique of the original. To Clara, it looked like it had been scratched out with particularly dexterous claws. But as she stared, she realized that although she had been taken by the likeness of the woman in the picture to Becca, albeit with that strange headdress, and to the calico at the picture's center, there was more to the image. Almost hidden in the crosshatching of the sitter's background—or maybe shaded—two other cats peered out. One large and pale, the other with the distinctive round head of a Siamese.

"The wise woman came to the aid of her community," Becca read quietly to herself. "With the aid of her familiars." Clara looked over at Harriet, but her oldest sister was focused on her pillow, clearly ready for her evening nap, while Laurel's faint snores let her know that their middle sister was also otherwise engaged. Even as she felt her own eyes start to close, Becca shifted again, this time reaching for her phone.

"Not that kind of detective," was all she said. But as Clara looked on, wide awake now, her person seemed to second guess the move, and put the phone away for the night.

Chapter 26

"I can't believe we're doing this." Maddy had met Becca in Central Square early the next morning at her friend's request. Sunny and clear, the weather was perfect for an outing, the sky that deep blue New England only gets in autumn, setting off the gold and russet of the trees around them. None of which had made Maddy happy about accompanying her friend once Becca laid out her plans. "You do realize that this is crazy? Not to mention the fact that the cop already warned you off."

"I shouldn't have told you about that." Becca led the way at a rapid clip that had Maddy, not to mention Clara, struggling to keep up. Clearly, admiring the fall foliage was not the purpose of this outing. "Besides, I'm not doing anything illegal. I'm helping my community. Looking into things."

Maddy's sigh might have been because of the pace, but Clara didn't think so. "I can't believe I'm taking personal time to do this. Speaking of, Reynolds would still take you on as a researcher."

Becca stopped at that and waited for her friend to catch up. "Oh, Maddy, I know you mean well. But can't you see what I'm doing now is what I was made for? I get to do research, but I can use my other skills as well." The slight pause before "skills" didn't go unnoticed. Maddy raised her eyebrows, but she was too good a friend to comment. "Besides," Becca added a little shyly, "this way, I have time to research my own family."

"Oh, Becca." It was the sympathy, rather than the scorn, that made Becca turn and start off again, her cheeks as red as the maples along the sidewalk.

"Maddy, I'm onto something." Becca lowered her voice, even though there was nobody around to overhear on the shady street. "The craft runs in my family, through the matrilineal line. We've long been wise women, serving the community."

Maddy only shook her head.

"You'll see," her friend said. "But that's not why I called you. I have a theory about who told the cops about me, but this time I want to make sure before I do anything."

The two fell silent as they continued walking. Clara, trotting to keep up, could feel the tension between them. What she couldn't figure out was how to ease it. Becca needed friends, the little cat felt strongly. Maddy might not agree with all of Becca's ideas, or even the path she'd chosen to pursue professionally, but she'd been there for her friend in ways that Clara could only envy. Even before Clara and her sisters had come to live with Becca, Maddy had been an integral part of Becca's life. Clara might not be able to define exactly why that made her more trustworthy, but it did. Maddy was more like a sister than a buddy. Or, she silently corrected herself, like one would want a sister to be—not annoying like Laurel and Harriet.

It was a pity Maddy couldn't believe in Becca. That seemed to be the sticking point between them, but, in truth, that made Clara trust her more. Maddy at least had the sense to know what was real. When Clara thought of that Gaia, with all her piercings and black, she knew there was a lot to be said for someone a little less fancy and a little more committed to hard work and honesty, even if she pooh-poohed the idea of magic and hurt Becca's feelings in the process.

Besides, she was here, helping Becca out, a fact Becca didn't seem to fully appreciate. As the two made their way down the street, the silence was growing increasingly awkward. Clara could see Becca stealing peeks at her friend, while Maddy fumed, so intent on staring at the ground in front of her that it was a wonder she didn't walk into a lamppost.

"So, where are we going?" Maddy asked finally. If Becca could hear the effort Maddy was making to keep her voice even, she didn't let on. And Clara was grateful. Not only should these two be on better terms, but the little cat was curious as well.

"Frank Cross's car lot." Becca smiled as Maddy gasped and came to a sudden halt. "Please, I'll explain."

Urging her friend along, Becca did just that, her voice rising with urgency and purpose. "It was what that cop told me," she said as they turned a corner into the industrial area that Clara remembered all too well. "That they knew I'd been down there the day that he was killed. It got me thinking."

Now it was Becca's turn to pause, and she met her friend's eyes. "How did they know I was at the lot? I didn't leave anything, and I never even spoke to Frank Cross, so it wasn't like he could have told anyone or written down that I was there."

"And you think that going back there is going to tell you something?" Maddy sounded incredulous, even as the two started off again, the brick beneath them giving way to concrete.

"I'm not sure." Becca smiled mischievously. "But with your help, I'm going to find out."

***

By the time they got to the lot, Clara was as curious as Maddy. She may have had more faith in Becca, but she still watched her intently, following her every move as she walked slowly around the perimeter. The lot was still a moonscape, though in the morning light she could see that the pitted asphalt was punctuated by a few dying weeds. Plus, the small building at its center had taken on some color. Yellow crime scene tape circled it, crossing that front window and running over the door that Becca had entered on her earlier visit—and which now looked locked tight.

That didn't stop Becca, who crossed the now-empty lot to try that door. Maddy followed, watching as Becca rattled the knob. From the way her head swiveled back and forth, it was clear the larger woman wasn't comfortable.

"Becca, I don't know if we should be here." She eyed the trees they'd left behind, like she would scurry up one if she could.

"We're not doing anything." Becca turned to circle the building. "This is a commercial property, so we're not trespassing. And we're not breaking in."

Maddy opened her mouth to protest, but no sound came out. Instead, she took off after Becca, who had darted over to the river side of the building. Before long, the heavier girl was panting like Harriet after a serious game of toss-the-mouse.

"How far do you think we are from the bike path?" Becca squinted up into the morning sun.

"A hundred yards? I don't know." Maddy shielded her eyes as she looked up and then out to the Charles. "Does the path even run here? I think maybe it's down below the level of the road, over by the river."

Becca considered. "So not from this angle."

"Becca." Maddy turned toward her friend, her round face serious. "What are you getting at?"

"I'm trying to figure out who might have seen me, and working out where I was seen from might help."

Maddy shook her head in confusion.

"The lot was nearly empty that day. Three cars, I think. I remember because I wondered if Frank was going out of business. His wife—widow—had implied that it was more of a vanity project than anything, but at the time I thought maybe she was just lashing out." Becca was scanning the roadway and the river opposite as she spoke. "It was late in the day, around dusk, but it was really dead, and I didn't hear any cars going by. But someone saw me. Someone must have, and then they called the police."

"Maybe it was someone who lives around here." Maddy made a sweeping gesture that took in the rundown triple-deckers behind the concrete monolith at the block's end.

"I doubt it." Becca crossed her arms. "What are the odds someone in one of those apartments would remember seeing someone who had simply dropped by, and even then, only for a few minutes? And I know someone who says he comes down here often for business. By bicycle."

"That guy Tiger." Maddy crossed her arms, too. "Becca, I knew he sounded like trouble. He's—"

"No, that's just it." Becca was still shaking her head, trying to puzzle it out. "I mean, yeah, I think it might have been Tiger. But why? He can't really think that I'd be involved in Frank's murder. Can he?"

"I don't know, Becs." Maddy began looking around again, as if she expected a score of strange men to suddenly appear. "But can we go now? Did you find out what you wanted?"

"Not exactly." She reached out to steady her friend. "Wait here."

"Wait, what?" By the time the question was out of Maddy's mouth, Becca had taken off, jogging across the lot and down the street to where a shaggy brown-leafed copse of trees hid her from view. Maddy looked like she was about to take off after her, but stopped, relief flooding her face as Becca raised her hand, palm out. Thirty seconds later, Becca was back, her cheeks flushed red from the run.

"I was right." She sounded triumphant. "If someone was coming down Putnam, they'd have a perfect view of whoever was standing out here, wondering if she should go in."

"But that could have been anyone." Maddy pointed out the obvious.

"It was someone who identified me to the police," said Becca. "So it was someone who knew me."

"So now what?" Maddy, at least, seemed amused. "Please don't tell me that you're just going to go talk to this guy Tiger again. Even if he didn't do anything wrong, it still sounds creepy."

"No, I'm not." Becca sounded thoughtful as she turned to take in the small concrete building before them. "I've done too much talking already, Maddy. In fact, I've spent all my time on this case talking to the participants in the hope of reaching some kind of agreement."

Before Maddy could respond, she continued. "In all fairness, that's kind of worked. I mean, Gaia hasn't admitted to stealing from the shop, but she did admit to having an affair with Margaret's husband. And she also admitted to trying to frame Margaret by putting the root in her own tea. So I wouldn't have thought there was anything else. Except that—"

She stopped mid-sentence, and then shook her head. "I can't believe I didn't think of that," she said. And before Maddy could respond, she was walking around the small building once more.

"Becca, what are you doing?" Maddy tagged along, following her to the compact structure's rear, but there she stopped, standing back, eyes wide as she scanned the empty lot. "That's...I don't think you should do that."

Clara couldn't have agreed more. Becca didn't seem to take any notice of her friend's hushed protest. Maybe she hadn't heard her, as all her attention seemed to be focused on an awning window, set high on a wall. Small as it was, it seemed to have been overlooked. At any rate, no yellow tape ran across its surface, and even from where Clara stood, it was clear that the bottom wasn't quite flush with the wall.

"I'm looking for clues. You know, like a proper detective." Becca, on tiptoe, picked at the opening with her fingertips, trying to get a grip on the metal frame. "Want to lend me a hand?"

"No, Becca. I don't think so." Maddy frowned. "And I really don't think—"

Her friend didn't even wait for her to finish. Instead, she'd pulled over one of the metal trash cans. Gingerly balancing on top, a sneaker on either side of the rim, Becca was able to grab the bottom of the window frame and pull it toward her, opening it outward.

"You sure?" Rather to Clara's surprise, Becca was smiling. "You're going to miss all the fun."

"Please, Becca." Maddy took a step forward, and Clara wondered if she were about to grab her friend, much like Becca would grab Clara or one of her sisters when they were about to investigate those intriguing bubbles that sometimes appeared in Becca's bath.

She wasn't fast enough. With a scraping sound, Becca slid the screen out of her way, then pulled herself up and, sneakers gaining just enough purchase against the textured concrete wall, climbed in.

"Becca!" Maddy's whisper sounded frantic as Becca's feet disappeared through the opening. Clara didn't know if Maddy's ears were sensitive enough to pick up the thud that followed, but for a moment the calico forgot to shade herself, standing on her hind legs as she attempted to peer through the wall.

"I'm okay!" The top of Becca's face appeared. "I had to kind of dive to not fall into the toilet. But, Maddy, if you're not going to join me, I need you to stand lookout."

Maddy sighed, closing her eyes in resignation, but then she nodded and even forced a smile. That's when it hit Clara how well the heavy-set woman knew her friend, and how much she loved her. Maddy had been arguing with Becca all day about her quest, as well as about her new profession, but when push came to shove, she did what she could to support her.

"I'll be over by the corner," she called back. "That way I can keep my eye on the street."

Maddy was a loyal friend. But she was still human. And as Clara watched her nervously looking around, her head moving so fast that a few strands of her neat dark hair shook loose, she pondered her own next move. She wanted to be with Becca, of course. But she knew well that cats are so much more attuned to the environment, so much more sensitive than even the most attentive human. No, she decided, weighing her desire against these factors, better to stay out here with Maddy. That way, if she heard or smelled someone approaching, she could alert her. How exactly she'd do that, she'd figure out later.

"How odd." Becca was speaking softly to herself. To Clara's sensitive ears, her voice from the other side of the building's concrete wall was as clear as a bell. Pitching her ears back to catch any other utterances, she began to patrol, leaving Maddy to make her own way around the small building.

"Though that doesn't mean..." Becca's voice was suddenly interrupted by a clattering. "Oh, that is strange."

Her person's exclamation, quiet as it was, along with that clanging metallic sound, proved too much for the cat. Smoothing the fur over her brows and pulling her head back into her ruff, Clara shimmied through the concrete and between pieces of rebar to find Becca hunched over an open desk drawer, a puzzled expression on her face.

As quietly as she could, Clara leaped to the desk, where only her natural grace kept her from colliding with the odd, flat objects piled there. Three of the strange sheets were stacked beside Becca, all smelling slightly of motor oil and the dust in the room, while a fourth appeared to have fallen by their side. Clara stepped delicately around them, noting their uneven painted surfaces. There was something cold about them. Something that made Clara want to retreat to the warmth of her person, who stood there, staring down.

Clara eyed the sheets with distrust. These could have made that horrible clatter, Clara thought as she reached out a sheathed paw to touch one cool surface. Metal, she realized, drawing back. Cold and dead. And yet, these weren't what Becca was looking at, not anymore at least, and so the calico stepped carefully to the edge of the desktop so she could gaze down at the drawer below. Even though she had a cat's eye view, improved by her superior vision in the shadowy room, it was hard to see what had captured Becca's attention. The drawer that she had apparently opened was completely empty.

As Clara watched, Becca pushed it back in an inch or two, and then released it. With a rattle, it rolled back out, almost like it was waiting to be filled.

"Now, now, don't get greedy." Becca must have had the same thought, Clara realized, as her person gently closed the drawer once more and turned to examine a miniature kitchenette.

Set next to the bathroom that had permitted Becca to enter, the kitchenette appeared to have been built into a repurposed closet. On the bottom sat a tiny refrigerator, with shelves above climbing up to the ceiling. Becca's search was methodical, starting with that fridge. But if she expected a bottle of poison, or even an interesting herb, she was bound for disappointment. The dorm-sized appliance held only an ice cube tray, empty, and a sad lime, brown at its edges. Becca ran her hand over the top of the fridge, but it came away so dirty she went into the bathroom to rinse it off.

Her examination of the shelves wasn't any more fruitful. The first held a microwave, but that, like the fridge, proved to be empty, if one didn't count a sticky film that even a human might notice. The second was also empty, and even from the desktop, Clara could see the fine layer of dust that had settled there. That left one shelf, above Clara's sight line. While she could have leaped up with a minimum of fuss, she didn't need to. Becca, on tiptoes and holding onto the shelf's lip for balance, had struck gold. With an exclamation of glee—"A-ha!"—she reached back to grab a mug that had been pushed back, apparently the only dishware of any kind left in the sad kitchenette.

"So you did sometimes take a break with—" Becca's head snapped back just as the acrid stench reached Clara. "Whoa!" Becca blinked as she stepped back reflexively, bumping into the desk with a thud and causing the empty drawer to rattle open. Clara didn't have to get that close to catch the reek of burned coffee and something sharper— whiskey?—mixed in. What she didn't smell was any of that bitter root or the sad, sick odor that had clung to Gaia. She looked at her person, wondering if Becca could tell that, too, or if there was some way she could share her insight. But Becca had shaken off the burned and bitter stench and had turned to push the desk drawer back into place. It rolled easily enough with a gentle rumble. But as soon as she released it, it once again slipped open, nudging against her like a hungry kitten.

"Oh, come on." She pushed it in once more. Only this time, the drawer didn't quite close. And as soon as she released it, the drawer rolled open once again.

"Becca?" Maddy's voice, tight with anxiety, reached her from outside. "What's going on?"

"Nothing." Kneeling now, Becca pushed the drawer shut deliberately. But this close even she could see that the metal front wasn't flush with the desk's frame. Something was keeping the drawer from latching.

"If it's nothing, maybe we should get moving." Maddy was keeping her voice low, but the tension had her pitch rising like a young bird's. "I did say I'd be in sometime before noon."

"Just a minute, Mad." Becca tried again, opening the drawer to its full extension before pushing it closed. But no amount of force that the petite young woman could exert would make it click into place. Then, as Clara looked on, Becca opened the drawer once more, pulling it out as far as it would go. Watching, the little calico felt her ears twitching, taking in the distant sounds of the traffic by the river as well as the anxious fussing of Becca's friend. The cat couldn't tell for sure what Maddy was seeing outside, but she could hear her breath quickening, just as she caught the rising fear in the other girl's voice. This was no time for Becca to keep trying what clearly wasn't working.

"If only…" Leaning on the opened drawer, Becca managed to tip the metal desk ever so slightly. As she did, she reached her arm back into the drawer. Alarmed, Clara rose from where she had been sitting. The slight tilt wasn't enough to dislodge her, but seeing Becca strain like that was concerning. And the way her arm disappeared into the desk brought to mind a small creature being devoured, one limb at a time.

"Hello there!" Becca even sounded like she was talking to a beast, although a friendly one, if her growing smile was any indication. "Come to Mama." Becca leaned even further in, the motion of her fingers rattling something inside the desk.

When she pulled her hand out, she was holding another flattened piece of metal. The back of the drawer, Clara thought. It was certainly bent and a little battered, as a broken piece would be, and although one side had been painted blue and white once, the colors were nearly scratched away. But the way Becca was eyeing it, turning it over in her hands, made her pet wonder. Standing on her hindquarters, the plump cat reached up to sniff. If only Becca would hold it a little lower…

"Becca!" Maddy's stage whisper was coming directly from the bathroom window, and Becca turned away from the desk.

"Just a minute, Mads. Reynolds can wait."

"I think someone's coming." The whisper became more of a hiss.

"Bother." Becca looked at the piece in her hand and then, holding it at arm's length, took several photos of it with her phone.

181

"Becca!"

A few more pictures, and then she slipped it back into the drawer, which closed this time with a satisfying click. Clara jumped noiselessly to the floor as it did and eyed the desk. It was metal, but she could shimmy through it if she tried. Only, she could already hear Becca in the bathroom. She was climbing up on the toilet tank to the window, and so the calico joined her, out on the pavement, where Maddy was shuffling anxiously.

"What is it?" She asked as Maddy ushered her off the lot. "Was there really someone?"

"I think so." Maddy dared a glimpse over her shoulder. "I'm not sure, but there was a big black car, like a town car or a limo, and I'm pretty sure I saw it twice. I think it circled back."

"Did you happen to see the plates?" Becca strained to see the road. Clara didn't think she sounded convinced.

"No, sorry." Maddy nearly pushed her friend along. "Please, let's get out of here."

Becca let herself be hurried, and after a long look at her friend's face, she picked up the pace herself. "You're scared," she said.

Maddy rolled her eyes. "Well, yeah." But the ice seemed to have broken. "So, did you find anything?"

"I did, but it's odd." Becca spoke almost as if to herself. "I didn't find anything in the office that I expected. No teapot or tea bags."

"I'm sure the cops took all of that." Maddy might have relaxed, but she wasn't slowing down.

"Yeah, but there's not even a kettle or a hot plate. Just a microwave." She slowed, lost in thought. "And they did leave one mug, but unless I'm very wrong, nothing was ever in that except for coffee and booze."

"Becca, please." Maddy had her arm know and was dragging her further up the street. "The police are investigating. It makes sense that they'd take everything."

182

"Everything? Even the kettle?" She paused. "Though I guess you could make tea in a microwave." The grimace that followed showed what she thought of that idea. "They sure cleaned the files out."

"You looked at the files?" Maybe it was the question, or that the two were simply over a block away by then, but Maddy had turned toward her friend. "What were you looking for, anyway?"

"I'm not sure." Becca stared off in the middle distance, reminding Clara of nothing so much as Laurel when she was trying to focus on a moth. "Insurance records maybe, or vehicle registrations. I mean, have you ever seen any cars down there?"

"Maybe one or two." Maddy shrugged. "It never seemed like the busiest lot, but I don't know the used car business."

"I did find some license plates. Dealer plates, for the most part. You know, the ones you put on a car when someone takes it for a test drive or has to move it? But there was also an old Rhode Island plate. It looked kind of beaten up."

"Great. The guy was a car dealer. Let's just get out of here."

"It was curious." Despite her friend's desire to move on, Becca was worrying the thought like it was live prey. "It seemed to have fallen behind a drawer, only the drawer was empty. I figure the cops must have gone through everything, right?"

Maddy shrugged. "I guess. I mean, I figure the authorities keep track of those."

Becca wouldn't let it go. "Only, Frank was a dealer here, in Cambridge, right? So why'd he have a Rhode Island plate?"

"Maybe that's where he got his stock from?" Maddy had started walking again. "I don't know where you're going with this, Becca. And, to be honest, I'm sure the police are looking into it."

"The police think Margaret poisoned her husband because he was cheating on her," said Becca. "I'm wondering if there was something else going on and Margaret was simply set up to take the fall."

183

"You do realize you're talking like someone out of a TV show, right?" Maddy had sputtered for about a block after Becca's pronouncement. Even now that she could speak, she didn't seem too happy with Becca's line of thought.

"I just think it's all tied together, and whatever happened to Gaia is in the center of it. You're the one who was seeing black cars circling."

"Car, singular." Maddy's head swiveled, but the tree-lined street they now walked along was quiet. "And I don't know if it was circling, exactly. I am pretty sure that it did come by more than once, though."

"Well, it's not here now." Becca took her friend's hand. "And we're out here on the street, where everything is perfectly safe. You sure you didn't see its plates though?"

"Becca!"

"I'm sorry, Maddy. Please, I was teasing. If you want to get to work, I understand."

"I'll feel better when you agree to drop all of this." Her friend squeezed her hand. Becca smiled back but didn't respond. "But until then, I'm coming with you."

Chapter 27

This time, Becca wasn't going to be stopped. All the way to the hospital, she'd been trying stories out on Maddy. The friends had hopped a bus in Central and, swaying from the hanger into Harvard Square, Becca rehearsed options.

"They're not going to let you in as her roommate." Maddy dismissed one after another, bending to look out the window. "And they won't believe you're her girlfriend."

"What if I say I'm Gaia's sister?"

Maddy only rolled her eyes.

"What?" Becca had protested. "I mean, I can say I usually dye my hair black."

"Please, Becca." Maddy had calmed down enough to laugh a little. "That girl sounds like enough of a drama queen on her own. And here's our stop."

The hospital was a few blocks away, and Becca kept peppering Maddy with possibilities as they walked the quiet streets up to Mount Auburn. As it turned out, no theatrics were necessary. When Becca asked for Gail Linquist's room number, she was directed to an elevator and went up to the fourth floor. As soon as they stepped out, the friends were greeted warmly.

"I'm glad she's getting visitors," the nurse on duty, an older, motherly woman told them. "We're keeping her company, but it's not the same."

"Thanks." Becca smiled and walked past the nurse's station toward Gaia's room, which had a window on the hall. Halfway there, Maddy stopped and turned, apparently gauging the distance between the room and the station.

"Becca?" Maddy called. "Does this setup seem odd to you?"

"That she's still in the hospital?" Becca shook her head. "I'm glad she's not in intensive care. You didn't see her, Maddy."

The pale face that looked up from the bed didn't bear much resemblance to the kohl-lined goth girl. With some of her natural color coming back, and none of the paint, she appeared younger and, in truth, prettier. "Becca! Thanks for coming."

"Hi." Becca walked around the bed and pulled up a chair. "This is my friend Maddy."

The two exchanged greetings, with Maddy eyeing the girl like she thought she might grow wings. While Clara jumped soundlessly to the counter, where a now silent monitor propped up a smiley face card, the visitors made small talk. Yes, Gaia was feeling better. Yes, she hoped to be getting out of the hospital soon.

"If they'll let me," Gaia said with a meaningful glance out the window, to where the motherly nurse stood guard.

"I'm glad they're taking care of you," said Becca. "Any security is a good thing if it keeps you safe." Maddy opened her mouth at that, but shut it as Becca leaned in close for privacy.

"I wanted to talk to you about Frank, if that's okay." Becca lowered her voice. "Because I think there's been a misunderstanding."

"I'd say." Maddy's comment, muttered under her breath, might not have reached Becca, but it brought a rash-like blush to Gaia's cheeks.

"Maddy." Becca turned on her friend. "We've got to take this seriously."

Clara wasn't sure, but she thought that Maddy and the girl in the bed exchanged a look. Becca, however, kept on talking.

"I need to know if you were down at his office the day he, well, the day he was killed."

"His office? You mean the lot? No." Gaia shook her head. "I thought I told you. I never went down there after the first time. I didn't like the guys he worked with."

"He had employees down there? Mechanics?"

Gaia snorted. "Those guys? No way. They were suits. Investors, maybe."

"I thought his wife supported him?"

Another laugh, almost like a bark. "Yeah, that was Frank." Her smile turned sad as she shook her head. "He wanted to be independent. I mean, he was never going to leave her, but he wanted so badly to stand on his own. And these guys, you could tell they had money. The way they talked. The big town car. One of them even had a diamond ring. Frank thought they believed in him, in his business. Maybe they did. I didn't like the way they looked at me, though. And Frank? Well, I think he'd have handed me over if they'd asked."

"Romantic." Becca didn't raise an eyebrow at Maddy's caustic comment, but Clara felt her tense at the interruption.

"That sounds awful, right?" Gaia didn't seem fazed. "I mean, that's what was so weird about what happened. I know Margaret was all bent out of shape. But, to be honest, our thing—okay, our affair—wasn't really that big of a deal. I had the feeling Frank had done this before. It wasn't supposed to be anything serious. I'd just broken up with Tiger, and it was pretty clear Frank wasn't going to leave his comfy life. Only that last day, he got all weird, telling me he was leaving town and that he wanted me to come with him. I said no. I mean, I liked my set up. I liked working at the shop and everything. Of course, seeing Frank soured that, too. Once my boss's loony sister found out, I knew I was going to get fired. That's when I, well..."

"The asafetida." Maddy bit her lip, but Clara could see the effort she was exerting to not chime in.

"That was stupid." Gaia must have picked up on Maddy's response too because she addressed this latest comment to the coverlet, which she'd started to pick at. Clara's ears twitched at the change of tone. The motherly nurse apparently noticed as well, and she looked over from her station.

"Are we doing all right?" she called, her voice kind but insistent. "Does anyone need anything?"

"We're fine." Gaia managed a smile. "Thanks."

"Becca..." Maddy's sotto voce carried the hint of a growl, but Becca held out her hand to silence her.

"Gaia?" She left it at that.

With a sigh that should have deflated her, the girl in the bed began to talk. "I've told them about that, and about how I wanted to get Margaret in more trouble."

"And they're thinking you tried again?" Becca spelled it out.

Gaia grimaced. "I guess I shouldn't have told them about the aconite. But I was scared. And I swear, I don't have it."

"That's why the fishbowl room." Becca nodded, taking in their surroundings with a fresh eye. "But also why they let us in. They think this was a suicide attempt—a real one this time. Gaia, this isn't good."

Gaia looked at Becca as she and Maddy exchanged glances. Neither seemed happy.

"Oh man," muttered Maddy.

"What?" A note of fear had crept into Gaia's voice.

"Someone tried to kill you, but the authorities don't believe there's a real threat. They don't think you need security." Becca put it as gently as she could. "You're the girl who cried wolf's bane."

Chapter 28

"I knew it." Becca spit the words out in an angry whisper. "I knew something was going on with Frank. Something besides him being a lousy husband. Money men, indeed. I told you I have sensitivities, Maddy."

Maddy opened her mouth to comment but, at a look from Becca, refrained. They were waiting by the elevator outside the ward. Becca had insisted on visiting the nurse's desk before they left, concocting some story about how she feared that too many visitors might upset Gaia.

"It was the first thing I could think of," she explained to Maddy once they were in the privacy of the elevator. "Because we don't know for sure who else might be involved. There's Margaret, of course. But even though she was angry, I just don't see her as a killer, and I don't believe she poisoned her husband either." Becca looked intent. "Besides, she knew about Frank. She's known for a long time. I remember something Elizabeth said when I met her."

"Elizabeth? That's the sister, right?" Maddy's tone hinted that she was leading up to something as she counted off the floors.

"Yeah, I want to speak with her again." Becca was also watching the counter with growing impatience. As the doors opened, she strode forward. "First thing."

"Speak with her?" Maddy almost squeaked as she followed her into the busy lobby. "No, wait! You need to report her to the police."

Becca stopped in her tracks and turned to her friend, uncomprehending. "What?"

"You're getting all worked up about Frank and some possibly shady characters, but that's all speculation, Becca. This Elizabeth knew what was going on. She was the one who had access to the poison, right? Didn't she 'confiscate' Gaia's plant?" Maddy made air quotes around the word.

"Well, we don't know what happened to it. She says it disappeared." Becca stopped and turned toward Maddy. "You can't think that she… that Elizabeth…"

"Come on, don't you?"

"No." Becca shook off the idea. "She's a wise woman. She's not going to use her knowledge to harm anyone."

"Becca, please. Listen to yourself. You're talking like she's a saint. She's not. She's a witch—okay, a Wiccan and an herbalist. But she's also someone who had access to a powerful poison. And she had motive." As Becca started to protest, Maddy kept talking. "She didn't like Frank. You said so yourself. She knew about his cheating before anyone. And she certainly didn't like that Gaia was collecting a paycheck while she was canoodling with her sister's husband."

"Canoodling?"

"Don't make fun." Maddy was trying to be serious. "As I see it, she probably figured Gaia would be blamed. I mean, she's the one who brought the nasty thing into the store, right? I bet this Elizabeth didn't even know that her sister was going to try to implicate Gaia in some embezzling scam."

"But she would have—"

"Don't say it's because she has the sight or something."

"I was going to say she would have known. Elizabeth knows her sister. And she's super protective of her."

"That's why she was so angry—"

"Wait, just wait." Even though the two had kept their voices down, their heated conversation was beginning to get stares. Suddenly aware of the attention, Becca grabbed Maddy's arm and pulled her into a corner.

"There are too many factors that still don't make sense," she said in an excited whisper. "For example, why did Frank suddenly want to leave his wife? By your account, he was a serial philanderer."

Maddy shrugged. "I don't know. Maybe he really loved Gaia. Or maybe he knew his sister-in-law was onto him."

"No." Becca shook her head, unsatisfied. "He was trying to make up with Margaret. I heard him. He was pleading. I think there's something else going on, something to do with those license plates."

"Becca, the police went through that office. If it was important, they would have taken it."

"One of them was hidden."

"No." Maddy spoke slowly and deliberately. "You told me that you bumped into the desk, and it fell behind a drawer. That doesn't mean it was hidden. It may have been in plain view in an upper drawer. We don't know, and that's the point— "

Becca wasn't having any of it. "Now, I know you don't believe me, but I do have some kind of sensitivity, Maddy. And there was something odd about that plate. It was almost like I was supposed to find it."

"Becca, do you hear yourself?"

"Problem is, I can't tell the police about the plate because of how I found it." Becca didn't even pause. "I don't even think I can make an anonymous phone call, 'cause then they'll think I planted it. No, I need to talk to Elizabeth."

"Talk to her?" Maddy's eyes were wide. "You want to give her a heads-up that we know she had means and motive?"

"I want to consult with her. She's got more insight into her sister than any of us, Maddy. I know enough to know that."

"No, no, no." Maddy had trouble keeping her voice down. "Please, Becca. You're too smart for this. We've got to go to the police and tell them what we know. We'll just tell them we were visiting Gaia. She's the one who told us about the plant and about Elizabeth–"

Maddy stopped short, like she was hearing her own words for the first time. "Wait, do you think that Gaia could be setting Elizabeth up? I mean, along with Margaret? Maybe she did poison herself, only she miscalculated or something, and it was all an attempt to shift blame." She shook her head, closing her eyes. "Now I'm sounding like you."

"No, now you're thinking about the possibilities." Becca took her friend's hands in her own. "And that's another reason I have to talk to Elizabeth. Please, Maddy. I know you don't believe, but trust me on this. Elizabeth has some kind of power."

"I don't know, Becs." Maddy sounded so sad that it was clear she had given up. "All I know for sure is that I don't trust her."

For once, Clara realized that she agreed with them both.

Chapter 29

"At the very least, let me come with you." Maddy wasn't happy with Becca's plan. The two had exited the hospital by that point.

"I can't. You know that." Becca tried to let her friend down gently. "Margaret approached me as a client. She has an expectation of privacy, and I have to respect that."

"But Elizabeth…"

"Is her sister, and she's got sensitivities." Before Maddy could object, Becca explained further. "She's going to know something's up anyway. It's better if it's just me. I mean, this is a delicate matter."

"Murder?"

"Infidelity," Becca corrected her. "But, yeah, maybe this is a case of two sisters looking out for each other. Besides, don't you have to get to work?"

Maddy was silent for a moment as she struggled to come up with a response to that. When she finally spoke, it was with resignation. "Promise me that if you do find out anything, you'll bring it to the police and call me, too. And promise me that you won't drink anything she gives you. Okay?"

"I promise." Becca knew she had won.

Maddy, visibly restraining herself, took her friend's hands in her own and clasped them hard for a moment before turning to walk away.

"Remember, Becca," she called as the bus pulled up, "nothing to drink!"

Becca smiled and waved as her friend's bus pulled away with a sound like a disgruntled pug.

"Nothing to drink?" She whirled around to see Tiger, on his bike. "Are you having a procedure?"

"What? No." Becca, flustered, laughed in a kind of confused, embarrassed way. "I'm—no. Tiger, you startled me."

"Sorry." He tilted his head as he grinned, making him seem more boyish. "It's none of my business anyway. I couldn't help overhearing."

"No, she was talking about…about something else." Becca took in the tall, dark-haired man as he dismounted, and Clara waited to see if she would mention their last interaction. "Oh, you must be here to visit Gaia."

"Yeah." He uncoiled the heavy chain that had been draped over his shoulder. "Are you going in?"

"We just came from there." She watched as he paused, open lock in hand. "Have you had a chance to talk with her yet?"

He bent over, focusing on the lock. "Not yet," he said, his voice strangely muted. "It's been weird."

"Because of Frank?" She spoke quietly, and Clara knew her person only meant well. Still, the cyclist seemed to shudder slightly.

"Yeah," he said after a moment's pause that might have been attributed to problems with the lock. "Maybe."

Becca turned away, giving him privacy. She was embarrassed, Clara knew. Her person had a tender heart and disliked causing pain.

"She wasn't serious about him, you know." When she started speaking again, she might as well have been addressing the no parking sign. "She said it was ending. In fact, I'm wondering if it was a bit of a rebound. You know, after you two…"

The exhalation could have been a laugh or it could have been a sigh. "Right. She wasn't serious."

"No?" She was giving him permission, Clara knew. Room to vent about his ex.

"I think she loved the idea of a sugar daddy. An older man with money to burn. You know they were planning on running off together, right?"

Becca bit her lip as Tiger turned and stood, the lock still in his hand. "Whatever she says now, don't believe it." He frowned at the lock, like it was to blame. "I'm not saying she loved him, but the idea of him? Or maybe it was just rubbing their affair in her boss's face."

"You think she intentionally let Margaret know?"

His dark eyes burned. "Is she playing all innocent now? She hates that woman. I mean, not that she deserved what happened."

"But Margaret didn't…" Becca caught herself. "I mean, we don't know what happened."

Tiger's eyes went wide and for a few seconds, he was silent. "You know she had access to wolf's bane."

"I heard that she recognized it. Or, well, her sister did." Becca looked around, as if she would see where to begin. "Gaia brought a plant in, but Elizabeth—that's Margaret's sister—got rid of it. Or made her get rid of it. That's a little unclear."

"Elizabeth." He said the name like it tasted sour. "Yeah, I know her, and she would say that."

"What?" Becca had to be thinking of her friend. Maddy's face had puckered up the same way at the mention of the widow's older sister.

"You just said it—Gaia brought in a poisonous plant and it disappeared. Right?" Tiger brushed his hair back as his tone changed to something softer. "Gaia never could resist picking up whatever she wanted, whether it was bad for her or not."

195

Becca had no response, and the cat at her feet felt for her. The cyclist's outburst was both too personal and too specific to ignore. The tension broke, though, as Tiger suddenly burst into a laugh, his teeth flashing in a wide grin.

"Listen to me!" He smiled at Becca. "I'm sounding like the wronged spouse, and I'm the one who thought we should split up. Maybe I'm dreaming up this whole conspiracy, and it'll turn out that she ate a bad chicken wing or something."

He sighed as he shook his head and then looked again at the lock in his hand. "But maybe this isn't the best time for me to visit Gaia," he said. "Anyway, I'm here, and it's a gorgeous day. Would you want to take a walk by the river?"

Clara waited for her person to say no. Becca had an investigation to pursue, after all.

"I was going to head into Central Square, if you'd like to join me." Clara whirled to look up at her person. "I don't know if that's what you were thinking of."

"I think a walk would do me good." He slung the chain over his shoulder. "Let me guess, you're going to interrogate Margaret?"

"Actually, I want to talk to Elizabeth," Becca confided. "Not about the wolf's bane, or not only, but she said some things the other day that I want to follow up on."

"Ah, now I understand why your friend was so worried." Tiger reached for his bike, holding its handlebars in one hand. "But never fear," he said, the smile audible in his voice. "You've got a tiger by your side."

"Don't you have to work?" Becca couldn't resist grinning back. Tiger's smile was contagious now that his dark mood had lifted. "I mean, I'm happy for the company and all."

"You mean these?" He motioned to his bike's panniers. "Nothing in there but my tools. I don't have any deliveries or pickups scheduled for today. Besides, I was planning on taking a break."

As if on cue, the device clipped to his belt flashed. With barely a glance, he thumbed a switch and it went black. "See?"

"If you're sure." Becca was smiling in a way that Clara didn't fully understand. "But what if you get other calls?"

"Not to worry. I only work for one client, and they know whatever it is, I'll get to it." He leaned in. "I'm kind of on call twenty-four seven."

"Maybe Gaia wouldn't be a great choice, then." The words slipped out, and Becca bit her lip, embarrassed. "I'm sorry. That was rude," she said.

His face was blank. "Gaia?"

"She told me that she might be coming to work with you, but with her habits…" Becca shook her head, flustered. "Anyway, I guess that's no longer an option."

"Yeah, I don't think so." Tiger looked down at his hands, like they could give him an out. "Not that she wouldn't be welcome, of course."

"Of course?" Becca was examining his face. For what, Clara couldn't tell.

Tiger's smile was back, as broad as ever. "Hey, the more the merrier, right?"

With that, they started out, Tiger walking his bike and Becca strolling beside him. Once the uncomfortable topic of Gaia was behind them, the two humans chatted casually. Becca, who seemed determined to avoid any mention of Tiger's earlier declaration, focused on her work and had explained about her coven by the time they passed through Harvard Square.

Becca showed no interest in catching a bus, not with Tiger asking for reading suggestions. And so the two kept walking, while Clara, unseen beside them, dodged the busy foot traffic as she did her best to tune into their voices. Laurel, she knew, would be better at reading the signals between these two. Yes, they were interested in each other.

Yes, the young man was being respectful. Any male human who asked Becca about herself was an improvement over Becca's cheating ex, she figured. It was only her own memory of Becca's previous heartbreak that made her nervous, Clara told herself. That made her wonder that his interest was so sudden and seemed so intense.

Whatever its impetus, the mood was broken when the two humans arrived at the colorful storefront to find the lights out and the closed sign posted in the window.

"I guess they couldn't get anyone to cover for Gaia." Becca peeked in, between a ram and a lopsided bull. Although she couldn't see any movement, the back storeroom appeared to be lit. "I could go to Margaret's apartment, but I was hoping to catch Elizabeth."

"You want to try around the back?" Tiger followed her gaze. "I'll stay here in case anyone shows up."

"Thanks." She flashed him a grin and took off toward the alley, her unseen cat at her heels.

"Elizabeth?" A minute later, she was knocking on the back door. "Are you in there? It's Becca." She waited, then pressed her ear against the gray metal. Being a cat, Clara didn't need such proximity to know that nothing stirred inside. "I'd like to talk to you, if you have a moment."

She stepped back and brushed her hair off her face. But nobody came to the door, and after another round of knocking, Becca retreated back to the street.

"I guess I'm going to have to try the apartment," she said, as much to herself as to Tiger. "I wonder if Elizabeth is avoiding me?"

"If she has something to hide, she might be afraid of you." The thought didn't seem to please her companion, and he frowned as he fussed over his bike. "I don't know if you should confront her, Becca."

"I'm not going to *confront* her." Becca stressed the word. "I want to talk to her. I want to find out what was going on with Frank. Elizabeth seemed to have some insight into her brother-in-law, so maybe she

198

knows why he was planning on running away."

"Isn't it obvious?" Tiger looked up in disbelief.

"You mean, to be with Gaia? I don't think so." Becca's stare fixed on a point somewhere beyond her companion. "I think something else was going on."

"Like maybe his wife was sick of him fooling around?" That earned him a scowl, and he put his hands up in surrender. "Sorry," he said. "Just pointing out the facts. But aren't the cops looking into all the angles?"

"I don't know," Becca confessed. "I mean, they warned me away from trying to help Gaia, but she's told me things. And I really don't want to get Elizabeth in trouble if she was just trying to protect Gaia from herself."

Tiger's brows went up at that. "Protect her from herself?"

"Yeah, didn't I tell you? It was Elizabeth who told Gaia that her plant was poisonous. Gaia didn't even realize what she had."

"That's what she told you?" Becca couldn't read Tiger's expression, and neither could Clara. Once again, she wished she had Laurel's power. "Well, I wouldn't be surprised if she's gotten rid of it now."

"What do you mean?" Becca put her hand on Tiger's handlebars to stop him as he turned away. "Gotten rid of it *now*?"

"Elizabeth's not telling you the truth—or not the whole truth," he said, his voice disconcertingly matter-of-fact. "She took the plant, whatever she says. I saw it in the back room of the shop the last time I went to visit Gaia. I guess Gaia didn't recognize it, or maybe it was after she was fired." He paused, his eyes going wide. "Maybe that's why Gaia was fired."

"You've got to tell the cops that, Tiger. This is serious."

He shook off the idea. "My ex gets fired and suddenly I'm accusing the owner of attempted murder? Besides, I was never supposed to be back there. Gaia used to sneak me in sometimes late at night—she had a way in through the window and showed me how. Anyway, it doesn't matter. That old crow probably got rid of it. But, hey, you could ask the cops to check it out."

To her credit, Becca took a moment, chewing on her lip as she considered the option. "No," she said at last. "They've already warned me off. Besides, I don't have any proof."

"But you're really resourceful." Clara could feel Becca flush slightly at the compliment. But Tiger wasn't done. "Maybe you could find a way to look for it. I don't think you'd be able to miss it. It's pretty distinctive, with those poisonous blue flowers and all."

"Maybe." Becca didn't look thrilled at the idea. "But now, I'd better go beard the lion—or the lioness—in her den. And I should do this alone."

Clara expected him to protest, but he only nodded. "Good luck. Let me know how it goes. On top of everything else, now I'm curious. If Elizabeth did dump that plant, when did she get rid of it? And if not, why do you think she's been keeping it? And where? You should be careful, Becca."

"I will be," said Becca, her mouth set in a determined line. "And thanks."

Chapter 30

Becca watched him pedal off before she headed down to Margaret's apartment. Clara might not have Laurel's skill, but she thought that her person looked a little wistful as well as curious. Wistful, the calico understood. This Tiger might be a tad odd, but he was trying to help, in his way, and he'd spent a good chunk of his afternoon with Becca. The curiosity was more than the cat could figure out. Her person was both sweet and warm, and to Clara it was no wonder why a man would want to get close to her. Surely, despite her searching gaze, staring back at the way Tiger had ridden, Becca must understand that much.

For now, Becca's thoughts were her own, and so Clara trotted along, tail up, when she rang the apartment bell and, soon after, made her way up those stairs.

"Becca!" Margaret's dark eyes widened with surprise. Clad in a velour track suit, she appeared even smaller than she had the last time Becca had seen her.

"I'm sorry to disturb you." She truly was, Clara could tell from her posture as well as her voice. "I know these last few days must have been difficult."

"Thank you." The widow collapsed against the doorframe, suddenly

201

appearing both older and smaller than usual. "It's bad enough that Frank is gone, but all the fuss." She bent her head, exposing the white roots of her part, and Clara could feel her person's resolve crumble.

"I am so, so sorry."

The widow accepted the condolences, the white line bobbing briefly.

"Are you—I'm sorry, you must be caught up in funeral plans?"

"No." One syllable shared with the doorframe. "Not yet." Margaret cleared her throat, her voice growing stronger. "We'll have a service, some kind of memorial, at some point. They—the police still have him. They're doing tests..." Her voice trailed off again as one hand waved her sentence to completion.

"That's part of what I was hoping to talk to you about," Becca ventured, the effort audible in her voice. "Or Elizabeth, really."

"Elizabeth?" Margaret's head popped up and those big eyes blinked. "Why?"

"I gather she might have some insight into what happened." When Margaret didn't respond, Becca kept talking. "With Gaia."

"You can't still think that I... That Frank..." A second wave of fatigue seemed to wash over her, deflating her once again as she stepped back, opening the door to her visitor. "Whatever," she said, her voice flat. "You might as well come in."

"Thanks." Clara slipped in alongside Becca and followed her through to the sunlit living room. The space appeared much as it had the other day, although Becca made a more careful examination of the plants on the sill. "Let me get my tea," Margaret said, her voice flat, as she walked through to the kitchen. "You want some?"

"Ah, no, thanks," Becca called back. "I really just had a few questions."

"What do you want to know?" Margaret returned holding a mug that smelled strongly of peppermint. She sipped, watching Becca over the mug, her eyes dry.

"Well," Becca took a moment to recalibrate. "I was wondering if you would tell me a bit about Frank's business."

"His business?" The tea seemed to have revived the widow. At any rate, Clara thought, if she was nonplussed by the question, she didn't show it. "He had that car lot down by the river. That was the extent of it."

Becca took this in. "Used cars? Did he buy them or bring them in from other locations?"

A frown rippled the little lipstick left on her lips. "I don't really know. Took them on consignment, I think. It was just a little thing, more a hobby than any kind of big going concern. I know he saw himself as some wheeler and dealer, but I doubt he had more than three cars for sale at any given time."

Becca paused, apparently storing the words away, as Margaret drank her tea. Before she could phrase another question, the widow continued, her voice taking on a tone of resignation. "That's not where he got his money from. You probably know that already, right?"

Clara could feel Becca holding her breath as she waited.

"I spoiled him." A sigh as she placed her mug on the table. "I know I did. The watches, the rings. The car lot itself." She peered up at her guest. "You've probably never been in love, have you?"

"Well..." A half smile from Becca.

"I thought we had a good relationship. No," she raised her hand, not that Becca had made any move to interrupt, "I know what you're thinking. But we had our ways. It had...he had never done anything like this before. I thought, well, it's just another phase."

"Maybe it was." Becca spoke softly. "Maybe he didn't mean to end it this way."

"You don't think... Is that why you were asking for my sister?" Her brow bunched together as she reached once more for her tea.

203

"Elizabeth didn't like him, but she wouldn't do anything to...to harm him."

"I believe you." Becca tried to keep her voice calm and even. "But I don't know if the police will, and I think she has information that could help us all."

The widow inclined her head over her mug. "You may as well talk with her, then. She's checking in on the shop."

"She is?" Becca leaned in.

A curt nod. "She got a call, probably a prank. That girl..."

Clara looked at her person. Becca appeared to weigh several responses, but wisely decided to hold her tongue. Or maybe she simply hadn't settled on one quickly enough as the sound of the front door opening had her craning around in her seat.

"Elizabeth." Margaret looked up at her older sister. While Becca had turned to face the newcomer, Clara could see the curious expression on the widow's face—eyebrows raised and mouth pursed. "Becca here was just looking for you. She has some questions."

"Of course she does." The taller sister breezed in, looking quite calm and collected, Clara mused. What Becca thought wasn't clear, but her pet could see that she had been taken aback by the older woman's response, if not by her sudden appearance. "I need to wash up, Becca. Would you join me?"

Becca rose and followed the other woman down the hall to a bathroom, where Elizabeth proceeded to roll up the sleeves of her corduroy workshirt. "So, where shall we start?"

"Your sister said you were at the shop?" Becca watched as Elizabeth lathered up her hands. "Is there anything going on?"

Elizabeth grinned in the mirror. "Very good," she said. "You're learning to gather information for yourself before you give it. But everything is fine."

Becca raised her chin. "Well, then, I've just got a few questions."

"Of course." Elizabeth focused on her hands. "I'm going to have some more cleaning to do. Gaia was a bit of a slob. Surely, that doesn't surprise you."

"No," Becca had to admit. "But I'm curious as to why you went down there."

"Why?" Their eyes met in the mirror. "Well, Margaret's not up for anything right now. And I don't think she should close."

"She was thinking of closing?" That appeared to hit Becca hard.

Elizabeth shrugged. "She's had a loss. And she no longer has a sales clerk. Plus, she's going to have legal bills."

That was Becca's opening. "Is she going to be charged in her husband's death?"

Again, their eyes met, but if Elizabeth was surprised by Becca's awareness of the latest development, she didn't show it. "What do you think?" she asked.

"I guess the police would say she had motive." Becca eyed the older woman curiously. "But as for means... Margaret already told me they're doing an autopsy. I'm assuming that they'll find that Frank Cross was poisoned with aconite—wolf's bane."

Elizabeth shook her head, staring straight into the mirror. "I don't know what they'll find."

"We know Gaia had a potted wolf's bane plant." Becca's voice was calm. "We know that you recognized it. You told her what it was. And then it went missing."

"Wait, you think that I took it and lied about it?" The white-haired woman turned toward her, hands dripping. "Or that Margaret...? No."

"I'm simply stating facts." Becca tensed, but if she thought of retreating, Clara couldn't see any sign of it.

"You're re-stating what other people have told you." Elizabeth took on a school-marmish tone. "Letting yourself be manipulated. Gaia, for example, is as careless with logic as she is with dangerous plants."

Becca didn't respond. Clara hoped it was because she wanted to draw the older woman out, rather than that she was stymied by this turn of events.

"Yes, I recognized wolf's bane." Elizabeth reached for a towel, shaking her head as if she could shed stupidity like water. "That girl pretends to study the craft, but all she saw were pretty blue flowers. Goddess keep her. I read her the riot act. Bad enough she had it. She was keeping it in the shop window. If anything had happened, we'd be liable."

"Something did happen." Becca studied the other woman's face. "Gaia was brought to the emergency room last night. She may have been poisoned."

Elizabeth started back, and then relaxed. "You know, she might not be the most reliable person to talk about being poisoned."

"I know she tried to fake something earlier," Becca confided. "This was real, though. I was with her in the emergency room."

"That doesn't mean..." For a moment, Elizabeth looked her age. "Poor girl. Poor, stupid girl. I assumed she took the cursed thing home."

Becca was shaking her head. "She says she doesn't have it. She thinks you took it."

Elizabeth's eyes narrowed, appraising Becca anew. "And you believe her."

"I believe that she doesn't have it anymore." Becca searched for an explanation. "And I don't even know if she knows how Frank died. Honestly, I don't know if she cares that much. From what she's said, the affair was basically over. She's just feeling sorry for herself because you fired her."

"And so she's looking to pin the blame on me." Elizabeth turned toward the bathroom mirror, her face unreadable.

"She's scared," Becca said.

"Sounds like she should be." Elizabeth was still holding the towel,

206

and now she looked down at it, as if it held the answer. "Sounds like maybe Gaia has begun to grow up."

Chapter 31

"You're going to tell that detective all this, right?" Maddy's relief was audible when Becca reached her at work. "'Cause you're done, right?"

"I don't know, Maddy. I'm not sure I see the point. I mean, I told him everything I know when he ambushed me at the hospital."

"Ambush?" Maddy's surprise must have gotten her a few looks, because her next comment was muted. "Becca, what are you talking about? You're involved in a suspicious death, and another person has been poisoned."

"Yeah, I know, only the police might not see it that way." Becca was walking slowly down the block as she spoke with her friend, her mind on the conversation she'd just had. "If they still think Gaia made herself sick, they might not be looking at all the implications."

"What implications? That woman Elizabeth said she was cleaning the place out, and I bet that means that stupid plant is gone. But don't they have tests? Can't they find traces of things like poisons?" Maddy watched a lot of TV.

"I don't know, Maddy." Becca stopped to look up at the late afternoon sky. "They might just dismiss that, or say that's where Gaia was hiding it. I mean, it was Tiger who told me Elizabeth took it. And honestly? I don't know how reliable he is on this. He's told me he's over Gaia, but I think there's still something there. He's more upset about all of this than he's letting on this, and I'm not entirely sure what to believe."

***

By the time they hung up, Becca had promised her friend that she would at least seriously think about calling Detective Abrams to fill him in on what Tiger had said. "Really seriously, Maddy," she vowed. "Even though it's all hearsay."

But by then, she'd lost her newfound equanimity. As Clara trotted alongside her, she could see that her person's focus had turned inward, bringing with it a frown and the kind of bunched brows that the little calico associated with ruffled fur.

When Becca slowed on the walk up to the library, Clara knew her worst fears were being realized. As much as she didn't want her person looking too closely into her family's long history with magical felines, she really didn't want her getting more involved with this case. Although Clara was loath to take any human's side against Becca's, for once, she had to admit that Maddy was right. A person had died, and this was no longer a case for an amateur. Becca needed to leave it to the police.

Once again, Clara wished she had Laurel's gift. Not for anything as trivial as her choice of clothing, but to make her see the sense in Maddy's words—and to make her as careful of her own life as she was of her pets'. Even if she could simply eavesdrop like her sister did on her person's thoughts, she'd be grateful. What was her dear person thinking about? Clara looked up anxiously, trying to read Becca's face, and almost collided with her as Becca's steps slowed.

Only then did Clara look around her with an almost imperceptible feline sigh of relief. Becca had come to a halt not ten feet from a familiar modern structure, its glass walls revealing the kind of benign busy-ness that Clara would wish her person engaged in full time. Even unable to read the words spelled out over the foyer in oversized letters, she recognized this as one of Becca's regular haunts: the Cambridge public library.

Eager for her person to enter, Clara gazed inside to where a young boy was checking out two books as his father looked on and an employee pushed a cart loaded with oversized hardcovers. All of this would usually be as irresistible as catnip to Becca, and Clara waited for her person to pull open the great glass doors.

When she didn't, Clara looked back with growing concern. Becca had her phone out, something she never did inside the building. Which, the cat told herself, must be why she had turned away.

"Tiger? It's Becca." Clara felt her whiskers sag. "I was wondering if you could tell me more about the plant you saw. Would you call me?" And with that, she hung up, but if Clara had any remaining hope that her person had put the matter to rest and would proceed inside the library, that soon dissipated. As she watched, Becca began to chew her lower lip and stare off into the distance. Since there was nothing out there beyond a rather drab brown oak, Clara began to fear the worst. When Becca turned her phone off and began to walk back toward the street, picking up her pace as she left the library behind, she knew what to expect.

"*Becca, no!*" Clara trotted to keep up. When it became clear that Becca was heading once more into Central Square, the calico began to panic. There was a reason Becca had been adopted by the three cats. She needed the gifts of all three, and just then, Clara felt the burden of being the only cat to accompany her person sorely.

"*Please…*" She did her best to project her thought, her ears twitching back with the effort. "*Laurel, if you can hear me, can you help us out?*"

Surely, her sister could pick up on her thoughts. She had already revealed her ability to travel shaded, much as Clara herself did. Ears up and every guard hair alert, Clara waited, hoping to get some sense that her slinky middle sister had heard her call and would respond. All she heard was the twittering of birds, though, and so she scurried to follow as Becca began walking even more quickly away from the library and the safety of the known.

Chapter 32

As the familiar storefront came into view, Clara let herself hope. While she didn't like the idea of Becca asking more questions—certainly didn't like the way that that woman Elizabeth seemed to know more than she should—at least she could understand such an action. Her person was thorough, a researcher at heart. Maybe Becca wanted something clarified. Maybe she had forgotten some important information. Maybe she had left her hat. But a quick glance to the velvet cloche that still topped Becca's brown curls killed that hope.

Still, as Becca approached the storefront, Clara dared to believe. The store's darkened interior showed no sign of life, and Becca knocked and waited—normal behavior, her cat told herself. Not rash at all. Only Becca wasn't giving up. After trying to peer inside, her face pressed against the painted glass, she tried again, rapping on the window, to no avail. And so when Becca ducked around the back of the building, hurrying down the alley like some small and timid animal, the little cat began to feel ill.

"*No, Becca!*" She tried once again to project her thoughts. To implant the idea of the library, so safe and warm. Or, even better, of the cozy sofa at home. Maybe she had too much imagination, however, and she could see all too well where this was all heading. Because Becca, despite Clara's fervent desire to warn her, appeared to be doing just what her pet feared most. She was going to try to duplicate her stunt of the previous day—only, this time, without a friend to stand guard. Not a friend who could call out to warn her, at any rate.

If she needed to, she would alert Becca somehow, Clara promised herself. Sure enough, as Clara watched, tail whipping in anxiety, Becca stared up at a high inset window with the intensity Laurel would use to gauge the jump to the top of the bookshelf. But Becca was no cat, and when her bottom didn't twitch in anticipation, Clara began to breathe easier. Until, that is, she saw that Becca's gaze had been distracted and she remembered. What Becca lacked in feline grace, she more than made up for in logic. Sure enough, a quick exploration of the back lot uncovered that plastic milk crate over by the dumpster, and it occurred to Clara that someone might have left it for just such an illicit entrance. Someone like Gaia, who wanted an easy way in and out. And although Becca was a good three inches shorter than the goth shop girl, when she stood on the milk crate and raised herself on tiptoe, she was able to reach the window.

"Now if only..." Clara's ears perked up as Becca spoke, more to herself than to any possible passerby, her pet realized. "Yes!" Her agile fingers, so much more flexible than any talon, had managed to raise the edge of the window and from there it slid easily. With a grunt and a bit of a squeal, Becca pulled herself up, her sneakers finding purchase on the brick. And a moment later, she was inside.

"I'm getting rather good at this." Becca's musing would have been inaudible to most, but Clara heard her self-congratulations with dread. As much as she wanted her person to learn new skills, breaking into locked buildings was not a good thing. Surely, Becca knew that. Her reluctance to alert her friend and onetime lookout was proof of that. In Maddy's absence, Clara hunkered down, determined to keep watch and to be ready to alert her person in case of trouble.

This late in the afternoon, the street was quiet, and Clara was grateful for the shadow of the building, which cloaked her spotted coat further even than her abilities allowed. Invisibility wasn't everything, however. Despite her abilities, the calico was a housecat by nature, only venturing outside to accompany her person. Not being able to see Becca or, even worse, smell her warm scent, was unnerving, making the little beast feel even more vulnerable. As much as she trusted Becca, she couldn't help but wonder if this entire venture was misguided and if, perhaps, the person she loved was in way over her head.

A muted crash made Clara jump. Here, in the rear of the building, she was protected from the street. Even if a car were to pull into the lot, she could duck behind the dumpster. Besides, that sound was from inside the building, she realized as she willed her fur back into its proper confirmation. That sound, more of a thud, had probably been occasioned by Becca knocking into something inside the darkened store. No cries of alarm or pain had followed, and none of that horrid squealing of bicycle tires that she could only too well remember.

"*Becca?*" Clara tried once more to reach her person. The only response was a thump and a soft grunt. The cat could stand it no longer and, bracing herself against what she might find, she shimmied through the brick wall toward her person.

The room Clara found herself in wasn't that dark. Granted, the afternoon sun was clouded by the glazing on the bathroom window as well as a rime of dirt. And while Becca had opted against turning on the electrical light, she had opened the door to the storefront, where the early twilight illumined the colored paint on the window, if not much else. Still, there was no reason for a creature to bump and flail, as Becca seemed to be doing. An upended side table explained the earlier crash, and even now her person shuffled slowly, hands out in some weak improvisation of whiskers.

Whiskers! Of course! Clara had forgotten how dull human senses were, and so as she sat back and watched her person fuddle, she tried to come up with a way to help her. Clara couldn't exactly turn on the lights for her. Cats simply didn't do that, and she was sure there was a good reason why. Nor could she guide her, as dogs seemed to do for their humans at times.

"*If only Laurel were here.*" She never thought she'd miss her sister. Only now it would be so useful to have her here. She could suggest that Becca close the door to the storefront. If she did that, she could turn on the overhead light. Surely, the slight glow that would leak out the bathroom window would not cause any alarm.

"*If only...*"

Her thought was interrupted by another crash and muted cursing as Becca reached down to caress her shin. But even as she did, hopping a bit as she rubbed the sore spot, she reached out her other hand for balance and soon found herself leaning on the open doorframe. As if a light had gone on in her mind, she stood, closed the door, and, running her hand along the doorframe, found the light switch. The light that flooded the room was almost too bright for Clara, who squinted as she ducked back into the shadow of the shelving. To Becca, though, it must have seemed wondrous. Clara looked up to see her person beaming back up at the fixture, like it had come to her aid by itself.

Newly empowered, Becca began a search in earnest. Working her way around the store room, she looked inside boxes and behind shelves. She opened canisters to check out their contents, and even though she sniffed some of the more pungent ones—Clara could smell ginseng and ginger, before the stench of asafetida filled the room—she was careful enough not to taste any.

When she moved on to the small kitchen area, Clara crept closer. Becca was concentrating too hard to notice the slight shadow she still cast, and the little cat wanted to observe her person at work. Becca

215

was methodical, moving slowly through the items on top of the tiny fridge one by one and replacing them with care. Opening the fridge, she made a point of sniffing at various jars and bottles, even when the rancid nature of some long-forgotten takeout nearly knocked her head back. For Clara, this was enlightening. She'd only seen Becca research in books or on her computer. Here she could witness for herself the disciplined and thorough nature of her work.

It wasn't quick, though, and Clara was aware of the passage of time as her person made her way around the room. Although it wasn't spacious, taking up maybe half as much footage as the tiny shop out front, the room was packed. And the lounge area that had been carved out of one corner, with that overstuffed couch and the coffee table, the tiny kitchenette and the bathroom, were the only areas not lined with shelving and boxes and paper. Clara didn't know much about inventory, but she had a sneaking suspicion that Margaret was as disorganized a record keeper as she was an employer. *Missing funds indeed*, the little cat thought with a disdainful sniff.

As she watched, Clara grew increasingly aware of the daylight fading outside—and increasingly alarmed that Becca was not. Becca still had not closed the bathroom door, and while the indoor light would not be that noticeable during the afternoon, as twilight descended, the illuminated window would certainly call attention to itself. Even if Margaret or Elizabeth came by to turn off a forgotten light, Becca could get in trouble, she realized with growing concern. If only her person would notice and shut that door. If only she had Laurel's power of implanting a suggestion in a human's brain. If only her sealpoint sister was here with her now.

Clara did her best, concentrating on the window, the light, trying to visualize the portal from Becca's viewpoint, only showing it as brighter and more obvious. When she failed at transmitting that image to her human, she pictured it instead as it might seem from outside, glowing

216

in the growing dark like a beacon. A clear indicator, if anyone was looking, that someone was inside.

It was no use. Becca was oblivious. And as her cat, all Clara could do was wait, which she did, with an impatience more akin to a hungry Harriet than her usual forgiving self. By then, Becca was working her way down the shelving behind the lounge area, and Clara could only hope she would soon turn and notice the bathroom light. Indeed, when Becca stopped and stared for a moment at the open door, her feline heart leaped. Either her thoughts were finally getting through to her person, or Becca had realized her error.

"The windowsill!" Becca exclaimed out loud, confusing her cat. "Of course!"

Following her person back to the small bathroom, Clara soon had her hopes dashed. Instead of flicking off the light, Becca simply stopped in the doorway and studied the long, high window. Open on one side, where Becca had made her way in, the window had a deep sill that ran along the top of the wall. Sure enough, down at the other end, three potted plants enjoyed the fading glow of the back room's only natural light. Two were succulents, the closest, an aloe, showing signs of a recent trimming. The third, however, had glossy green leaves and a dying blossom, a sad bruised purple, still hanging from its stem. As Clara watched, Becca climbed up on the toilet seat and, reaching, broke off one of those leaves as well as the limp flower. Wrapping them in toilet tissue, she slipped them in her pocket and washed her hands. Smart moves, Clara knew, but steps that kept her pet from giving the plant material the thorough sniffing she would have liked.

The running water also covered a sound that immediately put Clara's fur on edge. A sound that Becca's less sensitive ears were likely to miss. The scrape of metal on metal, followed by the slide of a bolt.

Someone was unlocking the shop's front door.

Clara whirled around as the door creaked ever so faintly, her tail

217

fluffing as her multicolored fur spiked in alarm. She and Becca would make a run for it. They would fight. They would…but Becca did not react. Whoever was out there was being careful, opening the door carefully so as to not cause the bells to jingle. Was it possible that Becca really hadn't heard anything? How could she not be aware, as the cat at her side was, of the slow footsteps making their way into the front room?

To Clara's horror, Becca appeared lost in thought—or in contemplation of the paper towel she was using to dry her hands—and no amount of concentration on her cat's part was getting her attention. To make matters worse, Becca had pulled her phone from her pocket and had begun fussing with it.

"*This is no time to check your messages!*" Clara's urgent warning went unheeded. As the footsteps approached, the calico considered her meager options. Should she run to the front room? Perhaps if she dropped her shading, she could startle the intruder into making some sound. Or better yet, trip the person and also slow her—his?—approach.

If only Laurel were here…

"*Move over!*" The hiss startled Clara so badly, she nearly fell. But as she scrambled back, she was able to see a chocolate-tipped shadow leap to the sink. Blue eyes blazed down at her for a split second, then turned upward to focus on the pale and distracted face of their human.

"*Becca! Listen! Someone's coming!*" Laurel's thoughts were so loud, even Clara could hear them. "*You've got to get out of here. Now!*"

It wasn't a tone Clara would ever take with Becca. Even as a silent suggestion, her sister's distinctive Siamese yowl was sharp enough to pin Clara's ears back. But whether it was that psychic caterwaul or Becca had finally come to her own senses, it broke through their person's preoccupied daze. Suddenly alert, Becca started, staring wide-eyed at the open bathroom door.

"She's going to close it." Clara began to panic. *"She's going to try and hide!"*

"No!" Laurel's silent cry stretched out into three syllables, and Clara could have sworn she heard the rasp of claws. *"Na-oh-wow!"*

Becca turned at last back toward the window. From the toilet to the sill, she clambered, almost as graceful as a cat herself. And then through the window and out.

"Thank you!" Clara turned to her sister once Becca was safely through.

"No more sense than a kitten!" Those blue eyes flashed, and then Laurel, too, was gone.

Chapter 33

Clara didn't even stop to smooth her fur before she leaped too, emerging in the lot behind the store in time to see Becca dashing for the dumpster. After a quick grooming—necessary for her nerves as well as comfort and appearance—Clara joined her, slipping behind the metal container to where her person was crouching.

"*Laurel?*" Clara cast about for any sense that her sister was still around. "*Are you here?*"

A faint shimmer in the air made her turn. But when neither Laurel's blue eyes nor her distinctive yowl emerged from the darkness around them, she settled back. Her sister had come to the rescue of their person, Clara told herself. She had heard her call and done what Clara could not. For that, the plump calico knew, she should be grateful.

If only she could get Becca to move on. Although her sensitive feline ears could pick up movement from inside the building, all appeared still out here. And yet Becca remained in what had to be an uncomfortable position for a human, squatting behind the dumpster like she was stalking prey.

"*Of course!*" Clara turned toward Becca with a new appreciation. Now that her person was out of danger, she would want to gather information and find out what was going on.

She didn't have long to wait. With a squeak like a frightened rodent, the back door swung open. Although Clara's eyes were trained on the entrance, she could hear the intake of breath as Becca saw the door swing open. Maybe it was the shadow that reached across the lot as the back room's light spilled out. Maybe it was the way the figure paused, scanning the empty space and seeming to settle, if briefly, on the dumpster, where Becca had frozen motionless following that one quick gasp.

Or maybe it was who had stepped into the darkness, holding the back door open behind her. Elizabeth Sherman, a scowl on her hawk-like face, stared into the darkness as if she could see the young woman and the cat hidden there. Then, without a word, she stepped back inside and closed the door. A moment later, the light went out, and all was still.

"Elizabeth." Becca said the name out loud, like she was trying out the taste in her mouth. "She can't know…" Her voice dropped off as her awareness of her surroundings grew, but Clara could fill in what her person left unsaid. Becca had been careful during her brief exploration of the store's back room. It was unlikely that the older woman would be able to tell if anyone had been there—a light could have so easily been left on by accident. There was certainly no way for Margaret's sister to know that Becca had been the trespasser. And yet, the way she had stared at the dumpster had been unnerving, reminding Clara of how the woman had apparently seen her the day they had first met, despite the magical shading that cloaked her from others' eyes.

After a few more minutes went by, Becca rose cautiously and, hanging close to the wall, made her way to the street. She walked slowly, and at first Clara wondered if the prolonged hiding had left her stiff. But a glimpse of her person's face revealed Becca's preoccupation. Clara couldn't be sure if Becca had been able to see how the older woman had stared, with almost cat-like focus, at their hiding place. But Becca was certainly mulling over the ramifications of that plant—proof, it seemed, of a dangerous lie.

A metallic shriek had them both spinning around, and Clara's back arched in fear.

"Tiger!" Despite her excitement, Becca kept her outcry to a whisper, for which Clara was grateful. Still, the little cat eyed the black bicycle, which had come to an abrupt halt by the curb, warily. "You were right!"

"You checked out the shop?" He sounded impressed. "They let you in?"

"I snuck in, to be honest." Becca sounded half ashamed and half proud of her feat.

"Wow, good for you!" Smiling, he lowered his voice to a conspiratorial hush. "You're getting good at this."

"Thanks." Becca didn't bother to hide her answering grin. "When you told me that Gaia used to sneak in, I realized it was possible to get in through the back window." She stood up straight, head back. "She's a little taller than me, but not by much. And you were right. I found the wolf's bane in the bathroom. Up on the ledge, where it could get some light."

"You think the cops will believe you?"

"They have to." Becca was beaming. "I've got proof. I broke off a branch for evidence."

"This is so great." He laughed, showing those white teeth. "You're brilliant, Becca!"

"Thanks." Becca looked down, blushing, though whether because of the young man's praise or the way he was looking at her, Clara couldn't tell.

"I couldn't have done it better myself." He reached for her hand. To Clara's surprise, Becca stepped away.

"I don't know…" Even in the dim light, Clara could see that her person had gone pale. "Maybe this wasn't such a good idea."

"What?" Tiger appeared confused by Becca's sudden change in mood.

"I'm wondering if it was foolish of me to take a sample. I mean, if I show up with some of the poisonous plant, that could make police suspect me, don't you think?"

He laughed. "You? Becca, come on. They'd know better."

"I don't know." She bit her lip. "I think maybe I've got to think about this a bit. Maybe go see Gaia again."

"Gaia?"

"Yeah." Becca's brow wrinkled in thought. "I want to find out more about when Elizabeth warned her about the wolf's bane and when it disappeared. I mean, maybe there's been a mistake. I'm getting the feeling that I'm missing something."

"But if you wait, then Elizabeth might get rid of it."

"Doesn't matter. I also took some photos of the shelf in the bathroom, but the light wasn't great." She held her phone over for Tiger to see as she clicked on the app. "See?"

He took the device. "Is this inside the store?"

She nodded as he thumbed through, growing more concerned as his face grew serious. "They're not great shots, are they?"

"I don't know." He sounded doubtful.

"Of course! They can still say it was a plant, so to speak." Becca leaned over. "Wait, that was from earlier. Here, this is the best one. Between this and the sprig, that's got to be enough for them to at least look into Elizabeth, right? Even if they also suspect me?"

"You know, maybe the police have a point. Maybe you should just let it go." Tiger sounded shaken. "The cops are already investigating Margaret, and Gaia's had a hard enough time. Besides, this could still implicate you."

"That's sweet of you." Becca didn't sound convinced. "But this is

223

what I do, Tiger. Or, well, what I want to do. I'm a researcher, and that means I'm an investigator, and Gaia is my client, so I owe it to her to find out what I can and bring her the results. Besides, I kind of have a friend in the department."

"Well, just leave me out of it, okay?" He chuckled, but there was a brittle edge to his laugh. "Gaia already thinks I'm kind of a nut. Next thing you know, she'll think I'm trying to get back together with her or something, and I, well, you know how I feel, Becca."

"Thanks, Tiger. I do." Becca smiled at Tiger as he righted his bike and rode off down the street. But even as she began to walk the other way, back to the square, it was clear to her cat that her mind was already a million miles away.

Chapter 34

"If only I could ask you three for advice." Becca appeared lost in thought. "Maybe you could help me decide what I should do."

Worried about any additional detours, Clara had stuck close to Becca's side as she walked home. Still, she managed to slip in moments before Becca unlocked the door to find Harriet and Laurel sitting there waiting.

"*What took you so long?*" Laurel's sharp Siamese yawp sounded like a question and an accusation all at once. "*Can't you manage her any better?*"

"*Now, now, Laurel.*" Once Becca had fed them, Harriet immediately became more conciliatory. "*We each have our tasks.*"

"*What tasks?*" Clara looked up at her oldest sister, but Harriet's round golden eyes merely blinked once before returning to her dish.

"If only you were really my familiars." Becca was leaning back on the counter. Although Clara's ears flipped back to catch the sigh that followed those words, it was clear that Becca was simply airing her thoughts. "My great-great-grandmother referred to her cat as her familiar, but maybe that was just a figure of speech. Or, I don't know, a convention of the time. She couldn't have actually conversed with her

225

cat, could she?"

Clara's ears flicked, but a heavy paw came down on hers. Harriet. *"No."*

Clara pulled back. *"But you were the one who started her on this whole magic thing. If you hadn't summoned…"* She stopped. There was no way to remind Harriet that it was her laziness that had prompted their person to believe she was a witch without insulting her. Besides, Becca had already shown an interest in magic by then.

"It's in the family," Harriet mumbled, her mouth full. *"It was going to happen anyway."*

"And you're the one who is supposed to look out for her." Laurel shot a glance Clara's way as she sat back and began to wash her face. *"Not lecture your elder sisters!"*

"I'm sorry." Clara dipped her head and stepped back from her food dish. Laurel eyed the leftovers, but wisely let Harriet dive in. *"But I don't understand."*

"Don't be such a kitten." Laurel sat back to wash her face, scrubbing at her tawny fur with one brown mitt.

"I just feel like you could help me sort this out." Becca was speaking to herself. Clara knew that. And yet she couldn't help reaching out to her person, which she did, batting at her leg with one gentle paw.

"What is it, Clara?" Becca roused to lift her pet, cradling her in her arms. "Did Harriet steal your food again?"

"Did not!" A faint grunt of protest as the marmalade cat looked up, her yellow eyes narrowing.

"I didn't say you did," Clara mewed softly. *"I only wanted to let Becca know that we're here."*

"So much for being discreet." Laurel's implication was clear.

"That's not fair." Clara squirmed in Becca's grasp, desperate to make her sisters understand.

"Whoa, okay!" Becca released her and she jumped to the floor, but even as she did, she turned toward her person with a plaintive mew.

"You three." Becca shook her head. "You're worse than the coven sometimes."

The three littermates froze. This was too close to home.

"Speaking of, I wonder if I should consult the coven?" Becca wandered back into the living room.

"*We have to be more careful!*" Clara did her best to keep the hiss out of her tone. It wouldn't help to antagonize her sisters more. "*You know the law!*"

"*I'm not the one who was squealing like a…like a…*" Harriet's short nose bunched up in thought.

"*Like a little mouse,*" Laurel purred. "*Clara, you're such a clown sometimes.*"

"*Clara the clown!*" Harriet echoed, her voice taking on a singsong quality.

It was all Clara could do to keep from snarling in her own defense. Instead, tail down in a dispirited droop, she followed her person into the living room and jumped up on the sofa beside her.

"Hi, Ande?" As Clara leaned in, Becca absently stroked her spotted back. "Do you have a few minutes?"

Clara couldn't hear the response as Becca shifted, reaching for her laptop. And as much as she would have liked to spread herself across the warm keyboard, she contented herself with leaning against Becca's hip as her person quickly typed out some notes.

"Thanks. I've been working on this case, and I've sort of hit an impasse." As Clara watched, Becca summoned up a familiar picture. The plant they had just seen, only set in what looked like a lush summer garden. "What can you tell me about aconite—wolf's bane?"

A slight squawk, as if from a startled sparrow, had Becca shifting. "No, I'm not. I'm trying to stay clear of what happened to Frank Cross. I promise." Clara looked up at her person. Becca rarely lied, but this

227

was stretching the truth. "Though I do wonder…"

More squawking, and Becca put the phone on the table.

"Hang on," she said. "Okay, I've put you on speaker so I can look it up. Yup, this looks right."

"What? Becca, what's going on?" The voice of the other coven member was tinny but recognizable. "You have an aconite plant there? With your cats?"

"No." Becca shook her head, although the other witch couldn't see her. "I mean, I have a cutting, but it's all wrapped up. I wanted to make sure it was from Gaia's plant."

"Wait, Gaia, who was having an affair with Frank? Asafetida Gaia? She has aconite, the real thing? Do the police know? Because aconite poisoning can look like a heart attack."

"I gathered that already." Becca's voice dropped. "I also think it might be what made her so sick. I don't know if you heard—she's in the hospital."

"She's—" Ande caught herself. "Becca, this sounds bad. You don't think it was some murder-suicide pact, do you?"

"I don't think so." Becca bit her lip, deep in thought. "Though someone told me that Gaia knew Frank had a heart condition. A 'bad ticker.' Only Gaia's plant was stolen. That's the one that I have a clipping from."

"Wait, I'm missing something." Ande's confusion came through loud and clear. "Back up. You have a cutting, but you got it from a plant that was stolen?"

"Yeah, it's a longish story, Ande. Gaia said Elizabeth Sherman, you know, Margaret Cross's sister, took the plant from her after telling her how dangerous it was. But Elizabeth said she didn't, even though I found it at Charm and Cherish, in the back room, and—"

"Hold on." Clara could almost see the taller witch holding up a long, slim hand to stop Becca from going further. "You went into the back room? I thought the store was closed."

"It is." Becca lowered her eyes even as she worked to keep the embarrassment from her voice. "But, Ande, I had a tip. And, well, this is what I do now. I investigate."

"You got a *tip*?" Clara's ears pricked up. The other witch sounded suitably disturbed. "Becca, why aren't you taking this to the police? This is serious."

The calico breathed a sigh of relief at this good common sense, but Becca was shaking her head. "I can't, exactly," she told her friend. "I mean, Tiger pointed out that it could make it look like I'm involved. You know?"

"Tiger?" Ande might not have been able to see the slight flush that crept over her cheeks, but she must have heard something in her tone. "I don't think I've heard about any Tiger."

"Oh, Tiger? He's, uh, he's Gaia's ex. He's been helping. Well, kind of…" There was no hiding the stammer now.

"Becca." Ande cut her off. "I don't need any special powers to know that something else is going on here."

"It's not…it's not what it seems." Becca rallied to complete the sentence. "They're broken up, but he still cares about her. She told me that herself."

"Uh-huh." Ande's voice dripped with skepticism. "And he's telling you all of this and not her, why?"

"Because." Becca was firm. "He doesn't want to talk with her. He feels he needs to keep his distance and not, you know, give her false hope."

"Well, then, that makes things easy for you." Clara looked up as Becca drew a breath. "I didn't mean like that, Becca. Though, if they really aren't together, well, why not? But what I meant was kind of the opposite. I may be wrong, but it sounds like this guy is getting your head in a muddle."

Clara looked at her person, but Becca didn't respond and Ande kept talking.

"Okay, I don't like any of this, but you want my advice, right? I say you should go to the cops. But if you're not ready to do that, and you want to know more about this plant and the sisters Gaia used to work for, then why don't you ask Gaia? She doesn't have to know her ex-boyfriend was involved. Does she?"

Chapter 35

"*I don't like it. But I never liked any of this.*" Laurel was grooming as Becca hurried to get dressed the next morning. Much to the sealpoint's dismay, Tiger hadn't called, and Becca had spent the evening online. Her one call in the morning had been to the hospital to ask about visiting hours. "*I blame that girl, with her fake hair and all those piercings. That girl is a liar.*"

"*If someone wasn't such a stickler for the rules…*" Harriet fixed Clara with her yellow eyes. For once, Clara felt she couldn't meet her gaze.

"*I know,*" the multicolored cat acknowledged, dipping her head. She had already let her fluffy oldest sister finish her breakfast, the uncertainty of the day having chipped away at the plump calico's own appetite. "*But we have to be extra careful,*" she murmured to her sisters in her own defense. "*Becca suspects something, I know it.*"

"*Well, of course. Because you let yourself be seen by that Elizabeth woman.*" Laurel wasn't letting this drop. But Clara didn't hear her. She was already shimmying through the door to follow Becca as her person hurried down to the street.

That didn't mean the calico wasn't mulling over what her sisters had said as her person set out at a brisk pace, her hat jammed down over her brown curls. Laurel's claim that Clara herself was responsible for the cats almost being revealed struck particularly close to home, she thought as she trotted down the sidewalk, careful to stay shaded in the early morning sun. Clara still couldn't forget how the store owner's older sister had looked at her—had *addressed* her—although Clara had thought she was being so careful, and she replayed the scene again and again as Becca made her way swiftly through the morning commuters. Clara had to dart to keep up, but the questions kept resurfacing, distracting the little cat as she ran. Had she let something slip in her concern for Becca? Was Becca beginning to suspect that her three cats were more than ordinary house pets? If their person kept up with her research, she was sure to uncover more about the long interaction between the women of her line and the cats who loved them.

That history, Clara knew, was why the rules had been initiated. Centuries may be long to humans, but to cats, who pass along memories from generation to generation, they were only a swish of the tail. And Clara knew as well as her sisters that when humans had last found out that their cats had the powers to protect and serve them, well, that had ended badly for both the pets and their people. Those bad old days were why the cats had the rules that now governed Clara's family.

But was it time for them to change? As Clara followed Becca back to the hospital, she thought about the coven that her person had joined so openly. Witchcraft was no longer forbidden, and while it seemed in some ways like magic had become devalued, it also appeared that any actual danger in practicing the old ways was past. Clara had always been so careful in how she observed the law, even taking on her sisters. Only now that she thought about it, about Elizabeth seeing her and how much easier it would make things for Becca if she could do the same, she couldn't help but wonder.

Would it really be that awful if Becca knew what her feline family could do for her and how much the three of them really loved her?

That is, assuming they did.

"I'm pretty sure Laurel and Harriet love Becca. They have to…" Clara barely voiced the thought. After all, Laurel had come to Becca's aid. Or was that only because Clara had called her? And surely Harriet had grown fond of the curly-haired young woman who had proved so reliable with the treats. *"Just because they complain…"*

The little cat was brought up short as Becca stopped suddenly before her. It took her a moment to realize they had already arrived at the main entrance to the hospital, and the law-abiding Becca was taking a moment to power down her cell.

Gaia was expected to be released today, she had gathered from Becca's earlier inquiry. That explained why she had rushed right down after feeding the cats and before even taking any coffee for herself. But Clara could see no sign of the slight, black-haired girl anywhere on the sidewalk or inside the big glass doors once Becca had stepped through them. In fact, she could only make out three people in the lobby, an elderly couple and an orderly, his eyes on the elevator as it pinged its way down.

"Hey there!" The voice made Becca turn. Gaia, looking pale but happy, was walking toward her, a white hospital bag under one arm. "Did your sensitivities let you know I was being released?"

"Not exactly." Clara could hear the happiness in her person's voice. "Admissions did. But I'm glad. Actually, I was hoping we could talk, really talk. I've got a ton of questions."

The other woman nodded. Without her usual makeup, she looked younger. Better, too, thought Clara. "Sure, I owe you, I think. Besides," she held up her phone, which, contrary to the posted regulations, glowed with life. "My ride's going to be a few. I'm not quite up to walking yet."

"I'm sorry." Becca backtracked. "I didn't even ask. How are you feeling?"

"A little weak. I'm glad you…well, you may have saved my life."

"I wish I could credit my powers, but I really just kept calling you because I wanted to get you to come down to the police with me."

"Stupid me, huh?" The pierced brow rose as she smiled. "But now I've told that fat cop everything I know."

"You told him about the wolf's bane?" Becca asked. The other woman dipped her head in a quick, embarrassed acknowledgment. "Did you tell him that you thought Elizabeth stole it?"

Gaia's expression turned equivocal. "I told him that it disappeared, but I don't know…"

"That's just it." Becca leaned in. "I do. I saw it. Tiger told me where to look."

"Tiger? How did he know?"

"I'm sorry, I shouldn't have brought him up. Though, to be honest, I have some questions about him, too."

"I know, you want him to talk to the cops, and I'll work on him." She sighed. "I think he's hoping that, after all this, we'll get back together."

Whatever Becca had been about to say appeared stuck in her throat. "Gaia?" After a moment's pause, she tried again. "How well do you know Tiger?"

A snort of laughter. "What's to know? He's a nice guy. Hey, he brought me a change of clothes." She hefted the white plastic bag. "I did not want to wear these home again. Not after being so sick."

Becca wasn't going to be distracted. "You don't think he's a bit too involved in what's going on? I mean, with Frank and all?"

"Tiger?" She didn't bother to hide her humor. "No way. He's sweet, but he's a straight shooter. I mean, his motives are clear."

"Poor Becca." As much as Clara wanted to, she couldn't rub against her person. She didn't really understand what Becca was getting at, but she did know she didn't want her person to be hurt again. *"And Laurel didn't see this coming."*

234

"I'm glad for you." Becca managed to sound normal. She even wrangled a smile as the other woman turned toward her. "I mean, if that's what you want."

"Yeah, I think so." A girlish shrug and another smile. "We'll see, right? Hey, you want a ride? We can talk to him together."

"Now?" Becca squeaked like a cornered mouse. "No, no, thanks."

"Okay." Gaia was too distracted to notice. "Well, thanks for coming by. I appreciate the visits, and, you know, everything you've done. Maybe that crazy Elizabeth is right." She flashed a wide grin. "Maybe you really do have some magic powers after all."

"Miss, are you feeling ill?"

The orderly hovered. Becca had stepped back as Gaia had headed out the door. She'd only closed her eyes for a moment, but the hospital staff was alert.

"I'm fine." Becca stood up straight. "It's just…personal stuff. Men." She was trying for brave, Clara knew, and loved her all the more for it.

"Tell me about it." The woman in scrubs turned toward the glass double doors. Gaia could be seen on the sidewalk, craning her head eagerly toward the street. "They go for the fragile type, don't they? She has that poor Tiger wrapped around her finger."

Becca's smile wobbled, only to give out entirely as she made her own slow way toward the exit. Clara couldn't blame her. As grateful as she was that her person found out about Tiger's duplicity before anything had happened between them, she still understood her disappointment. It might not be exactly the same as waiting at a promising mouse hole all night, only to realize it was really a crack in a baseboard, but it was similar. One got one's hopes up, and it hurt to reconcile with reality.

Clara kept her eyes on Becca as she ambled through the hospital lobby. Of course, Becca was dispirited, but she was moving so slowly her cat began to worry. Was she remembering her questions, the ones she hadn't asked? Or, no…as Clara caught her looking out through the lobby's glass doors, she understood. Becca was waiting for Gaia to be picked up, hoping to avoid an awkward meeting with the faithless Tiger.

"*She could have him if she wanted.*" An unexpected voice in her ear caused Clara to jump. Although she couldn't see Laurel, she would recognize her sister's distinctive yowl anywhere. "*He was seriously interested in her. I could tell.*"

"*She doesn't want him if he really wants to get back with Gaia.*" Clara turned toward the where a glint of blue betrayed her sister's presence. "*Even if he doesn't, he's nasty to lead Gaia on.*"

"*She was sad.*" A faint disturbance in the air signaled the flick of a tail. "*He wanted to make her feel better.*"

Clara wisely held her tongue. Besides, Becca had stepped closer to the windows that looked out on the entrance. If her person was braving the visual confirmation of her crush reuniting with Gaia, she was going to stand there with her, whether she could comfort her or not. She could feel the shuddering breath Becca drew as she watched Gaia raise an arm in greeting. A tan beater—a Toyota, easily twenty years old—pulled up, its fender held in place with a bungee cord. But it wasn't the re-appearance of the battered old car that made Becca gasp.

The young man who had jumped out of the driver's seat wasn't the tall, pale bike messenger Becca had come to know. This man wore a leather jacket with his jeans, and the blond tips of his black hair stood out as he reached for Gaia's bag.

Chapter 36

"Gaia, wait!" Becca broke into a run, plowing through the knot of people waiting for the revolving door. "Gaia!"

But even the haste that won her several hard stares and one loud complaint wasn't enough. By the time she was through, the car had driven off, with Gaia settled in the passenger seat. Becca pulled her phone from her pocket and stared at its blank screen in disbelief.

"Guard!" Becca whirled around and then raced back inside, looking for a uniform. An official. Anyone.

"That girl your friend?" A graying man stroked what looked like a day's growth of beard.

"Yes, and she just—that driver...she thinks it's her ride share, but he may be dangerous." She punched a code into her phone. "Come on!"

"She got in the car willingly?" the man asked, his voice thoughtful.

"Yeah, but..." Glancing up from her device, Becca looked once more out the window and then, turning back, she took in the slight, elderly man on crutches beside her. Purple bruising ran from the edge of his tonsure of graying hair down to his whiskery chin, but the dark eyes that peered into hers were clear, their gaze piercing.

"I'm sorry," she said with a sigh of resignation. "That was rude of me to push through like that. Pointless, too."

He shrugged and a smile brightened his features. "You were scared. I'm used to it. Nobody sees us old folks. 'Specially not girls like that. I wouldn't worry too much about that one, though. Like I said, she got into that car with her eyes wide open."

"I really am sorry." Beck paused to take in the man before her. It wasn't just the beard that gave him a slightly scruffy appearance. His khakis, which dragged as if sized for a taller man, were stained, and that cheery smile revealed several missing teeth. "Do you need some assistance?" Her voice, as she asked, became soft, like she was afraid of offending.

"Me? Nah." He waved her off with hands chapped rough. "I'm doing better than anyone expected. Charmed, I am. One vet helps another." He chuckled at some private joke.

"Mr. Harris?" a worried male voice called across the lobby. "There you are. Come on, Bill, we've been waiting." A tall orderly in lime green scrubs was loping toward them.

"My valet," the ragged man said with a wink to Becca.

"Bill Harris." The orderly took the older man's upper arm. "You're due in PT. You weren't trying to walk out again, were you?"

"Just keeping an eye on the young lady here." That smile again. "Sentry duty."

"More like an old sailor's tricks." The orderly looked over at Becca, his wide face creased with concern. "He wasn't bothering you, was he, miss?"

"No, not at all." She shook off the suggestion as comprehension dawned. "Wait—Bill Harris, are you the man who was hurt in the hit-and-run? They said a veteran…"

"At your service, miss." A dip of the tonsured head. "Only it may be a while before I'm cleared for duty again. Gotta watch out for those waves."

"Mr. Harris?" The orderly tugged gently, turning the man. "Don't you remember we talked about this? You're not in the Navy anymore."

"We're still at war, son." The bruised face gone serious. "And this young lady, she's on the front lines. You remember what I told you, missy," he said as he was led away. "Eyes wide open!"

***

"What was that about?" Becca mused as the two slowly ambled off. "Maybe he thought I was USO? I mean, I've heard of the WAVEs but…" Although she wasn't addressing Clara, the calico took her question seriously. Becca was mostly concerned with Gaia and with the identity of the man who had driven her off, the little cat knew. But the stranger who had accosted her person was of more interest to the little cat.

"I wish I understood." Clara looked up to see Becca chewing on her lower lip, a sure sign that she was deep in thought. When she once again consulted her phone, Clara breathed a sigh of relief. Surely, her person was going to call for aid or a consult. As much as her cats were not fans of Becca's coven, there was a place for other humans in their person's life. But when Becca simply stood there, staring at the device, she realized something else was going on.

"Is it possible?" Becca's voice was too quiet for any but her cat to hear. But lacking Laurel's particular skill, the shadowed feline could do nothing but wait.

The hospital lobby, however, was not a safe place for a small creature. Although Becca was standing by the door, Clara soon realized that she needed to take cover. The same craft that enabled her to virtually disappear could all too easily cause even the most careful pet lover to trip over the little feline. So after the third near collision, Clara scooted over to a bench that ran along the window. She might not be able to hear everything that Becca said from here, but she could keep an eye on her and keep herself safe.

"Watch it!"

Clara whirled at the unmistakable hiss. *"Laurel?"*

A slow blink made the almond-shaped blue eyes disappear and then appear again in the shadow by the bench's legs. *"I was wondering when you'd have the sense to get out of the way."*

"What are you doing here?" This was the second time Laurel had surprised her, and as much as she welcomed her sister's assistance, Clara had to admit the sealpoint's sudden appearance had unnerved her.

"What aren't *you doing is more like it."* Laurel's distinctive voice wound her own question up into a caterwaul, and Clara looked around in concern. *"Oh, don't be such a clown, Clara! You think these people can even hear themselves think?"*

That stopped her, and she looked toward where her sister's shadow could be seen as a vaguely lighter area against the bench. *"Laurel, can you hear what Becca's thinking? The way she was staring at her phone has me a little concerned."*

The eyes went wide in mock surprise. *"But I thought you didn't want me listening in on Becca. Now this is interesting..."*

"Please, Laurel." Clara was at a loss to explain. *"Something is going on, and I'm worried."*

"Why don't you just go back out there?" Her sister blinked, her shade retreating into the darkness. *"And listen for yourself?"*

Sure enough, Clara saw, Becca was no longer staring at her phone. Instead, she held it up to her ear. But even feline senses were no match for the cacophony of the lobby, and so Clara made her way back to her person, darting around a family of four and a large man on crutches to stand as close to Becca's feet as she could without touching.

"Detective Abrams, please." She kept walking, the phone up to her ear. "It's Becca Colwin returning his call. Calls, I guess. He's...what? He's looking for me? I'm—no, you don't have to pick me up. I'm going to Charm and Cherish. I should be there in about fifteen minutes. If he can meet me there, I expect to have something to show him."

Chapter 37

Clara looked around for her sister, but Laurel's blue eyes didn't peer back from under the bench. When the calico's sensitive nose failed to catch any hint of another feline in the crowded foyer, she realized her sister had slipped away without her.

For one awful moment, Clara thought Becca had, too. Then she saw her person on the sidewalk and with a leap made it through the glass of the front window to land on the sidewalk beside her. But even had Clara not been shaded, Becca might not have noticed the sudden appearance of her pet beside her. As she walked through the small crowd of a taxi line, Clara's person seemed to be focusing on another world. Almost, the cat thought, as if she could see the unseen.

Could it be? As recently as a week before, the little cat would have thought this to be impossible. As much as Becca wanted to have magical powers, such abilities were solely the province of cats, or so the little calico had always believed. And although Becca's research had brought her perilously close to the truth about her ancestors— those brave women who assisted their felines in the application of the craft—her approach was all wrong. As much as she loved the three littermates she'd adopted, Becca still viewed them merely as pets, rather than guides and teachers, a mistake that Clara had blithely assumed doomed any attempts at magic to failure.

In the last few days, however, Clara had found some of her core beliefs about her beloved person, and about her own powers, to be challenged. She simply didn't know.

To be on the safe side, Clara kept herself cloaked as she tagged along after her person. Although they had cleared the crowd immediately outside the hospital, the little cat was concerned. Becca seemed to be lost in thought, oblivious to the city around her. Trotting alongside her person, Clara saw that she was frowning, her sweet face intent on something beyond the little cat's perception. But since Clara could not smell any predators in the immediate vicinity, all she could do was fret over what was occupying her person so.

Hearing, however, was different. Clara was a city cat, and from her earliest days in the shelter she had become accustomed to the sounds of people and their machines. As a reasonable creature, she had an aversion to cars, and thus she was grateful when Becca turned down a residential street. She had a sense of where her person was heading—the store where she had asked that big detective to meet her was not that far away, especially if she took the bus from Harvard Square. Still, she stuck close by Becca's feet.

As they turned down another corner, Clara realized that Becca was retracing her path of the other day, when she and the bike messenger had walked to the nearby square. This route was not only quieter, it was, Clara suspected, what her person would term a "shortcut," a very human concept, but one that she accepted as her person's choice.

As one tree-lined block followed another, Clara began to relax. The roar of the city's traffic never totally disappeared, but as she trotted alongside Becca, she could hear other sounds that recalled different times. A bird sang somewhere unseen, and two squirrels squabbled over the first of the season's acorns. In such a setting, the click of a bicycle gear merited no more than the flick of an ear. The squeak of a brake, though, that caused the cat to turn, as a sudden whiff of a familiar scent made her fur begin to rise.

"Becca!" The voice, friendly if a bit breathless, startled Clara's person, who whirled around with a gasp.

"Sorry." He smiled as he jumped off his bike and walked it up to her. He reached to embrace her and Becca almost tripped as she scrambled out of reach. "I didn't mean to startle you."

"Tiger! Goddess bless." Those were strong words for Becca, and for a moment Clara worried that her person had fallen harder than her pet knew. Only, there was a note in Becca's voice that Clara couldn't place. What was her person thinking? "It's Gaia. I think she's in trouble," she started to explain, her face clouded with worry.

"Gaia?" He stepped back, considering.

"Yeah, I came by to talk to her. Only she left with someone, and, well, I'm heading over to meet with the police now." Becca could have been talking to herself, she seemed so preoccupied. "But I think you were right. I think maybe Elizabeth was behind the poisoning."

"I knew it." Tiger nodded, a grim half smile spreading across his face. "I bet they'll tie the poison in with Frank's death, too."

"That's right." Becca looked up at him. "You said Frank was poisoned from the start. Back before any of us had heard anything."

She paused ever so briefly, lost in thought, and began to walk once more, heading, Clara knew, into the square. "Before Gaia had heard anything, come to think of it. Although, didn't you say Gaia knew he had a bad heart?"

"Yeah, she did." His face was unreadable as he walked beside her, rolling his bike by his side. "I remember her telling me. She must've forgot."

"Funny thing for her to forget." Becca could have been addressing the bricks of the sidewalk. "Come to think of it, you knew about Gaia being poisoned before anyone else, too."

"Well, yeah. I was with her." Those blue eyes went wide with innocence as he strode beside her.

"No, you weren't." Becca shook off his assertion as she kept walking. If her pace picked up a little, it was barely perceptible to any but the small cat who trotted by her side. "I was on the phone with her when she started getting sick. She was alone. I'm the one who called 9-1-1."

As she talked, Becca turned a corner, and Clara saw the traffic of Harvard Square ahead. His bicycle at his side, Tiger lengthened his stride to move slightly ahead, a tilt of that handsome head as he tried once again to catch her eye. "And am I ever glad you did, but she called me first, and then I came by." The assertion came out with force, like he was claiming the sick girl. "Truth is, I thought she was just being dramatic. Trying to get my attention."

Becca shook her head again slowly and sighed, Clara thought, with a trace of sadness. "She wouldn't do that. She broke up with you. She's told me you're the one who's been trying to get back together."

"Well, yeah." That grin as he sped up, moving slightly ahead of Becca. Trying to get in front of her. To catch her eye. "The girl has some pride, after all. Good old Gaia. Crazy girl."

"Not like her buddy Gail Linquist, huh?" Becca's voice was flat. She was waiting as she walked, Clara realized, though for what, the loyal calico couldn't tell.

"No way." He was laughing, a broad chuckle that matched the slight rattle of his bike, as he shifted his grip on the black metal frame. "I never understood that friendship."

"You don't know her, do you?"

"Excuse me?" A burst of laughter followed, but when Becca finally turned to face him, she didn't join in.

"Gaia—Gail—they're the same person, and you don't know her. You're not her ex-boyfriend." She said it simply, her voice a trifle sad.

245

The noise of the traffic would have drowned out her words if they hadn't stood so close to each other. "Your name isn't Tiger."

"I'm not?" One look. A laugh, and he gave it up. "Yeah, well..." With a tilt of his head, the tall, lean man smiled down at her. "You made that assumption, didn't you? I just went with it. Come on, Becca. It was no big deal."

"No big deal?" Her voice had taken on a steeliness that Clara didn't recognize. "Why did you pursue me?"

Neither, apparently, did the cyclist beside her. "Why?" He chortled as if she had told a joke. "Why does a guy like me usually pursue a girl like you?"

"Why?" The steel replaced by ice. Another laugh, but something had shifted. He leaned back, straightening the bike. Becca started toward the intersection ahead, then stopped once more. "It had to do with the photos, didn't it? The plant I saw, or..."

She paused, her eyes going wide. "You were the one who suggested I go back to the store. You egged me on, hoping I'd get caught. You called Margaret to tell her that you saw someone breaking in, only I hadn't done it yet. But then, when I was foolish enough to break off a branch..." A gasp as the implications of that call—the missed messages, the police looking for her—hit home.

"Now wait a minute." He reached out to take her hand, but she jerked her arm away. To Clara's relief, Becca began to walk again, heading swiftly toward the noise and bustle of the busy street ahead. Taller than her by a head, the bike messenger had no problem keeping up, wheeling his black-framed bike by his side. They were almost at the corner. Clara lashed her tail, unsure what to do or how to intervene. "I never told you to climb in a window—"

"You knew I would." Becca pulled her phone from her pocket and peered down at it as she walked, talking all the while. "You knew, because you saw me break into Frank Cross's office. You must have been the one who told the police. Only you didn't know what I'd found, did you? Until you saw…"

She slowed as she began poking at her phone.

"I'm sending that photo to the police."

What happened next was too fast for Clara to react. Like a real jungle beast, the man they knew as Tiger lunged, grabbing for the phone in Becca's hand. But Clara jumped as his bike clattered to the ground, tripping him as he surged forward.

"No, you don't understand!" The fake Tiger struggled to his feet, reaching for Becca as she stumbled backward. Stumbled to the curb, desperate to get away. "I was trying to protect you. I would have if I could—"

To Clara's dismay, Becca stopped. "What?"

"My bosses." He stood and brushed off his knees as two women in suits pushed by. When he looked up, his face was sad. "They are not people you cross."

"His new business partners…" Becca could have been talking to herself. "The ones Ande knew about but Margaret didn't. The ones Gaia didn't like…"

"I'm just the messenger," he said, taking a careful step forward. "I pick things up and I drop them off. Sometimes, they have me clean up the mess."

"Like Frank Cross?" Becca took another step backward. Already, the noise of the busy traffic was enough to nearly drown out her quiet query. "You knew about his affairs. About how he'd died before anyone else did."

He nodded, coming closer. "He had a sweet deal, but he panicked. All he had to do was change out the plates and keep his mouth shut."

Waves. The Ocean State, the symbol of Rhode Island. Clara didn't know if she was picking up Becca's thoughts or if she had heard this. Only that it was true.

"The hit-and-run?" Becca must have made the same connection. In the midst of the square's bustle, she was a point of quiet inquiry.

The man before her nodded once again, his pale face sad. "It was an accident. One of the boss's sons. He was drinking." He shrugged. "We could get rid of the car, but we needed clean plates right away to make the trail disappear. All Frank had to do was keep quiet."

Pedestrians parted around them. Behind her, the morning traffic was only beginning to die down.

"That's all you have to do, too, Becca." His voice was soft. The warmth had returned. "I don't want to hurt you. Never did. Honest. I really like you. Now, just give me the phone."

Time stood still as Clara looked from the man back to her person. Surely, the little device wasn't worth the trouble. As the calico looked on, Becca held it up and took a step back.

He lunged. Grabbing the arm that held the phone, he wrestled it from her grasp. Only then did Clara see the cold glint in his eye as he pulled it free and pushed her backward into traffic.

"*No!*" Clara yowled. She was too small to push Becca to safety, too small to take down this predator with the assumed name. But appearing out of nowhere, she had the element of surprise. As Becca's hat went flying, the calico leaped, making herself visible as her person stumbled after the little cloche, into the street.

"Clara?" Crying out the name, Becca caught herself, and, turning, fell to her knees beside the curb as a passing pickup truck crushed the hat into the pavement. "How...?"

But whatever she was going to say was caught up in a thunderclap of pain and noise, and Clara knew no more.

Chapter 38

"Wake up, little one." A kind voice, long remembered. *"Wake up!"* The rough warmth of a tongue. *"Wake up!"*

"Mama?" Clara struggled to open her eyes, only to find Laurel's steely blues glaring down at her.

"Move it!" Her sister's hiss had an edge of—could it be?—fear, and Clara struggled to her feet. *"Quickly!"*

She was in Harvard Square, with Laurel's shaded body, the merest hint of milky coffee in the afternoon light, propping her up against a curbstone.

"What happened?" Clara took a step and nearly fell as her right front leg gave out. Before she could hit the pavement, however, she felt herself pulled upright. Laurel had her by the scruff of the neck. Despite the pain—her paw was throbbing—the grip was strangely comforting, and Clara relaxed.

"Great Bast, you're heavy!" Laurel muttered, her breath warm on Clara's neck. *"All righty, then. Off we go!"*

Clara felt herself being lifted into the air, and the strange tingling of her guard hairs that signaled a passage through an earthly barrier. *"Wait!"* she managed to yell as she felt her sister begin to take flight.

"*We can't leave Becca!*"

"*Becca's fine.*" Laurel growled through clenched teeth. "*See for yourself.*"

She turned, maneuvering Clara like a kitten. Sure enough, Becca was standing on the sidewalk, alone. The man she had known as Tiger appeared to have fled, leaving her gaping, her head swiveling between the sidewalk and the hat that now lay squashed flat in the road before her. But it wasn't the cloche she seemed to see.

"Clara?" She was blinking at the traffic, which sped past unabated. "Clara kitty?"

"*She can't see us.*" Laurel muttered. "*Not now.*"

"*But she'll be worried.*" Despite the pulse of pain, she yearned to be back on the ground with her person.

"*She's about to be very busy,*" said her sister. Sure enough, a siren added its wail to the noise, causing Becca to turn in its direction and set off at a run. "*Now are you content, you silly clown? Because I've got enough to do to get us both home without having to answer all your questions.*"

With that, Laurel began to purr, and the rising and falling vibration lulled Clara, who closed her eyes and felt herself a kitten again. She was carried like this once. She recalled a storm and a sudden exodus. The abandoned shed where she and her sisters had been born was no longer safe, a soft voice purred. They were going to a new home and to a new responsibility. They were to take up the mantle of the cats before them, joining forces to assist a young woman who was also just beginning to make her way in the world.

"*You'll be fine here.*" She recalled a gentle push. A nudge with a wet nose sending her waddling after her sisters into the box trap the shelter worker had set out. "*Look out for each other, girls!*"

"*We will, Mama,*" Clara called. And her sisters? They must have been there before her. All she could remember was that rough, warm

250

tongue.

"There we go. Almost all better now."

It felt so good. The pain was almost gone, and Clara looked up to see not green eyes but gold. Harriet's warm bulk towered over her as she groomed Clara's injured leg. They were on the sofa, in Becca's apartment. Safe.

"Harriet?" Clara blinked, confused.

"Hush, little one." Between Harriet's warm bulk and the reassurance of her purr, Clara relaxed. Strangely, she did feel better. She didn't know Harriet could heal.

"There's lots you don't know, Clown." Laurel, washing her own booties, murmured from her perch on the sofa's back. *"Not that you'd ever listen..."*

"Hush." Harriet looked up. Clara felt it too, the rapid patter of footsteps running up the stairs. A moment later, the sound of a key in the lock, and then Becca, *their* Becca, was racing in. She scooped Clara up in her arms.

"Clara! I was so worried." She hugged the calico close. "I thought I saw you outside. I thought you were hit by a car. I was so scared."

Clara mewed softly and squirmed to be put down. The affection was lovely, but the embrace was making her leg ache.

"Clara?" Becca held her pet before her, then gently placed her on the floor. Clara stepped gingerly. Yes, her leg no longer throbbed, and it bore her weight. Still, she lifted it ever so slightly. "You're limping," her person noted.

As if to prove her wrong, Clara walked over to Harriet and nuzzled her oldest sister. It was the least she could do. *"Thank you."*

***

"I don't understand. I was sure..." Becca shook her head. Without her new hat, her curls sprang free. Clara had never seen a more welcome sight. "Anyway, you're here. All three of you, and now I've got to go. I've got to meet Detective Abrams and explain everything. The minute this is all settled, though, I'm taking you to the vet."

"*Good job.*" Laurel's retort lacked its usual bite, and Clara looked over at her sister. "*Little Miss Know-it-all.*"

Harriet, settling back on the carpet, simply closed her eyes and continued with that self-satisfied, healing purr.

"*I have to say, this one is coming along rather well.*" Laurel watched as, after another round of pets and some treats, Becca found another hat and, with a last backward glance, locked the door behind her.

"*Coming along?*" Clara looked at her sister. "*You mean, she can learn?*"

But Laurel only gave the feline equivalent of a shrug. And since Harriet was now sound asleep—snoring, in fact—Clara lifted her tender paw, shimmied her hind quarters, and leaped through the wall to follow their person back down to the street.

"*Oh, don't be silly.*" The voice beside her startled Clara, and she landed hard on the sidewalk. Laurel's presence was unnerving. Even more so was the feel of teeth on her skin as her older sister once again lifted her by the scruff. Sleepiness and that strange tingling, and then they were in Central Square, outside Charm and Cherish, as Becca came up the block.

"*How did you...?*" Clara twisted around to face her sister.

"*Quiet, silly! Listen and learn.*"

"Elizabeth!" Becca was banging on the door.

"Calm down, child." The older sister was opening it, still in her cleaning clothes. "I knew you'd be back. All of you."

"All? Never mind, I'm here to warn you. A plant, a poisonous plant, has been planted...I mean, someone is trying to frame..."

"Ah, Ms. Colwin." She stopped talking as a large, familiar man stepped out of the back room. "Why am I not surprised to see you again?"

"I left a message that I'd meet you here." Becca sounded a bit defensive. "I had to make a stop first."

"And you thought you'd warn Ms. Elizabeth?" His voice rumbled like a growl. "Tell her to get rid of evidence?"

"It's a plant." Becca caught herself. "In both senses. I don't think Elizabeth took it. I think Tiger, or whatever his real name is, did. He's had it all along. The real Tiger said he'd seen someone hanging around. He must have stolen it from the shop after hearing Elizabeth lecture Gaia. He thought it might come in handy while he was keeping an eye on Frank Cross. Maybe he knew Elizabeth did some gardening—she had an aloe plant. Maybe he'd seen that and it gave him the idea, and when questions came up about Frank's death, he tried to frame Margaret and Elizabeth."

"I think you're forgetting someone."

"Gaia? She was an afterthought. Part of his 'cleanup,' in case she knew anything. Though I guess he might have wanted it to look like a guilt-ridden suicide attempt."

Abrams was shaking his head. "No, Becca. You."

"Me?" Becca blanched, and her hand went to her bag.

But the detective only smiled. "An over-eager amateur poking her nose in where it doesn't belong could get in trouble, you know."

Becca's color turned from pale to pink. "You wouldn't have known about the license plate without me. Or the wolf's bane, for that matter."

"We have Frank Cross's financial records," he said gently. "We have a description of the car. We knew he was in over his head."

"But I gave you Tiger."

"And I'm not going to prosecute you for soliciting as a private investigator without a license."

Becca didn't need Laurel's suggestion to let the detective have the last word.

Chapter 39

The next few days were crazy, with phone calls and visits from Detective Abrams and his colleagues. Harriet was permanently fluffed with annoyance, and Laurel had taken to sleeping on her perch on the bookshelf, what with all the interruptions. Clara, however, kept closer to her person than ever. She'd seen the hat and remembered all too well how close she'd been to losing her. The plump calico was on the back of the sofa, nuzzling up to Becca's neck, when Maddy came by with the news.

"They've found him. Tiger, that is." Maddy held out her phone. "Your Tiger, I mean. That's him, right?"

"Yeah." Becca's voice went soft as she read out loud. "That's him— Thomas O'Hara. 'A onetime bicycle racer, O'Hara had been disqualified for betting on his own races.'"

On the small screen, Clara could see that wide grin and the jet-black hair that fell over his eyes. Before she could examine the photo more closely, Becca let out a small cry.

"He's dead," she said. "Found unresponsive and later pronounced dead. Traces of the same toxic substance that have been linked to both an earlier homicide and an attempted poisoning of a potential witness were found on the victim." Becca looked at her friend, eyes wide. "The wolf's bane."

"Read on." Maddy's voice was grim. "They're calling it an apparent suicide."

"Suicide?" Becca didn't sound convinced. "I remember what he said about his bosses. 'Men you don't want to cross.'"

"Either way, good riddance."

Becca didn't respond to that, but Clara could see how sad she was, even if her friend chose not to, and leaned in, purring. Sometimes, all you can offer is love.

***

When the carrier came out later that same day, Clara stared at it, confused. Surely, Becca didn't think that her attentiveness, those extra cuddles and purrs, signaled something wrong. But before Clara could object, she was bundled inside the box-like contraption.

"*Have fun!*" Laurel looked at her through the metal grid. "*Remember to howl like you're suffering.*"

"*Maybe they'll give you treats.*" Harriet pushed her sister aside to stare into the case. "*Maybe I should come, too.*"

"*Too late, Fatso.*" Laurel ducked as Harriet's big paw came swinging.

"Kitties! Cut it out!" Becca was putting on her coat. "I promise, your little sister will be back soon."

"*Like we care,*" said Laurel. But Laurel, Clara was beginning to understand, talked a very different game than what she felt.

***

That realization, as well as the growing idea that perhaps her sisters were less useless than she had once thought, kept Clara distracted during the bumpy T ride that followed. Accustomed to moving freely, the little cat found the so-called cat carrier particularly uncomfortable. She knew, however, that sidling through its plastic sides to take a seat beside her person would cause more trouble than it was worth, and so she settled in as best she could, thinking about her strange deliverance as the subway rumbled along.

"*Look after each other.*" The voice, so warm and strangely familiar, didn't belong to Becca. Even as her eyes closed in thought, Clara felt that to be true. Felt, as well, that Becca was part of the larger story, one that was only now being revealed. "*You must all help each other to learn and to be strong.*"

"Hello." The deep male voice that broke into Clara's reverie sounded vaguely familiar, as did the plain but friendly face that looked through the carrier's grill.

"What happened to you, Miss Kitty?"

"Her name's Clara." Becca's voice was tight with concern. "And I'm not exactly sure. I thought I saw, well...I thought maybe she had an accident, and then she was limping, so I thought I should bring her in."

"Always better to check." Warm hands lifted Clara out of the case and deposited her on a metal surface. "You know, if it's an emergency, you can come in right away."

"I know. I thought about it." Clara glanced up, concerned. She had never meant to worry her person. To her surprise, Becca looked slightly flushed. "But I heard the hospital had a new feline specialist, and I really wanted you to see her."

"Well, we can do some X-rays." Those warm hands ran gently down her leg, which, by this point, barely ached. "Though she isn't reacting like a cat ordinarily would to a break."

"She's very special." The catch in her voice made Clara look up. The vet, too, apparently.

"Of course she is." That deep voice sounded sympathetic, the brown eyes wide with concern. "Ms. Colwin? Didn't we run into each other...I'm sorry, bad turn of phrase."

Becca summoned a flash of a smile. "Yes, you pulled me out from

256

under a cyclist. You told me to be careful, not that I listened. Wait…" She blinked, looking rather cat-like, Clara thought. "You're the one— the vet who helped the homeless man."

That smile at last, with the dimples. "Yeah, I guess I should be glad that all emergency medicine is pretty much the same."

"They said a vet, but I figured…never mind. I spoke with him, you know. I guess he's going to be okay."

"I'm glad." Silence fell as their eyes met over the cat. "I gather he was living rough," said the vet as the moment passed. "Maybe now he'll get some support. Speaking of which…"

While the two humans had been speaking, Clara had stood and begun to explore the metal table. Sure enough, her leg now took her weight without any pain at all. Tail up and ears erect, she stood at the table's end, looking from the vet to her person.

"Mew," she ventured.

Chapter 40

"Frank Cross was mobbed up." Becca's bombshell elicited the expected gasp from Marcia, who sat back and stared, wide-eyed, at her host.

Ande, however, seemed unnaturally involved with the tea, fussing with the measurements as if they were rocket science.

"Ande, you knew?" Becca reached out to still her friend's hands.

"I told you what I could." She looked up, her face sad. "I'm sorry. I didn't know for sure, and I didn't want any trouble. I told you I wasn't doing his books anymore."

"I thought that was because he acted inappropriately." Becca bit her lip. "Gaia said he was in league with some sleazy guys, and all the while Margaret kept insisting he worked alone. I should have figured it out."

"You're not psychic." A trace of a smile lit up her dark eyes. "Even if you are a fine witch detective."

"Yeah, but I thought…" Becca fondled the lapis pendant. "I guess I should trust my instincts more, and the magic less."

"Man, this doesn't look good for Charm and Cherish." Marcia had recovered, though her eyes were still saucer-wide.

"No." Ande's voice was firm. "I made very sure that the store's accounts were not involved with Frank's. Money went out to him for his allowance, but that was it."

"That's good news." Becca looked from one friend to the other, a grin spread across her face. "Because I've taken a part-time job there. Elizabeth insisted, and, honestly, I can use a regular income. She seems to think I have real potential—as a sales girl at least."

Becca shrugged, and Clara looked from her to her sisters. The gray-haired woman had implied more than that, she knew. And for once, the little cat wanted her person to believe. Becca was good at what she did. She had figured out that Tiger was involved before her pet had. More to the point, there was more to their shared history than Clara had ever before considered.

Maybe some of that cautious optimism got through to Becca. Or maybe, the calico realized, there were other powers at work, because Becca looked around and then down at her favorite pet.

"Besides," she said as her grin grew wider, "Charm and Cherish is a great resource—and I'll get an employee discount."

Chapter 41

"*Dear Becca.*"

Laurel was right! If she concentrated, she could "hear" Becca's thoughts.

"*How lovely to hear from you. I've been hoping you would contact me. I have so much to tell you, but, of course, I had to wait for you to ask…*"

Clara's eavesdropping was interrupted by Harriet.

"*What's going on?*"

"*She's reading.*" Clara tried to step around her sister. Contact, it seemed, was necessary for her to exercise this particular skill. "*Something about her family.*"

"*Huh.*" Harriet plopped down and began grooming her snowy belly fur, blocking her calico sibling.

"What's up with you two?" Becca turned to look. "You'd think you want to read over my shoulder." She paused and looked back at the screen. "Aunt Tabby does say I should pay attention to my cats. Funny, Elizabeth says that, too."

"*What are we doing?*" Laurel appeared on Becca's other side and stepped over her lap.

"Watch the..." Becca grabbed up the laptop. "Well, I guess that's the universe giving me a clue."

She set the computer aside and reached to rub Clara's ear, even as the two older cats nudged her for a position.

"*Laurel, it worked.*" Clara looked up, excited. "*I wonder if I could try...*"

"I know what you three want." Becca extricated herself from the fur pile. "Treats, coming up."

"*Wait.*" Clara looked from Laurel to Harriet. "*Did one of you do that?*"

"*Family meeting.*" Laurel lashed her tail and then, distracted by the movement, began to lick it. Hours later, the treats had all been eaten and Becca gone to bed. All three cats had accompanied her, of course, and now lounged around their person in various stages of repose. "*It's time!*"

"*Ahem.*" Harriet, who had been napping, puffed herself up. Turning from Laurel to Clara, she pulled her large head back into her considerable marmalade ruff and began. "*It has come to my attention that perhaps we have been lax in our lessons. Granted, we've had other concerns.*"

"*Like the pursuit of treats.*" Laurel's muttered aside was nearly muffled as she dug into one brown bootie.

Clara, who lay by Becca's side, felt her whiskers twitch. Harriet didn't often speak of anything at such length—anything but food, that is. Something was up.

"*While we have been hoping that your natural feline intelligence would clue you in, it has become increasingly obvious that you have missed our role in your adventures.*" Harriet's voice rumbled with an almost growl-like solemnity that alarmed her baby sister.

"*Your role? I've seen Laurel, but...*" Clara turned to her littermate, but Laurel only shrugged, her café au lait fur shimmering in the

261

moonlight.

"*Our role,*" Harriet repeated, slowly closing her round gold eyes for emphasis. "*While you certainly have incipient powers, Laurel and I have been doing our best to boost those powers. Partly to aid you in your work, and partly to foster your independence.*"

"*My independence?*"

A true growl, or it could have been the start of a furball, cut her off.

"*Clearly, our person has chosen you as her familiar. For reasons of history and heritage, this makes sense. However, you must understand that the care of a human is a serious obligation, and all three of us must do our bit. So, while we've tried to encourage your strengths and your independence, it will not do for you to disparage or try to disown your family. We are your family, Clara, for good or ill. Your sisters.*"

"*So... you've been helping me?*" Clara nearly squeaked. So much began to make sense—the failures of her shading, Laurel's aid. Even Harriet's magical grooming, which had healed her wounds. A warmth that could not be attributed only to her sleeping person's proximity began to fill her, and she could feel the purr begin to start, deep in her chest. "*Both of you?*"

"*Of course we've been helping you.*" Laurel focused on her bootie and refusing to meet Clara's eye, even as Becca sighed in a dream and nestled closer. Harriet, by her feet, was once more sound asleep. "*We're family.*" Laurel's distinctive yowl, softer now. "*And that means we love you, Clown.*"

Acknowledgments

It may take three cats to help one witch detective, but many more are required to get a book out. Readers like Karen Schlosberg, Brett Milano, Lisa Susser, and Chris Mesarch; editor and Polis publisher Jason Pinter, who took a chance on my quirky cats; Frank Garelick, Lisa Jones, and our beloved Sophie Garelick for boundless support and encouragement; the Sisters in Crime/Mystery Writers of America community, and all the readers who have reached out over the years. Gratitude and love as well to my friend and longtime agent Colleen Mohyde and her wonderful spouse John McDonough, himself a source for all things police procedural, for your continued, sustaining belief. And always, always my beloved Jon S. Garelick, without whom none of this would be any fun, if it were even possible at all.

About the Author

A former journalist and music critic, Clea Simon wrote three nonfiction books, including the *Boston Globe* bestseller *The Feline Mystique*, before turning to a life of crime (fiction). Her more than two dozen mysterious usually involve cats or rock and roll, or some combination thereof, including the first Witch Cats of Cambridge mystery, *A Spell of Murder.*

A native of New York, she moved to Massachussetts to attend Harvard and now lives nearby in Somerville.

Visit her at www.CleaSimon.com or at @CleaSimon.

Don't miss the new Witch Cats of Cambridge mystery
A CAT ON THE CASE
Available now from Clea Simon and Polis Books!

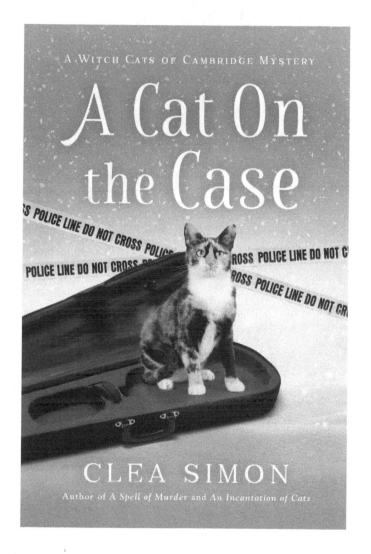

CPSIA information can be obtained
at www.ICGtesting.com
Printed in the USA
LVHW090723240221
679764LV00001B/1